Skating
on the Edge

ALSO BY JOELLE CHARBONNEAU

Skating Over the Line

Skating Around the Law

Skating on the Edge

Joelle Charbonneau

Minotaur Books
A Thomas Dunne Book ✖ New York

A THOMAS DUNNE BOOK FOR MINOTAUR BOOKS.
St. Martin's Publishing Group.

www.minotaurbooks.com

www.thomasdunnebooks.com

Library of Congress Cataloging-in-Publication Data

Charbonneau, Joelle.
 Skating on the edge : a mystery / Joelle Charbonneau.
  p. cm.
 "A Thomas Dunne book."
 ISBN 978-0-312-60663-3 (hardback)
 ISBN 978-1-250-01745-1 (e-book)
  1. Women detectives—Fiction.   2. Roller-skating rinks—Fiction.
3. Attempted murder—Fiction.   I. Title.
 PS3603.H3763S53 2012
 813'.6—dc23

                                                    2012026815

First Edition: October 2012

10 9 8 7 6 5 4 3 2 1

To Joe Blanco with much love.
Your inspiration lives on.

Acknowledgments

With every book I write, I find I am more and more grateful for the support I receive during this process. First, as always, I have to thank my family for their laughter, patience, and unfailing confidence in me, especially my mother who is a wonderful source of roller skating information, my son, who makes me see the world through new eyes, and my husband, who provides me with sugar, caffeine, and a joke when I need a boost.

I would also be remiss if I didn't thank my incredibly talented agent, Stacia Decker. Your belief in me and my writing means more than you can know. Also thanks to Donald Maass, the rest of the DMLA gang and Team Decker—I don't know how I got so lucky to be in such a great club. You guys are the best.

To the Thomas Dunne team—thank you for continuing to love and support Rebecca, Pop, and the gang. Thanks to Andy Martin for his leadership. To my wonderful editor, Toni Plummer, thank you for your belief in my writing. Also, much gratitude to my incredible copy editor, India Cooper, for sharing your passion and keen eye with me. And last, but not least, huge applause to David Baldeosingh Rotstein for the jacket design and Doron Ben-Ami for the jacket illustration. My covers are wonderful. Thank you!

Finally, my heartfelt gratitude to the readers, booksellers, and librarians who pick up this book. Without you none of this would be possible.

Skating
on the Edge

One

I needed to learn to say no. Saying no wouldn't make me a bad person. Entire ad campaigns devote millions of dollars to explaining why "no" is a good thing. No to drugs. No to drinking and driving. No to saturated fats. Okay, no doughnut-loving American followed that one. Still, I hadn't gotten the "say no" message. Otherwise, I wouldn't be scheduled to take my turn in the Indian Falls Native American Days dunk tank sponsored by the town's senior center.

"Are you ready to climb in?" Agnes Piraino asked. Her voice sounded sweet and reassuring. Her smile was warm. It was just what you'd expect from a retired librarian. I was onto her, though.

Agnes was the one who'd conned me into saying yes to this event in the first place. One of her volunteers, Jimmy Bakersfield, had been told by his doctor that he had to take it easy. That meant falling into a tank of cold water was out of the question. Jimmy was a friend of my grandfather's and had always been nice to me. I felt all warm and fuzzy when I agreed to take his place. Of course, that was before I saw him strap on a pair of roller skates and zoom around my rink last night. Now I felt like a chump.

"Come over here, dear." Agnes took my hand and led me toward the tank.

The fiberglass red, white, and blue dunk tank loomed in front of me. The seat suspended above the water had several holes in the vinyl fabric, exposing the stuffing and wood underneath. My butt clenched in anticipation of a splinter invasion.

Agnes's bright smile said she was oblivious to my angst. "We should probably get you in there. The line is getting a bit long. You're lucky. We didn't have many customers yesterday."

"That's because no one wants to dunk a senior citizen." My grandfather's voice cackled from behind me. "It's hard to feel good about sending someone plummeting into freezing cold water when they have a pacemaker. Threat of death takes all the fun out of it."

I turned and reached into my pocket for my sunglasses. Pop was decked out in an open-collared white satin jumpsuit decorated with sparkly red and black rhinestones. His normally white, wavy hair was covered with a black wig. A red and gold scarf hung from his neck.

Pop's Elvis act was headlining tonight's festival entertainment. After the music, the town was shooting off fireworks. At the moment, I was hard-pressed to say which would be more flamboyant.

"You look wonderful, Arthur." Agnes gave my grandfather a smile and blushed. "I can't wait to hear you sing later."

Pop smoothed his fake black hair and grinned. "I've added a bunch of new dance moves to the act. I think you'll like them."

My grandfather executed a double pelvis thrust, which looked painful in the sparkly skintight unitard. Agnes clapped her hands together with delight and batted her eyelashes. I took the opportunity to scope out the best escape route.

The food booths containing everything from corn and pulled pork to deep-fried candy bars blocked off the path to my right. The line waiting to dunk me stretched from the front of the booth clear over and around to the left. To the back of me were other games, a petting zoo, and the large muddy hole where the Indian Falls Bicentennial Fountain was supposed to be bubbling. For once, the political machine wasn't to blame for the slowdown. The project was approved and ground was broken. Then the mayor's wife got a look at the design and threw a fit, which meant construction came to a screeching halt. Good for marital harmony, but bad for the park. The hole was an eyesore, and it wasn't deep enough for me to take cover in. Damn! Unless I wanted to hide in a porta-potty, I was stuck.

"Rebecca, who's running the rink? Did you close for the day?" My grandfather stopped gyrating long enough to give me a quizzical look.

"George was in charge when I left," I explained. "He said he would hold down the fort until I got back." My mother's death over a year ago left me the default owner of the Toe Stop Roller Rink. I had come back to Indian Falls in May to sell the rink. Only it hadn't sold yet. Until it did, I was in charge of scheduling staff, ordering concessions food, and promoting the rink's newest attraction: Roller Derby girls. So far I'd been here for almost five months. Yikes.

Pop grinned and hitched a finger toward the still-growing dunk-tank line. "I think George changed his mind."

I peered around my grandfather and groaned. George was in

3

line, along with almost every other member of my staff. Most of them were high school students. No doubt a few of them had good aim. Icy water, here I come.

"Rebecca, do you want to change clothes before getting into the tank? We really should get started." Agnes gave me a firm but gentle shove toward the tank. I took a step forward and caught my foot on a cord snaking along the wet ground.

Oof. I hit the ground with a squish.

Yuck. My hands, my knees, and the bottom of my jean shorts were coated with a combination of grass and mud.

Agnes looked like she was ready to cry. "Oh dear. I didn't see that cord. I'm so sorry, Rebecca."

"I'm fine, Agnes," I pushed myself off the ground and brushed away some of the grass. "Just a little muddy."

"One of the food vendors must have needed more power." Pop held out his hand and helped me up. "There just aren't enough electricity outlets to go around. We're having problems over by the stage, too. That's why I came to find you. Your father has disappeared, and I need a manager to help straighten things out. Otherwise we'll have to cancel the show."

My father, Stan Robbins, was Pop's current—albeit reluctant—band manager. Two months back, Pop lent Stan some money. Stan was now playing tour boss for free until his debt was paid off. Only my father wasn't the most reliable guy around. Not a surprise. He disappeared from my life when I was nine and didn't reappear for years. Still, the one thing he excelled at was selling the almost unsellable. Pop's Elvis act fell into that category.

"Oh, you can't cancel the show, Arthur." Agnes clutched her hands against her chest. "Everyone at the center is coming."

Pop grinned. "Don't worry. Rebecca will handle everything."

I had no idea what I was supposed to handle, so I wasn't sure I deserved the ringing endorsement. Still, if it got me out of dunk-tank duty, I was game. "Sorry, Agnes," I said, trying to keep the relief out of my voice. "Pop needs my help."

Agnes looked at the growing line. Her tiny shoulders slumped. "What am I going to do? We have to have someone sit in the dunk tank. No one wants to throw balls at an empty seat."

She had a point. Still, as much as I wanted to make Agnes feel better, I wasn't about to give up my Get Out of Dunk Tank Free card. Pop needed me for God only knew what, and I was going to help him. Too bad leaving Agnes in the lurch made me feel like a rat.

"Hey, Little Orphan Annie! When's this show gettin' on the road? I paid five bucks to send you plunging into icy waters."

I turned toward the sound of Sherlene Patsy's booming voice. The derby girl ditched her place in line and crossed the sodden grass to harass me.

Pop's jaw dropped.

Agnes looked like she was going to pass out.

I just sighed.

Sherlene's outrageous ensemble made even my grandfather look normal. Bleached blond and six foot one, Sherlene was sporting white leather hot pants with a wide stainless steel belt. Her ample torso was shoehorned into a pink leather bustier with ESTROGENOCIDE etched out in metal studs. To top off the look, about a hundred metallic bracelets tinkled up and down her arms. Sherlene, also known as Sherlene-n-Mean, was one of my rink's most colorful derby girls. To her it was more than a sport. Roller Derby was a way of life.

Sherlene propped a hand on her hip and said, "Hey, Red, the crowd is starting to get restless."

"Agnes doesn't have a volunteer to sit in the tank," I explained. Agnes let out a sad sigh and hung her head.

Sherlene's dramatically shadowed eyes narrowed. "I thought Rebecca was going to be in the tank. That's what everyone in line is saying."

"She was going to, but I need her help with the band." Pop took a step closer and smiled up at Sherlene. "I won't be able to do my show unless Rebecca straightens things out with the sound guys."

Sherlene chewed her bottom lip. "The right sound can make or break a show. The sound system at the rink is killer. It's part of what the team likes about the place."

"The system here at the festival isn't half as good. There isn't enough power for my band's microphones." Pop waved his arms and stomped his foot, sending his wig careening dangerously to the left.

"Okay, Rebecca has to fix the sound problem." Sherlene reached over and adjusted the wig. She then reached into her hair, pulled out a bobby pin, and used it to secure Pop's rug. "That means I'll have to take her place here."

Agnes clapped her hands in delight. "Oh, that would be wonderful, dear. How can I ever thank you?"

"You can let me make an announcement about our match this Friday against the Quad City Queens. We want a sellout crowd screaming for us while we stomp them into the ground and make them cry for mercy."

Agnes took three steps backward and did a little hand motion in front of her chest. I think she was warding off evil spirits. I didn't blame her. When Sherlene was in Roller Derby mode, she was more than a little scary.

"Are you sure you want to do this?" I asked.

"Of course she's sure. Aren't you, dear?" Agnes stepped forward and turned Sherlene toward the booth before she could change her mind. "Everyone is going to be so excited to hear we have a real celebrity in the dunk tank. This will be the biggest event of the festival. People will be talking about it for years. Do you want to change into something different before we start or are you ready to go?"

Sherlene must have been ready. She climbed up the back steps and folded her tall frame into the tank. In a matter of seconds, the derby girl was seated on the suspended bench and waving to the crowd.

"Hello, Indian Falls!" The crowd fell silent at the low, gravely tone of Sherlene's voice. Sherlene had a voice phone-sex operators would kill for. "Make sure you come to the Toe Stop Roller Rink this Friday. EstroGenocide is going to blow the roof off the joint!" She pumped her fist in the air, and a bunch of high school kids cheered.

"You gotta admit she knows how to put on a show." Pop adjusted his spandex crotch. "Maybe I should add her and a couple of the other derby girls to the act as backup dancers. I'll bet they'd put butts in the seats."

Scary, but Pop was probably right. Adding the Roller Derby team to the rink's schedule had brought a flurry of new business in the door. The team didn't even care that for the past two months the rink had been under renovation due to a large gaping hole in the back wall created by my former rink manager. This Friday we were holding a bash to celebrate the end of construction dust and the disappearance of all evidence of the explosion. Thanks to Sherlene and her team, I was certain to have a wall-to-wall crowd.

Pop and I walked away as Sherlene shouted additional adver-
tisements. I think she even promised the one thousandth fan a car,
but I was too far away to be certain.

"So, what happened to Stan?" I asked my grandfather as we
dodged cotton-candy-carrying kids playing tag. "I thought he was
starting to get into the idea of being a band manager. You even said
he was doing a good job." That said something, too. Pop and
Stan's mutual dislike was legendary.

Pop shrugged, sending the rhinestones on his shoulders into
prismatic ecstasy. "Got me. I woke up this morning and he was
gone. He left a note. It said he was helping a friend paint today and
to call if the band needed him."

"Did you call?"

"His phone service was shut off last week. He even left the
phone sitting on the table right next to the note. The man is a
pimple on my butt."

Yuck.

I shook off the image and waved to three of the members of
Pop's band. They were milling around the stage, decked out in
red and gold rhinestone-studded bowling shirts. The rhinestones
were added when they decided to back up Pop's Elvis act. Who
knew Elvis and a mariachi band could work so well together? If
Pop could actually sing, they would be great.

"So." I turned to my grandfather. "What do you need me
to do?"

"The sound guy is over there. We need power for two more
microphones for Eduardo and Miguel, and they say mine is
overloading the system. My fans won't be happy if they can't
hear me."

I wouldn't bet money on that. Still, I told Pop I'd do what I could to remedy his problems. He smiled and said something to Miguel and Eduardo. To me it sounded like *"Nieva adonde ayudame. Sí?"*

The band guys nodded and laughed. So I had to ask, "What did you say, Pop?"

"I told the guys that my granddaughter was going to be a big help. They've been teaching me Spanish."

Not very well. I didn't take Spanish in high school, but I'd lived in Chicago long enough to have lots of friends who spoke the language. "I think the word for granddaughter is *nieta*, Pop."

He looked at Eduardo for confirmation. Eduardo's eyes twinkled as he nodded.

"Well, damn." Pop frowned. "I guess I'm going to need a few more lessons."

A scream echoed across the park. Then several more. Cries of "Oh my God" and "Get a doctor" rang out. Instinct had my feet in motion, and I raced toward the voices. I could hear Pop huffing behind me, but I outdistanced him and reached the crowd surrounding the dunk tank in less than a minute. I couldn't see what had caused the uproar, but my heart clenched as I pictured kindhearted Agnes. She'd had a rough couple of months. I just hoped they hadn't caught up to her.

"Is she okay?"

"How could this happen?"

"How terrible!"

I pressed through the clumps of freaked-out people and finally got to the front, where my sometimes archnemesis, Deputy Sean Holmes, was leaning over someone. I was relieved to see it wasn't Agnes. She was standing nearby looking pale and stricken.

Sean stood up and raked a hand through his ash blond hair. He

9

looked stunned. Pulling out his cop phone, he hit a button and said, "I need the sheriff at the festival dunk tank, and you need to call Doc and the paramedics. We have a woman not responding."

Sean took a step to his right and turned his back as I looked down at the ground. The world tilted. Sherlene Patsy, Roller Derby diva, was sprawled out on the muddy ground. Her clothes and hair were soaking wet. Her makeup was smeared.

And unless I was mistaken, she was dead.

Two

I raced over to Sherlene and put my hand on her neck. No pulse. I gave a couple of pumps to her chest and did the CPR breath thing into her mouth. Deputy Sean had probably done this already, but I had to try. It hadn't been that long since we heard the shouts. Which meant there was hope, right?

Nothing.

I pushed harder.

Still nothing.

I was going to try a third time, but a strong arm pulled me back.

"I'm sorry, Rebecca." Sean Holmes pulled me upright and gave me an awkward hug. "She's gone."

The sound of approaching sirens rang in the air, mixing with the laughter of happy merry-go-round-riding children and the cries of scared dunk-tank patrons. The scene was surreal, to say the least.

"I don't understand." I stepped away from Sean and brushed

away two stray tears. "How could Sherlene die in a dunk tank? Were you here? Did you see it?"

"Of course he was here." Pop stood next to me, huffing and puffing. Running in tight pants required a lot of effort. Sucking in air, he asked, "Who do you think was first in line?"

I looked up at Sean. He gave me a halfhearted shrug. I sighed. Of course Deputy Sean Holmes would be the first in line to dunk my butt in freezing water. We had that kind of relationship.

Oh God. "Did you dunk Sherlene?"

Sean shook his head. "I missed on the first try and gave the rest of my baseballs to the kids behind me."

His interest in the dunk tank had disappeared when I did. Go figure.

I looked back down at Sherlene's lifeless body. "I still don't understand. How does a person die in a dunk tank? Did she hit her head when she fell in?"

Several members of the Indian Falls Fire Department raced onto the scene. The minute they saw Sherlene on the ground, they stopped dead in their tracks.

Sean immediately took charge, barking orders. In a matter of minutes, the scene was taped off and the emergency workers had pushed the onlookers to a respectable distance.

That included me and Pop.

Sean instructed all witnesses to stay nearby while the para-medics confirmed what we all knew. Sherlene was dead. Sean clicked some pictures of the ground. He took some of the dunk tank. Then he whispered something to our head firefighter and the two of them disappeared behind the tank. Where I couldn't see them.

Crap.

At this rate I would never find out what happened to Sherlene, and I needed to know. I had finked out of dunk-tank duty and had left her to take my place. Now she was dead, and I had no idea how or why. I needed answers. Clearly, Sean wasn't ready to share. Still, I was surrounded by witnesses. One of them might have the answers I was looking for.

I spotted my main skating instructor, George, sitting on the grass near the popcorn stand. Crossing the grass, I plopped down next to him.

George looked at me with red-rimmed eyes and sniffled. "I can't believe she's gone. It's so unfair."

"I know." I put my arm around George and gave him a hug. "I can't understand how this happened. Did you see it?"

He nodded and swallowed hard. "She was yelling out announcements about the match and flexing her muscles. When someone missed the target, she laughed and insulted them. Classic Sherlene-n-Mean. The crowd shouted for Rick to take her down. And he did. He hit the . . . the . . . target."

Tears leaked from George's watery blue eyes. He sniffled again and dragged the back of his hand across his nose. My throat began to burn as I held back tears of my own. I gave George another hug. He hugged me back and didn't let go.

I understood George's pain. George was the coach of the Toe Stop's Roller Derby team and was its unofficial mascot. He loved the action and the Oscar-worthy stunts the ladies performed. As coach, he believed his job was to understand what made every member of his team tick. So, over the past two months, he'd made a point of befriending each and every one of "his girls." Most of the girls had loved the attention. Sherlene-n-Mean had been a tougher nut to crack. Which made George all the more determined. As of last week, she still hadn't opened up to him. Now she never would.

George finally let go of me, so I asked, "What happened after the ball hit the target?"

"She fell in. The crowd cheered. Everyone was congratulating Rick on sending her into the water." George hung his head. "Even me."

I patted him on the back. "Sherlene would have approved."

He gave me a sad smile. "I know. During practice, she would congratulate other team members who sent her headfirst into a wall. She appreciated skill."

"So what happened?" I asked. "Did she drown?" I had a hard time imaging the statuesque Sherlene drowning in a dunk tank, but stranger things had happened in this town.

"I don't know." George shrugged, and his eyes misted over. "She hit the water, and we all cheered for Rick. Her head came up out of the water. I remember that she smiled, and then everything just seemed to stop. Her eyes rolled back, her face turned white, and her shoulders started to jerk."

George took a deep breath. "At first everyone thought she was just putting on an act. Deputy Sean was the first one to run over and help. There was a problem getting her out of the tank. I don't know why. A few people tried to help, but Sean told everyone to stay back. After a few minutes he hollered that it was safe, and a couple of guys got Sherlene out of the tank. Sean tried to revive her, but I guess it was too late."

I looked back at the dunk tank and tried to picture what George described. I'd assumed Sherlene had hit her head on the way down and drowned. It made the most sense, except that George said her head was above water when she died.

Weird. Weirder yet was the way George described Sean's attempted rescue. Why wait to pull Sherlene out of the water? Knowing Sean, I knew there was a reason. I wanted to know what it was.

After giving George one last hug, I went back to the taped-off area. Sherlene's body had been moved. Since there was nothing left to see, most of the nonwitness crowd had wandered off.

Pop was over to the right, his hip perched on the ticket-taking table. No doubt he was getting the gossip from the senior set on hand. Later I'd ask him what they saw. For now, I had my sights set on another source of information.

Deputy Sean was next to the dunk tank. He was deep in discussion with two new arrivals, Sheriff Jackson and the handsome Indian Falls veterinarian who was my sometimes boyfriend, Lionel Franklin. Lionel spotted me on the other side of the tape and waved.

Okay, I knew he was just waving hello. Still, I decided to translate his gesture into a request to join him. How else was I going to justify being in the middle of a roped-off police scene?

Crawling under the tape, I crossed the grass to the threesome. Lionel gave me a mildly amused look. Sheriff Jackson waved. He had several smudges of dirt on his overalls and a gardening glove flopping out of his pocket. Clearly, the sheriff had been pruning his roses instead of attending the festival.

"Rebecca, good to see you." Sheriff Jackson gave me a smile. "Were you here when this unfortunate incident took place?"

Saying no would get me banished back to the other side of the tape. Instead, I said, "Agnes, Pop, and I were with Sherlene before she got into the tank."

Sheriff Jackson nodded and scratched his chin. "We've got a lot of witnesses who saw what happened up front. It might be helpful to have your take on things. You have a sharp eye for detail. Just like your mom."

Sean glowered at me but said nothing. He hated it when I had anything to do with police business. If he'd been in charge, my butt would have been drop-kicked to the other side of the park. Lucky for me, Sheriff Jackson was the ultimate authority—at least until the next election.

I ignored Sean's angry expression and turned to Sheriff Jackson. "Agnes and I met behind the dunk tank about fifteen minutes before it was set to open. I was the scheduled volunteer for tank duty."

Lionel choked.

Sean stopped looking irked. Now he looked worried.

Sheriff Jackson just smiled and asked, "Did you notice anything out of the ordinary?"

"The ground was wet, but I don't think that qualifies as out of the ordinary."

He nodded. "Looks like you rolled around some in it."

"I tripped on a cord behind the dunk tank. Agnes was surprised to see it. I guess it wasn't there earlier."

Sheriff Jackson shot a look at Sean. Sean looked over to Lionel. Lionel nodded. It was like watching a game of telephone in action—and I was being left out.

My tripping over the cord must be important. Right? So I walked around the dunk tank to take a look.

"Rebecca, stop right where you are." Sean's voice boomed behind me. "Otherwise I'll arrest you for tampering with a crime scene."

Crime scene. The words stopped me cold. If Sheriff Jackson and Deputy Sean were treating this as a crime scene, then that meant Sherlene's death wasn't an accident. I looked over at Lionel. His expression was part concerned and part nauseated. Yikes. I finally understood what he was doing here. Doc Truman, our resident physician and coroner, was on a cruise with his wife. Lionel was his backup, which meant he was in charge of examining the dead body. No wonder he looked upset.

I was starting to feel a bit freaked myself. This was looking a lot like a murder scene, and I had put Sherlene right in the middle of it.

A sick feeling wedged into the pit of my stomach. "Listen." I took a deep breath. "I think it might be a good idea if I looked to see if anything has changed since I was here."

Sean wasn't impressed. His hands twitched near his handcuffs as though daring me to make a move.

I sighed. "You can come with to make sure I don't disturb anything. What possible trouble can I cause if you're watching over me?"

Sean cocked his head to the side and studied me for a moment. Finally, he nodded and off we went.

We took a wide path to the other side of the dunk tank. Sean put a hand on my arm. His expression was one that parents give their toddlers. *Look. Don't touch.*

Duh.

The back of the tank looked like I remembered it. Patriotic paint. Fiberglass structure. Wet ground. An electrical cord.

Wait. The cord wasn't leading off to the food vendors like Pop had assumed. It was going straight to the tank.

I took a step closer and felt a hand clamped over my arm.

"Don't make me arrest you, Rebecca." Sean sighed. "I really don't want to."

That was strange. Sean always wanted to arrest me. Dead bodies normally heightened that desire. It was a constant in life I had begun to count on. Not that I wanted to be arrested. Still, the fact that he wasn't salivating to throw my butt behind bars was troubling, to say the least.

"It looks like the cord I tripped on is leading to the tank," I explained in my most reasonable tone. "I wanted to see what it was hooked up to."

I waited for Sean to tell me that it was none of my business. To say that the police would handle this and that I should go off and run my rink like a good girl.

Instead, he blew out a loud breath and said, "It's hooked up to what we think are two small appliance cords. The appliances have been stripped and the wires exposed."

Yikes.

"And the wires were . . ." I looked over to the dunk tank and swallowed hard.

Sean tightened his hold on my arm. "They were in the water. The water and the metal Sherlene wore acted as conductors. Sherlene went in the water and ended up electrocuted."

Holy crap! The world around me went in and out of focus. My mouth went dry. Someone had gone out of his or her way to turn the dunk tank into a death trap.

A death trap that could have been meant for me.

Three

I blinked open my eyes. A camel was staring down at me, and he was wearing a black Stetson cowboy hat. Not that the camel or the hat was surprising. Elwood was Lionel's ex-circus camel and one of my favorite animals ever. The fact that he saved my life once only made me love him more. What I didn't understand was where I was and why he was watching me sleep.

Elwood leaned down and nudged me with his nose. I'm no Doctor Dolittle, but I thought he looked concerned. I patted his cheek, struggled to a seated position, and looked around.

"How are you feeling?" Lionel squatted down and offered me a bottle of water.

I took a big swig. "What happened? The last thing I remember was talking to Sean."

He took my hand, which made me feel safe and jittery at the same time. Lionel was sexy, smart, and a wonderful guy. Problem was he actually wanted to live in Indian Falls. I didn't. Getting too attached was just masochistic.

"You fainted." Lionel gave me a lopsided grin. "Scared the hell out of Sean. His face went whiter than yours."

I looked down at my shorts and sighed. More mud. "So where am I?"

"Elwood's trailer. He and I were giving camel rides to the children. Elwood was playing cowboy to the kids' Indians. We stopped when I got the call about Sherlene. Sean and I thought it would be best to get you out of public view before anyone thought you were dead, too." He chuckled, but it was that tense kind of laugh that told you a person didn't really think something was funny. Lionel was freaked out.

Come to think of it, so was I.

I took another sip of water and sighed. "Sean said Sherlene was electrocuted when she hit the water."

Lionel's hold on my hand tightened. "She was electrocuted in the water. Just when and why it happened is still to be determined."

Hearing cop-speak come out of my favorite vet was disconcerting. "What do you mean?"

"Cause of death won't be determined until the autopsy, which I'll have to observe." He shrugged, but his face took on a slightly green cast. As far as I knew, this was the first time Lionel had been called upon in his capacity as backup coroner. I'd be queasy, too, if I had to watch someone get cut open. He swallowed hard and admitted, "She might have been electrocuted when she first got dunked, but other things could have contributed to her death."

"What kinds of things?" The question popped out. I couldn't help it. I'd had pretty good luck with investigating crimes in the past. The guilt burrowing into my gut and the fact that a homicidal maniac might be on the loose and after me compelled me to take a whack at solving this. While I trusted Sean to do his job, I wasn't sure I trusted him to keep me alive. Alive was a good thing, and I planned on staying that way.

"Lots of things." Lionel let go of my hand and stood up.

"Like?" I scrambled to my feet. My legs trembled underneath me. Fainting was definitely bad for muscle control.

Lionel gave me a stony look that said, *Stay out of it*.

So I did the only thing I could do. I played the victim card. "Look, Sherlene was only in that tank because I bailed. I could be the one you have to watch be autopsied. I think that gives me the right to know what happened."

Lionel's jaw tightened, and his hand fisted at his side. I could see the anger, frustration, fear, and love in his eyes. Love! Yikes. I swallowed hard and pushed away the mushy feelings welling up inside me. I needed to focus.

The moment passed, and Lionel admitted, "Minerals in the water could have been a factor. Same with Sherlene's clothing. She might have also had a medical condition we don't know about that was exacerbated by the electricity. We'll know more after we examine her."

The whole mineral-in-the-water thing was beyond my scientific knowledge, but the clothing factor made complete sense. Sherlene's ensemble would have set airport metal detectors off in orgasmic alerts, and even unscientific me knew metal conducted electricity. If I knew that, I was betting the killer did, too. Which meant Sherlene-n-Mean might have been the actual target. My fashion statements erred on the side of cotton and denim. Metal accessories weren't my thing.

I brushed mud off my knees and took a couple of steps to test my wobbly legs. They were spongy but functional.

"Thanks for taking care of me." I stood on tiptoe and pressed a kiss to Lionel's cheek. "I should probably get over to the rink and make some calls." Sherlene's team needed to hear the news, and maybe they would have a few ideas about who might have wanted to kill her.

I started to walk away, but Lionel caught my hand and pulled me back. My still-shaky legs gave out. I went stumbling into his blue cotton shirt and his well-muscled chest. Not a bad place to be.

Lionel tilted my face up, and his lips met mine. Yowzah! The man could kiss. Little shivers traveled up and down my spine as his tongue did a dance in my mouth. His hands clutched my back. One of his legs tucked in between mine so we were as close as we could get without removing clothes.

Someone moaned. I think it was me, but it was hard to tell in a camel trailer. There was an echo.

Finally, after several minutes of serious make-out time, Lionel put a gentle kiss on my lips and took a step back.

"What was that?" I asked, gasping for oxygen. "I thought we aren't technically dating anymore."

Lionel ruffled my red hair and gave me one of his smiles. "Maybe we are. Maybe we aren't."

He turned and walked out of the trailer, leaving me behind with cowboy camel Elwood. Which was probably a good thing. Debating my love life wasn't on my current agenda. Solving Sherlene's murder was.

It was still daylight, so I felt brave enough to walk the seven blocks from the park over to the rink. I kept my cell phone in my hand just in case a madman jumped out of a bush. The minute the rink came into view, I stopped in my tracks. There were people everywhere. As I got closer I realized that not only were dozens of people milling around, but a makeshift memorial had been started near the front door.

Flowers, Rollerblades, photographs, and a variety of leather and metal arts-and-crafts projects were strewn about the sidewalk near the entrance. A number of lit candles lined the memorial. A couple of signs expressing admiration for Sherlene were also on display.

Scattered around the parking lot were red-eyed people mourning the loss of a Roller Derby great. Some wore EstroGenocide T-shirts. Others were sporting leatherwear with metal accessories and fishnet stockings in honor of their fallen hero.

Resisting the urge to warn them about the conductivity of metal, I skirted around them and went to the front door. A large sign said the rink was closed today for the Indian Falls Native American Days Festival. George's handiwork, I guessed. Earlier, I might have been annoyed that he closed the rink in order to get a chance to dunk me. Now I was grateful for the quiet space.

Without fanfare, I let myself into the rink, careful to lock the door behind me. I hit the light switch, then waited as the fluorescent blubs flickered to life. Once the shadows were banished, I went to get my skates. I started a Chicago CD blaring from the sound booth, laced up the heavy white boots, and rolled out onto the smooth, polished wood floor.

Pumping my legs, I built up speed and zipped around the rink. Wind whipped my face. The music pounded in my ears, and all the fear and sadness I had stomped down came flooding to the surface. Tears streamed down my face. I had a hard time catching my breath. Still, I worked my legs to go even faster. It made me feel alive. Something I was very grateful to be. I had no idea if

Sherlene was the intended victim today or if someone wanted me dead, but I was going to figure it out. I had to.

I rolled off the floor and into my office. The room was just as my mother left it. The scarred wooden desk took up most of the space. Shelves of trophies from the glory days and a whiteboard with the rink schedule decorated the walls. My only additions were a wheelie leather office chair and the most recent picture I had of my mother. Seeing her smiling face made me misty all over again.

I wiped the tears from my cheeks and pulled off my skates. I dumped them in the corner and pulled out a piece of paper. Okay. Who was annoyed enough with yours truly to want me boiled alive?

No one. I would never be voted Miss Congeniality, but murdering me was a tad extreme. There were only a couple of people from my past who might be holding a grudge, and none of them was the murderer type. At least I didn't think so.

I clicked the end of my pen for a few minutes. Finally, I scribbled *Sinbad Smith* on the top of the page. Sinbad had every right to be annoyed with me. I was the reason his kid was cooling his heels in the county jail while waiting for trial. Sinbad didn't appear to blame me for his son's circumstances. The last time I went in his coffee shop, the guy gave me a free cookie. That didn't sound like a man intent on murder. Heck, giving me a strychnine snickerdoodle seemed a lot easier than electrocution by dunk tank.

Still, I made a note to pay Sinbad a visit. He did work around small appliances all day long. Maybe two of them made their way into the dunking water.

Next on the list was Guy Caruso, the town bowling alley's owner and a genuine pain in my ass. The man threw a fit when I started renovating. The new arcade area in the rink really pissed him off. He claimed I was poaching his customer base. His arcade included Tron, Pac-Man, and a few dilapidated pinball machines, so I guess he had a reason to be worried.

I stared at the paper for a few more minutes and sighed. No one else popped into my head. If a crazy killer was after me, I had no other ideas as to his or her identity. I'd have to make do with the list I had.

Now what?

I drew a line down the middle of the paper and wrote Sherlene's name at the top of the right half. Since I didn't know who the intended victim was, I really needed to investigate both fronts.

Only I didn't have any names to add. George was right. Sherlene was a closed book. I decided to call the Roller Derby captain, Typhoon Mary, to see if I could open Sherlene's life.

Mary Decker answered on the first ring. The sniffles on the other end of the line told me she had already gotten the news about Sherlene's demise.

"Oh, Rebecca," she wailed. "I can't believe this is happening. Sherlene-n-Mean was so alive. How can someone that alive be dead?"

Good question. One I'd been asking myself for the last hour.

I gave her my condolences and listened to her extol Sherlene-n-Mean's virtues for several minutes. When she was done, I said, "The police are looking into her death. They're investigating it as a possible murder."

The person who broke the news must not have known that

part. Mary went silent on the other end. For a second I thought we'd been disconnected. Then I realized I could still hear her breathing. "Mary?"

"I knew it." Mary's voice sounded almost triumphant. "Sherlene-n-Mean could take out an entire line of skaters with one shoulder bump. There was no way water alone could take her down."

That was one way to look at it.

"How well did you know Sherlene?" I asked. "I liked her, but I never heard her open up. Did she ever talk about where she was from or her family?"

Mary sighed. "Sherlene and I talked, but mostly about team stuff. She had a lot of ideas about uniforms and our team image. I hate to admit it, but I don't know much about her life outside the roller rink. Why do you ask?"

"Her family needs to be told about her death. I'd rather the news come from one of us than have them get a call from the police." Not the whole truth, but it was a part of it. Deputy Sean did lack social skills. Sympathy just wasn't his forte.

"I agree," Mary said with fervor. Clearly, Mary had met Sean. "Let me look at her team application. I have the team members provide family and hometown information for public relations purposes. I bet there's something useful there. Hang on."

There was a thunk and the sound of papers shuffling. "Hello?" No response, but I could hear Mary blowing her nose in the background. Guess I was on hold. At least there wasn't any bad instrumental music keeping me company. The last time I was on hold it was with the cable provider. Twenty minutes of digital cable commercials and Muzak was enough to make me want to swear off television forever.

"Here it is," Mary said, a little breathless. "Says she grew up in Moline, Illinois. Under the family section she lists her mother, Joanne. No last name is listed, so it must be the same as hers. She never mentioned being married, but she might have to one of the other girls."

"Who was she closest to?"

"Kandie Sutra and Sherlene-n-Mean were pretty tight. You should check with her."

I planned on it. I got Kandie's number and her address from Mary and asked, "Was there anyone on the team who had problems with Sherlene? I'm sure the cops will be asking."

"Laurel Loveless got in a shoving match with Sherlene-n-Mean last week." Mary's voice took on a hushed tone as though she were worried someone would overhear. "It took fifteen minutes for George and me to break it up and get practice back on track. I don't think Laurel could have killed Sherlene, though. She just isn't the type."

I added Laurel's name to the list and sighed. I had no idea what the killer type was, but I was going to do my best to find out.

After saying good-bye to Mary, I grabbed my purse and my list and headed for the front door. The crowd had grown even larger. More signs with tearful slogans. More flowers and a lot more leather.

Navigating around the mourning fans, I walked to my sunshine yellow Honda Civic parked on the far side of the lot. I opened the car door and heard, "Wait!"

I turned to see a wigless Pop hurrying toward me in his sparkly spandex jumpsuit. In the tight outfit, Pop's run looked more like a strange interpretive dance.

Finally, a panting Pop stopped next to me. He pulled at the

fabric near his butt. "Damn Lycra material. Running always gives me a wedgie." Pop gave another tug and sighed. "That's better. My gig got canceled, so I thought I'd see how you were doing. Where are you headed?"

"To Sinbad's for a latte."

"Excellent." Pop went to the passenger side and opened the door. "I could use a good cup of coffee. The stuff at the center gives me the runs."

I winced and got into the car. Pop looked at the paper in my hand and asked, "Did you bring your grocery list along, too? I could use a trip to the market. You father is like a goat. He eats everything."

Before I could protest, Pop grabbed the list out of my hand. I tensed as he read the names. His eyes turned serious. "Good idea. I knew you'd realize the killer might have been after you. No one at the center thinks that, though. They're all betting Sherlene-n-Mean pissed someone off. They might be right, but I knew you wouldn't sit around and wait for the cops to figure this mess out. That's not your style."

He was right. I wasn't the type to hide inside with the curtains drawn, waiting for someone else to solve my problems. It was a personality trait that got me in a lot of trouble.

"Guy Caruso is a good suspect," Pop said after reading the list again. "He's got killer written all over him."

"You think so?"

Pop nodded authoritatively. "The guy is a crook. He always 'forgets' to give senior citizens a discount. Thieves turn into murderers all the time on those TV cop shows. It's called escalation."

My grandfather had a point. People went to Ten Little Pins to bowl, not because they were fond of the owner. In fact, I couldn't name one person who called Guy Caruso a friend. I don't know if he was a killer, but he was shady. He had made no bones about his dislike of me, either. I made a mental note to pay him a visit during business hours as I pulled into a spot out front of Sinbad's coffee shop.

"Hey," Pop said. "You're missing someone on this list."

"Really?" The more suspects, the better chance I had of finding the right one. "Who?"

Pop's eyes narrowed. "Who benefits if you die?"

Aside from Guy Caruso, I didn't have an answer. "I don't know."

"If you die, the rink will pass to your living relatives—and only one of us needs money."

My keys fell from my hand as the pieces fell into place. Pop was right. I did have a relative who needed money, and he would probably get some if I died.

My father.

Four

I took several deep breaths. Stan was lousy in the dad department. He disappeared for years on end, tried to bum cash off me, and was always looking for the next great, albeit fishy, business scheme. None of that added up to murder. At least, not the way I did the math. Still, it wouldn't hurt to check out his alibi for today. Earlier, Pop had said my father was painting. That should be easy enough to verify. Once I did, my stomach lining would stop crawling.

Bolstered by that logic, I got out of the car and headed into Indian Falls's only coffee shop, Something's Brewing. Sinbad Smith stood behind the counter. He smiled as Pop and I walked through the door. The grin made his large build less intimidating. His white teeth gleamed against his tan Egyptian complexion. Only his smile wasn't as bright as it had been a few months ago. Having a kid awaiting trial for grand theft auto, arson, and manslaughter had taken its toll.

"Rebecca, it is good to see you. Do you want your usual?" Sinbad fired up the espresso machine before I said yes. He turned to Pop, took in the outfit, and blinked.

"My grandfather was supposed to sing at the festival today," I explained. "The concert was canceled due to extenuating circumstances."

"Extenuating my ass." Pop stomped his foot, causing the spandex to shift again. He reached around to yank at the riding-up fabric. "You know, someone could have killed Sherlene to shut down my act. Marvin Hanson tried to get the gig, but the committee wasn't interested in his saw playing. He draws blood every time he plays. Losing a limb in public only works if you're in professional wrestling."

Sinbad looked at me and raised an eyebrow. I just shrugged. Pop was probably right about the wrestling thing.

"Did you go to the festival today, Sinbad?" I asked.

Sinbad shook his head and grabbed a large cup. "I thought about closing up, but a couple of families came in to get cookies and hot cider. So I decided to stay here. I heard about the murder, though. Deputy Holmes told me."

I blinked. Sean wasn't the world's worst detective, but he normally went for the obvious answer. I thought it would take him longer to make the leap from Sherlene as victim to me. "What did he say?"

"He said a woman had been electrocuted in the dunk tank and wondered if I knew anything about it." Sinbad grabbed a gallon of milk out of the minifridge.

"Do you?" Pop shot him a hopeful look.

"Of course I don't, which is what I told Deputy Holmes." Sinbad frowned and began steaming the milk for my latte. I was impressed at his restraint. Personally, I would have chucked the milk at anyone who accused me of murder.

"Did Sean say why he was questioning you?" I asked, before Pop could open his mouth again. "Did you even know Sherlene?" If Sinbad was taken aback by Pop's outfit, Sherlene's typical getup would have blown his mind.

Sinbad shook his head. "Not really. I served her coffee once or twice. Not enough to know her usual drink."

Okay, that fact might not mean much in the city—I used to go to the same coffee place every morning, and no one ever remembered what my usual was—but this was Indian Falls. If you had a five-minute conversation with Sinbad, he'd find out your favorite coffee drink and he'd remember it. If Sinbad was the killer, he probably wasn't after Sherlene. Gulp.

"Sean must have had a reason for talking to you about the murder."

"Yeah." Pop sauntered up to the counter. He jabbed his bony finger at Sinbad and said, "Like maybe you were trying to off my granddaughter and got Sherlene instead."

"Why the hell would I do that?" Sinbad dropped my cup of coffee. It hit the ground with a splash.

Sinbad was big and he looked pissed, but Pop wasn't backing down. "Rebecca had your son thrown in jail. If she's out of the way, she can't testify at his trial. He might get off. Sounds like a pretty good motive to me."

"I wouldn't hurt Rebecca." If Sinbad's stunned expression wasn't genuine, he was one heck of an actor. "She didn't make my son break the law. He chose to do it, and he's right where he belongs—in jail."

I let out a sigh of relief. The man could be lying, but I didn't think so. Sinbad wasn't looking to do me in. Which made me wonder, "So why did Sean question you about the murder?"

"He thought I tried to murder Jimmy Bakersfield and got the wrong person."

A lightbulb flickered in the back of my brain. Jimmy had volunteered for the dunk tank before backing out yesterday. If the murderer knew that and wasn't clued in about the change, Jimmy might have been the intended victim. Wow. I hadn't made that connection. Sean had improved in the investigation department.

Only now I was really confused. "Why would you want to murder Jimmy Bakersfield?"

"I guess I can tell you." Sinbad sighed. "Most of the town already knows. Jimmy decided I should be held accountable for my son stealing his car and blowing it up. He came in last week and demanded I pay him ten thousand dollars. He threatened to lead a boycott of my business if I refused."

The seniors in Indian Falls had an almost unionlike hold over the businesses. When they boycotted something, everyone paid attention. No one wanted to cross the picket line for fear of looking disrespectful to their elders. If Jimmy had the support of the other seniors at the center, his threat had substance.

Which meant Sinbad had a motive for murder.

"That was weird," Pop said, climbing into my car. "We got another potential victim, but no coffee. On top of that, now I need a shower."

After dropping the first latte, Sinbad had tripped on the mat behind the counter and sent Pop's iced coffee drink flying. Right at Pop. His white spandex jumpsuit now had wet streaks of mocha-frappa-something, whipped cream, and sprinkles from top to bottom. I hoped Sinbad was cleared as a suspect soon or I might never get a cinnamon latte again.

"Do you think the dry cleaner can get the coffee out?" Pop dabbed at the stained fabric with a napkin. "The ladies love this outfit. What will I do if the stain can't be removed?"

Burn it. Personally, I thought the ladies would be happier not seeing Pop pull spandex out of his ass. I knew I would.

I steered the car toward Pop's house. "So Jimmy was organizing a boycott against Sinbad?"

"That's the news around the center." Pop pulled a sprinkle off his shirt and popped it into his mouth. "But it ain't going to happen. Last week, a delegation let Sinbad know we were on his side. We like to use our power against real injustice, and most of us think Jimmy's just taking advantage of the situation. His car was a heap of junk. Someone should have blown it up long ago."

True enough. And since Sinbad knew Jimmy's threat was empty, he had no reason to kill Jimmy. I pushed talking to Jimmy off my to-do list and pulled into the driveway of Pop's colonial. The garage door was open, which meant only one thing: Stan was home.

Pop's eyes narrowed. He hopped out and stalked up to the house. Pop was a man on a mission.

I walked into the kitchen to find my father and Pop in the middle of the room, glaring at each other.

"Where the hell were you today?" Pop puffed out his chest. "I need a band manager I can count on."

Stan crossed his arms in front of his chest. "I got you the gig, didn't I? What more do you need me to do?"

"I need to you to throw your weight around. The sound guys gypped us on microphones."

"They've probably heard your act."

Pop sucked in air. His face turned red and splotchy. Finally, he sputtered, "You wouldn't know talent if it crawled up your hairy chest and bit you on the nose. I have fans, and they want the best show I can give them. It's your job to see that they get it. Unless you don't want the job anymore."

My grandfather dropped the words like a gauntlet. I held my breath, waiting to see if my father would pick it up. No band job meant no place to live. Which meant he'd want to come bunk with me. While I wasn't wild about Pop and Stan rooming together, it was better than the alternative. Besides, in a warped kind of way, the two of them enjoyed their fights. Neither would be happy to lose the excuse to have them.

"Maybe Stan had a good reason for not being at the festival," I offered.

Pop and I waited.

Finally, Stan blew a strand of dark auburn hair off his forehead and sighed. "Look, I had a friend who needed help painting. The gig was supposed to be a no-brainer. Everything was spelled out in the contract. I shouldn't have been needed. Had I known there was going to be a problem, I would have been at the festival to fix it. Honest."

"Do you think I'm going to believe that cockamamy story?" Pop yelled. "You don't have friends in this town."

"I think he means me."

We all turned. A skinny, short, pasty-looking kid with large glasses and a paint-speckled T-shirt appeared in the doorway. Something about the kid was familiar.

"This is Alan," my father said with a smile. "He gave me a ride home."

The kid had a driver's license? He looked twelve years old.

Alan blinked and pushed an oily lock of hair out of his face. "Hi."

"Alan and I met last week at the diner. Turns out he's an entrepreneur in need of a little mentoring. I decided to give him a hand." My father patted Alan on the back, sending the little guy staggering forward.

The kid regained his footing and gave us a tentative smile. "Stan has a lot of great advice on getting a business up and running."

"And getting you arrested," Pop quipped.

My father wasn't amused. The muscle just above his eye twitched, and his shoulders stiffened. "Are you insinuating that I'm a crook?"

"I'm not insinuating anything. I'm saying it. You're a crook, a swindler, and a rotten band manager to boot. You're even a terrible roommate." Pop gave a punctuating nod.

Stan took a step forward. "At least I manage to take my clothes out of the dryer."

"Are you saying I'm a bad roommate?"

"There's no food in the refrigerator."

"Because you ate everything I bought. It's your turn to do the shopping, but if I wait for you to do it, I'll starve. Old people need their nutrition. I'll bet you're eating the food on purpose so I'll starve to death."

"Yeah, right. You're like a vampire. You live forever and suck the life out of everyone near you."

Alan watched the tennis match of verbal insults with wide eyes and an open mouth. Pop was balling his hands into fists, and Stan was daring him to throw a punch. They were having the time of their lives—and scaring the geeky kid in the process.

"Don't worry," I told him. "They won't hurt each other."

The kid swallowed hard. "Are you sure?"

A sense of déjà vu hit me. This kid was really familiar. "Have we met before?"

He gave me a sheepish smile. "Yeah. My family owns the Presidential Motel. You came by a few months back looking for a couple of guys."

Eureka! I pulled memories of the sad, run-down motel on the edge of town out of the recesses of my brain. "Are you still running the place by yourself or have your parents come back?"

Alan had been working on revamping the joint since his parents split in an RV. After my one visit, I would have recommended torching the place. It was a disaster.

His smile grew wider. "The RV broke down in Canada last month. That gives me a chance to finish my improvements before they get back. Then I can start on my marketing plan. Your father has been helping me with that."

"I thought he was helping you paint."

"Stan's doing both. Isn't that great of him?" Alan said my father's name as though Stan were a rock star and a video game programmer all in one. It was a little strange to see such hero worship for a guy who had played ding-dong-ditch with his only child. A child my grandfather believed Stan might want dead.

Since Alan had spent the day with my dad, maybe he'd be able to put that particular thought to rest. "So my dad was with you all day?"

Alan nodded. "He was helping me paint the last two guest

rooms. We would have been done sooner, but I didn't buy enough paint. Stan was nice enough to go get more."

My heart sank a little. "When was that?" Sherlene's murder occurred around noon.

"Sometime before lunch. On the way back he picked up lunch for us at the diner. Their meat loaf is really good."

The kid smiled big. He had no idea he'd said the wrong thing.

"You even left the toilet seat up this morning," Pop yelled. "I almost fell in and broke my tailbone. How would it have looked to have the paramedics come fish my bare butt off the pot?"

"You'd have looked pretty silly." My father grinned. "The guys would have been talking about it for days at the diner. Might have been good publicity for the band."

Pop frowned. "Crap. I didn't think of that. Maybe we could stage something like it without making me go bare-assed. The band could use some ink."

Stan nodded. "I was thinking about a reality show kind of thing. They do that with musicians all the time on MTV. We might not get to network, but we could think about an Internet version."

"There aren't any dating shows on the air for people my age," Pop said with a grin. "It's an untapped market. Say, Sherlene-n-Mean getting killed will draw a lot of media interest. We might be able to use that angle."

Stan paused and then looked at me. "Sounds like one of your derby girls. What happened?"

"Someone tampered with the dunk tank." I watched my father's reaction for signs of guilt.

Nothing. The knot in my esophagus grew larger. No shock. No horror. No fatherly concern. Not a flicker of anything.

Alan, however, looked fascinated. "She died in a dunk tank?

38

And you knew her? That's so weird. How could you rig a dunk tank so it kills someone?"

"I was wondering that, too," Pop said. "Guess it'll be in the paper tomorrow. Maybe we can clip the article and use it with our reality show pitch. Couldn't hurt."

Stan gave an enthusiastic nod. "I'll make sure to look for it tomorrow." He patted me on the shoulder and flashed a sympathetic smile. "I'm sorry your Roller Derby friend got hurt, Rebecca. This is going to be hard on you, and I want you to know we'll only use that angle if we need to."

I swallowed hard. The idea of a reality show made me want to hurl, but the sympathy looked and felt real. Maybe because I wanted it to be.

"Your dad's the greatest," Alan said, adulation beaming from his eyes. "My dad always said that we couldn't fix up the motel, or we couldn't find ways to bring tourists into town, but Stan sees the possibilities in life and works to achieve them."

Wow. It normally took longer for my father to hook a mark and reel him in. Come to think of it, I couldn't figure out the angle on this one. What was in it for Stan? His foray into selling hot musical instruments I understood. His desire to pimp Pop in reality TV might be profitable, albeit utterly disturbing. This mentoring project baffled me.

Stan put his arm around Alan and gave him a hard squeeze. "Alan here is the one with the great ideas. I'm just helping him find the confidence to put them into action. Alan's parents didn't realize what a smart businessman they had."

Alan's face reddened. "Gee, thanks." He pushed up his glasses. "Um, I probably should get going. Do you need me to drop you anywhere, Stan? Maybe we could do dinner at the diner? My treat." Alan looked at me and quickly added, "Unless you think you should stay here. You're Rebecca's dad. She probably needs you after everything that happened."

"Nah." Stan waved off the suggestion. "Rebecca is indestructible. She can take care of herself just fine. Can't you, honey?"

"Of course she can," Pop chimed in before I had a chance to open my mouth. He gave me a proud smile. "Rebecca knows how to roll with the punches. Nothing gets her down for long."

My father nodded. "I'm sure you're right about that, Arthur."

Stan put his arm around Alan again and started toward the door. "Come on, son. We'll talk about implementing your marketing plan over a couple of hamburgers and some chocolate shakes. A brain like yours needs a lot of fuel to keep it working."

My stomach clenched as I watched them walk out of the house. I had the icky feeling I'd just been displaced as Stan's offspring. In fact, it felt like Stan had just kicked me to the curb. My stomach rolled. Now that Stan didn't need me, I had to wonder if he might actually mean to get rid of me. Permanently.

Five

Pop invited me to stay for dinner. Turned out he had a small refrigerator hidden under a tarp in the garage where he kept his secret stash. Stan hadn't found it, so there was plenty of food. Only I wasn't hungry. Suspecting my father might be plotting to do me in was a great appetite suppressant.

Then again, maybe it was just the idea of being replaced in Stan's life that had me in knots. Stan wasn't going to win any Father of the Year awards, but he was the only dad I had. Knowing he was calling some kid "son" and spending quality time with him tugged at emotions I didn't know existed.

Either way, I was going to make a point of watching Stan's movements. Which is why, when I left Pop's, I found myself cruising by the Hunger Paynes Diner.

Sure enough, I could see Alan and Stan at a window booth, and they looked like they were having a great time. If Stan had attempted to kill me today, I doubted he'd be celebrating his mistake with malts and french fries. While that should have made me feel better, it didn't. Strange.

Unsettled, I went back to the rink. In the fading sunlight, I could see the memorial had grown. So had the number of people. At least fifty folks were milling around the parking lot in their Roller Derby fan gear. They were busy telling stories, laughing, crying, and praying. I saw a small group of women huddled to the right of the entrance. The remaining EstroGenocide Roller Girls were here.

Typhoon Mary waved me over. "I hope you don't mind us being here. We hated sitting at home and didn't know where else to go."

Coming to the rink made sense. Where else would a Roller Derby team go to mourn their friend? A few fans started edging closer. One clicked a picture of the group with his cell phone. Another dug a pen and a piece of paper out of her purse and started asking for autographs.

"Do you want to come inside?" I asked, stepping to my left to block the view of another picture taker. "You'll have privacy."

Mary looked at the group. They nodded, and inside we went. In the bright light, I got a good look at the women's faces. They were vulnerable and sad. The opposite of the confident, take-on-the-world expressions I was used to seeing. Something told me I would see the same thing if I looked in a mirror.

I spotted Laurel Loveless chatting with Fatal Fiona. I'd have to find a way to talk to her about her fight with Sherlene-n-Mean. I also wanted to talk with . . . huh. "Where's Kandie?"

Mary clasped her hands together. "No one can get ahold of her. Dharma Gheddon called her to tell her practice was canceled, but no one answered the phone. I hate to think of her alone. She must be heartbroken. Sherlene-n-Mean helped Kandie get through her last breakup, and it was a doozy."

Kandie had had an affair with a married rink owner a couple of towns away. The wife gave an ultimatum, and the Roller Derby team hit the road, looking for a new home. Turned out mine fit the bill.

"Did Dharma tell her Sherlene was dead? Maybe Kandie doesn't know."

Mary brightened at the thought but then sighed. "Kandie would have wondered why practice got canceled. We never cancel practice the week of a match. She knows that."

Good point. Kandie Sutra was a dedicated member of the team. She took speed lessons with George, she was here for team practices, and I saw her doing drills on her own almost every day. Kandie had to know about Sherlene. So why hadn't she contacted any of the other team members? It felt off. I wanted to check it out.

I went into the office and googled Kandie's address. Armed with instructions, I headed out to the rink. George was there looking tired but dry-eyed. He dispensed a few hugs and then blew his whistle. "I think you should all grab your skates and hit the floor for practice. Sherlene-n-Mean wouldn't have wanted us to sit around crying. She'd want you to knock each other on your asses and get ready for Friday's meet."

The woman cheered and made a dash for the new locker room in the back of the rink. George watched them go, wiped a tear from his face, and headed off to get his skates.

With George in charge and Laurel Loveless too occupied to chat, I left in search of the absent Kandie. The directions led me to a run-down house about twenty minutes away. In these last vestiges of sunlight the place looked like it might have been painted white. Or maybe gray. There weren't any streetlights to help me decide. More disappointing, there weren't any lights on inside.

Drat.

Since I'd come all this way, I decided to go up to the house and ring the bell.

Nothing.

I gave it one more try and knocked. The door inched inward with a creak.

Holy crap. I took a step backward and tried not to freak. This wasn't the city. An unlocked door in the middle of western Illinois wasn't a big deal. Still, an unlocked door belonging to the best friend of a murder victim was worrisome.

I pulled out my cell phone and hit number six on the speed dial. A moment later, Sean answered. "Hey, Rebecca. What do you need?"

For a second I wasn't sure what concerned me more—Kandie's open door or the fact that Sean had my number programmed into his phone. "Hey. I'm at Kandie Sutra's place. There aren't any lights on, but the front door swung open when I knocked."

"And?"

"And she was Sherlene-n-Mean's best friend. Don't you think that's a little strange?"

Sean sighed. "A lot of people forget to lock their doors out here. This isn't the city."

No kidding. "Look, I'm worried about Kandie. None of her friends can get ahold of her, and there's a murderer on the loose. Now, do you want to come out here and help me look inside or should I do it myself?"

Okay. That came off more confrontational than I'd intended.

But the more I stared at the ajar front door, the more concerned I got.

I could almost hear Sean grinding his teeth as he said, "You're going to do whatever you want to do no matter what I say. I have evidence to log in tonight and some other leads to run down. If you can wait an hour, I'll head over. If not, don't do anything stupid."

He disconnected.

I could drive into town, get a Happy Meal, and wait for Sean to arrive. There was something appealing about letting a man with a gun go into the house first. Only the idea of Kandie Sutra bleeding on a floor somewhere inside wouldn't go away. What if she needed help and I waited an hour because I was too chicken to go in alone?

Keeping my finger poised on Sean's speed dial number, I pushed the front door open wider. "Hello? Kandie? Are you here?"

No whimper for help or sound of footsteps creeping toward me. I stepped across the threshold and felt along the wall for a light switch. Eureka! Recessed lighting blazed to life, giving me a good look at Kandie's living room. Two blue armchairs, a dilapidated brown sofa, and a scarred and very dusty coffee table were stuffed into the tiny space. There was a hallway jutting off to the left and what looked like a kitchen toward the back.

No sign of Kandie.

Trying to avoid touching anything, I walked through the living room and found the kitchen light. All the knives were in the knife block. I considered that a promising sign.

The message machine on the counter was blinking, so I hit PLAY. The first was a weeping Dharma Gheddon. Practice was canceled. Sniff. Sniff. Pause. Call if you get a chance. Sob.

If Kandie had gotten that message, she would have called Dharma immediately. I would have. The next caller on the machine didn't bother to leave a name. A female voice just said, "We need to talk. Call me back immediately. Or else."

The voice wasn't familiar, and the "or else" raised the hairs on the back of my neck. I checked caller ID for the name or number of the caller. Dharma was listed. So were George and a blocked caller. Unless George was in a Marilyn Monroe phase, the voice on the machine was the latter.

Crap. So much for my first real lead.

I backtracked to the living room and headed down the hall. Bathroom. No one there. Just a couple of empty medicine bottles for pain pills prescribed by a Dr. J. M. Salkin and a mirror that needed copious amounts of Windex. Guest bedroom. Nothing but dust. I hit the switch on the last room and stopped in my tracks. The rest of the house needed a good spray of Pledge but was otherwise tidy. This room looked like a tornado had whipped through it. Twice.

Drawers were hanging open. Clothes were strewn across the floor. A small nightstand in the corner had papers scattered all around it. A lamp that must have sat on the nightstand now lay on the floor. Strangely enough, the bed was made—albeit rumpled near the foot.

Wait. I poked around the closet. No suitcase.

A quick trip to the guest bedroom. No suitcase in that closet, either, but there was an empty spot in the corner that had a rectangular pattern of dirt around it. Bingo. Kandie's lack of housekeeping abilities was actually useful. I was guessing Kandie had taken an unexpected trip out of town.

I rummaged around in the clothing debris and the papers by the nightstand, looking for a clue to her destination. A few latte receipts, a sticky note with her next doctor's appointment scribbled on it, and a grocery list reminding Kandie to buy cheese, bananas, milk, and vitamins were all I could find. So much for my detective abilities.

After shutting off the lights, I turned the lock on the front door and shut it tight. It was the least I could do.

I arrived back at the rink as the Roller Derby girls were heading out. They looked tired, sweaty, and a whole lot happier than before. The workout gurus were onto something with the whole endorphin thing.

George was waiting for me in the office. He had changed into a multicolored striped, form-fitting turtleneck and was running his hand through his sweaty hair, making it stand on end. George looked stressed. In fact, his eyebrows were so close together he was starting to bear a remarkable resemblance to *Sesame Street*'s Bert. Muppet wasn't a good look for George.

"What's up?" I asked.

"The girls and I had an idea, but I'm not sure you're going to like it." He shuffled his feet and sighed. "Sherlene wasn't religious. At least, we don't think so. So having her funeral in a church doesn't seem right."

I had to agree. Sherlene's leather and metal hardware weren't normal sacramental attire.

"We want to do what Sherlene-n-Mean would want," George explained, "and we think she would want to have the funeral here." I must have looked as stunned as I felt because George hurried to add, "I told Typhoon Mary that potential buyers might not like the idea of the rink being used as a funeral parlor. So we understand if there is a problem. Sherlene wouldn't have wanted to hurt the rink's sale."

To be honest, the sale of the rink wasn't my first or even my second thought. Having a funeral in the rink gave me the creeps, but it made a warped kind of sense. Still, I probably should check in with my Realtor just in case the funeral on wheels would cause any problems.

Beyond that, there was still another issue. "Has anyone talked to Sherlene's family? They might have their own ideas about her funeral."

George shrugged. "No one knows how to get ahold of her family. Everyone was talking in the locker room about how Sherlene-n-Mean was a mystery. She never talked about her past."

Holy crap. The locker room. I'd completely forgotten that every Roller Derby girl had her own combination locker to store stuff here, and I was the keeper of the combinations just in case. This sounded like a just-in-case moment to me.

"Tell you what," I said, almost pushing George out the door. "I'm going to track down Sherlene's family. If they want a roller rink funeral, I'll be honored to host it here at the Toe Stop."

George smiled as a fat tear rolled down his cheek. "Your mom was right, Rebecca. You are the best."

He grabbed a Kleenex and walked out the door.

I looked at the picture on the corner of my desk and sighed. Mom smiled at me from the middle of the frame while her hand rested on the red curls of a ten-year-old me. Almost a year and a half had passed since she died, and I missed her more than ever. Maybe it was being in the rink she loved that made me miss her more every day.

Was George right? Would my mother approve of what I was doing? I was pretty sure she'd like the rink renovations. They had been forced upon me by my car-bombing ex-manager, but I was proud of them. Selling the rink, though? Trying to build some kind of relationship with Stan? Tracking down murderers?

Mom's picture didn't give me an answer, so I rifled through my files and pulled out the list of lockers and their lock combinations. Time to get to work.

Crossing the rink floor, I headed to the back where the new locker room had been constructed. I didn't go into the locker room much, although I did have my own locker equipped with derby attire and speed skates. George insisted. He said having the rink owner skate during the occasional practice with the team was good for morale. So far, I'd skated with the team three times. I wasn't sure I'd earned the team's respect, but I'd walked off the floor without any broken bones. That had to count for something.

I walked into the locker room and hit the switch. Lockers lined the length of two walls. A small bathroom with shower was at the end, along with a full-length mirror per the team's request. The Roller Derby girls liked to look their best before beating the hell out of one another.

According to my records, Sherlene's locker was the last one at the back end of the room. I dialed the combination and popped it open. Yowzah! Someone could open up an Indian Falls S and M shop with the stuff in here.

Black leather tanks, black leather pants, and several black sports bras were hanging from hooks. A couple of pairs of black and silver fishnet tights and lots of silver chains, along with six studded leather collars of varying colors, were stuffed into the top shelf.

A bunch of papers and team T-shirts with SHERLENE-N-MEAN on the back were stuffed in the bottom along with two silver crosses—weird—and a pair of steel-reinforced leather boots. I'd watched a mildly annoyed Sherlene do damage to frisky fans with a tiny tap of those boots. God only knows what pain they could have caused if she had been in a bad mood.

I hung the boots on a hook to get them out of the way, then grabbed the papers and shuffled through them. Looked like a bunch of fans leaving phone numbers. They must not have known about the boots.

One page had two sets of numbers scribbled on it. One was the locker combination. The other was the letter *P* followed by a series of three numbers. Two were divided by a dash. I had no idea what the numbers represented. Still, I pocketed the page just in case it was important.

Time to invade Kandie Sutra's privacy.

Being a social butterfly, Kandie had chosen a locker in the middle of the room. I knew from my halftime forays into the room that Kandie had an entire beauty shop in her locker, along with half her wardrobe. She'd even requested a second locker, a request I'd turned down.

Bracing for the smell of perfume and hair spray, I flung open the door and blinked.

The locker was empty.

Or empty by Kandie standards. Gone were the glitter body spray cans, the hot pink hooded sweatshirts, and the bags and bags of makeup. A few gum wrappers were scattered on the bottom of the locker, and a pink scrunchy sat on the top shelf. The rest had been cleared out. I wished I knew when.

I was about to close the locker when something near the bottom caught my eye. I stooped down. Sure enough. Something had fallen in between the metal slats. Ten minutes and two broken nails later, I had a photograph of a sullen-looking Kandie and a tall dude looking very happy to be plastered against her. The picture was pretty fuzzy, but I could tell that the guy had dark hair and was tall. He also had twenty years on Kandie. No wonder he was so happy to have his hand on her ass.

After pocketing the picture, I headed back into the rink, trying to decide if Kandie's trip was as unexpected as I'd originally thought. The rink had been locked most of today. That meant she had to have cleared out her locker before Sherlene's death. Something told me that at the very least, Kandie knew something about Sherlene's death. I wanted to know what that something was. Determined, I picked up my pace across the rink floor.

Suddenly, there was a loud whoosh behind me and a huge echoing crash. Holy shit! I jumped as sharp, painful pinpricks hit my ankles and the backs of my legs. My heart whacked the walls of my chest as I turned to see what the hell had just happened.

The rink's disco ball lay scattered across the floor in at least a million pieces. My legs had a few of those tiny pieces embedded in the skin. I looked up into the rafters, trying to see where the disco ball used to hang, and almost fainted for the second time that day. Five feet behind me, a loose cable dangled from the ceiling. Had I not been in such a hurry to cross the floor, my legs might not be the only part of me bleeding.

I might be dead.

Six

My nerves were shot. I'd barely escaped being electrocuted, and now I'd had a close encounter of almost the worst kind. Two near-death experiences in one day were enough to put anyone on edge.

I took several deep breaths, got my heart rate down to a non-hyperventilating status, and reached for my cell phone. Five minutes later, Deputy Sean walked through the door. He took one look at me and frowned. Shaking his head, he pulled out his walkie-talkie phone and called for an ambulance.

I looked down and grimaced. The cuts on my legs were bleeding, and they stung. Now that Sean had drawn my attention to them, they stung a whole lot more.

I hobbled over to the sidelines and grabbed a towel off the rail. It was probably laden with derby girl sweat, but I was beyond caring. My mother's disco ball had just been decimated. I wasn't about to bleed on her floor, too.

I leaned down and carefully dabbed at the blood on my legs.

Ow. Meanwhile, Sean holstered his walkie-talkie and ran a hand through his hair. "How close were you to the disco ball when it fell?"

"About five or six feet away." Actually, it was more like two or three, but saying that out loud was too scary.

Sean raised an eyebrow and waited for me to change my story. I just stared back. It was childish, but I needed a victory and this was going to be it.

He opened his mouth as though ready to argue but then shook his head and shrugged. A point for me. Not that I was keeping score.

Sean walked to the middle of the rink and looked up at the area that once housed my disco ball.

"It was probably just an accident, right?" I asked. The sound of the ambulance siren grew closer. "Calling you was probably an overreaction on my part."

He didn't say anything. He just kept looking up into the air.

"Earth to Sean." No change. The muscles in my shoulders pulled tight, and my head started to pound. "Hey, I'm ready for you to read me the riot act about wasting your time. You were busy tracking down leads, and I shouldn't have called you over a simple accident."

Sean didn't take me up on my offer. That was bad. Sean loved to tell me when I was wrong. He lived for it.

Two of Indian Falls's paramedics pushed through the front door and raced into the rink. Sean pointed to me sitting on the sidelines. They changed course and made a beeline in my direction.

I wasn't sure I wanted them to touch me. One of the guys looked like he hadn't slept in days. The other was a teenaged rookie named Robbie. Robbie and I had crossed paths before. He was a dark-haired kid, on the chubby side, with pimples and a penchant for leering down women's shirts. No way was I going to let him put his hands on my legs. I'd take my sweat-stained-towel treatment over these two any day.

I scooted back a couple of inches. "Robbie, I didn't know you were a paramedic."

Robbie gave my legs the once-over and said, "Doc is on vacation. Chuck is off tonight, and Warren wanted company since he's been on call for the past thirty-six hours. He wasn't sure he could stay awake on his own. So I got to ride along. Isn't that cool?"

Nope. It was the exact opposite of cool. An overtired paramedic and his hormonally challenged sidekick. Not exactly my idea of reliable medical care.

"You know, I think Sean overreacted when he called you. Soaking in a hot bath is all the medical attention I need." I started to stand up and felt a hand push me back onto my butt.

"Sit." Lionel loomed above me. He looked both handsome and angry, but his tone was measured and reasonable when he said, "Warren, why don't you let me have a look at Rebecca's injuries? I'll let you know if I need help."

Lionel kneeled down beside me. "What the hell did you get yourself into now?" He pulled some antiseptic and a pair of tweezers out of a bag.

I was about to get indignant. Then I felt the antiseptic hit my wounds and I was too busy feeling the burn to do anything but close my eyes and pray for mercy. Holy crap. That really hurt.

"Okay. There are several pieces of glass I have to remove. It might sting a little, but you were lucky. The glass doesn't look like it's very deep."

Lucky was the last word I'd use to describe myself right now.

The glass removal was less painful than the antiseptic, but it still hurt. By the time Lionel was finished, my legs were aching for pain relief.

"Is she okay?" Sean hunkered down and rested a hand on my arm.

"She's fine." Lionel raised an eyebrow at Sean's solicitous behavior. "Nothing a bath and a good night's sleep won't fix."

Sean patted my arm. "Well, we'll have to see she gets both."

Lionel gave Sean a flat stare. Sean stared back. It was weird.

"So, Sean," I said, interrupting whatever strange male ritual this was. "Did you decide this whole thing was an accident?"

While Lionel was pulling glass out of my leg, I had come to the conclusion that the disco ball's plunge had to be the result of an old wire and bad timing. The pulley system suspending the ball was the same one from my childhood. Mom always liked lowering and raising the ball by hand. She thought it gave the rink a nostalgic feel. Which is why I hadn't changed the system during my recent renovations. And probably why the ball almost clocked me.

I mean, no one else had been inside the rink with me. Jury-rigging the thing to fall just as I passed under it would have taken a lot of effort and a pair of eyes watching my every move. The fact that it happened on the same day Sherlene was murdered was odd, but coincidences did happen.

Sean wasn't ready to commit. "It might have been an accident, but I'm not comfortable making a ruling without a little more information. Who was in the rink tonight?"

I told him about the impromptu Roller Derby practice. "I unlocked the rink and let the girls in, and George was here watching them while I was gone."

Sean made a note in his book and nodded. "Why don't you go upstairs and clean up? I'm going to take a closer look at the pulley system."

I pointed Sean in the direction of the rink's ladders and then booked outside. I headed around to the side entrance for my apartment with Lionel trailing up the stairs behind me.

"You really think the ball falling was an accident?" Lionel asked as I unlocked my apartment door. "That seems like a big coincidence after Sherlene-n-Mean's murder this afternoon."

I flipped on the living room light. The tension in my shoulders eased as I stepped into my home. The three-bedroom apartment ran the length of the roller rink. The living room had the requisite couch, love seat, and television. It also came equipped with a window that looked onto the rink floor. The window was a constant torment to me in my youth. My mother would watch me practice from above while shouting out advice and encouragement. Every time she yelled a skating tip, my butt hit the floor. Startling a not-so-gifted skater is never a good idea. Still, I'd give anything to have my mother yell advice to me again.

Glancing though the observation window, I saw Sean climbing up the ladder to examine the pulley.

I turned back to Lionel and shrugged. "It's the only thing that makes sense. No one else was in the rink."

"How can you be so sure? The rink is a big place, and a lot of people have been hanging around outside since Sherlene's death. Someone could have slipped inside without anyone knowing it."

Damn it. He was right. I was fairly certain the rink was empty when I let the Roller Derby team inside. Still, I couldn't say for certain that no one had entered the rink while I was at Kandie's place.

I pulled out my cell and hit George's number. George was anal. He noticed everything. If someone entered the rink while I was gone, George would know.

He picked up on the third ring. "Rebecca, I was just going to call you. The team and I are at the diner. You should come join us. We're telling Sherlene-n-Mean stories."

"Sounds like fun, but I can't. There's been a little accident at the rink. The disco ball fell, and Sean is here looking at it." I tried to keep my voice light.

Apparently, it wasn't light enough. George yelled, "I'll be right there," and hung up.

I flipped shut my phone and sighed. "He hung up on me."

Lionel grinned. "I'll bet he's here in less than five minutes."

I took that bet and got us some sodas. Then we waited for the telltale sound of feet on the stairs. Nine minutes later, George burst through the door looking red-faced. His eyes were more than a little wild. I gave Lionel a smile that said, *I won.*

"Deputy Sean wouldn't let me inside the rink. He didn't want me destroying evidence. I thought you said it was an accident." George leaned over with his hands on his hips and panted. He must have run all the way from the diner.

"I'm sure it was an accident." I handed him my drink, wishing it contained something stronger than caffeine. "Sean is just being careful. After today, you can't blame him."

George chugged the soda and leaned against my sofa. "You're right. Sherlene-n-Mean's death just has me on edge." I patted him on the shoulder, and he gave me a weak smile. "I guess I'm not the only one. The team is pretty shook up. Especially Kandie Sutra. She was really out of it."

I blinked. "You saw Kandie today? When?"

57

George blinked back. "She came into the rink while you were gone. No one had been able to contact her about Sherlene's death, so we weren't sure if she'd heard."

"Did Kandie skate with you guys? I didn't see her with the team when they left." Which meant she might have been lurking somewhere inside just waiting to drop a glass ball on my head.

"Kandie wasn't in the mood to skate. She said it felt wrong to skate without Sherlene on the floor. None of us wanted to push her. She looked awful."

"Awful how?" The Kandie Sutra I knew lived up to her sultry stage name. Even during a derby meet, it was rare to catch her with a hair out of place.

George shrugged. "No makeup. She had dirt on her knees and a scrape on her arm, and she didn't want to talk about either. I asked if she was okay, but she didn't really answer. I was going to ask again after practice, but she disappeared."

My Spidey sense started tingling. "So you didn't see her leave?"

"Nope." George's breathing had finally slowed, and his cheeks and ears had lost that bright pink tint. "The last time I saw Kandie, she was heading into the locker room. Maybe she felt closer to Sherlene in there."

Maybe she was clearing incriminating evidence out of her locker before dropping a glass ball on my head and booking it out of town. Kandie might have tried to take me out at the dunk tank and then had to try again. If that was the case, she'd missed. Thank God.

Still, Kandie had no reason to want to take me out. We said hello and good-bye, and once in a while she gave me a tip on applying makeup. She might have had a strong desire to attack me with a mascara wand, but she didn't have a reason to kill me. At least not that I knew of.

"Hey, what happened to your legs?" George pointed to the cuts, which were already starting to scab over.

Lionel waded in before I had a chance to answer. "She was in the middle of the rink floor when the disco ball fell. She'll be good as new in the morning."

"I hope you're right. Well, I guess I should get going." George headed for the door and then stopped. "Oh, I forgot. Guy Caruso stopped by the rink tonight to talk to you. Old Man Leerschen did, too. He yelled that you were ruining everything and left. I meant to leave a note on your desk, but I forgot. I'll be at the rink early tomorrow in case you want to sleep in."

And out the door George went.

I turned to see Lionel leaning against the mantel, watching me. "What do you think?"

Lionel raised one eyebrow. "About which part?"

Good point. "Kandie Sutra. I was at her place earlier. She wasn't there, but the front door was ajar."

"So, of course, you went inside."

I chose to ignore his exasperated tone and said, "Her suitcase was gone, and it looked like she'd packed in a big hurry. I also checked her messages and caller ID. No one who called today broke the news about Sherlene's death. So how did she know?"

"Maybe she went to the store and someone mentioned it. You know how that works."

True enough. Pop's friends had been great sources of information in the past. The CIA had nothing on Indian Falls's gossips.

They could ferret out a secret and tell the world about it all before the Showcase Showdown on *The Price Is Right*.

Still, finding Kandie Sutra was my top priority. She was acting strange, and she had been in the rink before the disco ball fell. According to George, so were two other people: Old Man Leerschen and Guy Caruso.

I put visiting both of them on my mental to-do list and sat down on the couch with a thunk. Ow. My legs really hurt. "I hate this. I have no idea if I should simply be worried that a murderer is on the loose, or if I should be scared out of my mind that the murderer is after me. How do I deal with that?"

"You lock your doors and let the police handle it." Sean stood in the doorway, looking sweaty and thoroughly annoyed. "Do you realize you left your door open?"

I ignored the question and asked a more pressing one. "Was it an accident?"

"Hard to tell." Sean puffed out his chest and did his best television-cop impression. "The hardware holding the ball is old. The clasp holding the chain in place might have just failed. Or someone might have helped it along. I dusted the mechanism for fingerprints, just in case, but I don't think anything will come of it."

Lionel stood beside me. "So you don't think someone is trying to kill Becky?"

Sean smirked. "She's irritating, but I don't think anyone is ready to kill her for that." He gave me a stern look. "Yet. You should still take precautions, just in case I'm wrong. Start with locking your door."

Sean turned and tromped down the stairs. When he was gone, Lionel said, "He's right. You should be more careful. Maybe you should rethink living alone until the murderer is found."

I shook my head. "I don't want to live at Pop's place. I don't think I could survive the *Odd Couple* thing Stan and Pop have going on over there."

Lionel crossed the carpet and put his hands on my shoulders. "I wasn't talking about you moving out. I was thinking more along the lines of someone camping here at night."

He leaned down and placed a lingering kiss on my lips. Suddenly, the pain in my legs faded as the rest of my body heated up.

I pulled back and looked up at his handsome face. "Does this mean you want to officially start dating again? I mean, nothing has changed. I'm still planning on selling the rink and moving back to Chicago."

He gave me a crooked smile. "Let's just take this one day at a time and see what happens. Are you game?"

Lionel pressed his lips to the side of my neck, sending a shiver of excitement up my spine. All thoughts of Chicago and the rink flew out of my head. I wrapped my arms around his torso and snuggled against his muscular chest.

"Does that mean yes?"

My lips curved into a smile. "Yes."

Lionel smiled back as his head descended toward mine. My heart thudded, and my every nerve ending tingled with excitement—or maybe fear. My lips met his and I threw myself into the kiss, trying to block any doubts about this decision.

In the five months that Lionel and I had been sort of dating, we had never had sex. Not that I objected to the idea of sex. In fact, I liked the idea, even though I didn't have all that much experience. I'd only done the deed with two guys. Neither of whom impressed me much. The first was my college boyfriend, who after a year of dating finally coaxed me out of my clothes. The other was a jazz trumpet player whose soulful playing I fell in love with. Unfortunately, his lips were only skilled at making his trumpet sing. Sex thus far hadn't been unpleasant, but it hadn't rocked my world.

The sensations Lionel was currently causing with just the tip of his tongue and his hands told me that sex with Lionel Franklin wouldn't be merely pleasant. It was going to have a serious impact on me and tip the delicate balance of our relationship.

I pulled Lionel closer and pushed all relationship dos and don'ts to the side. Lionel made me feel cared for and alive. Two things I desperately needed after today. I wanted him. I'd just have to deal with the fallout later.

My fingers fiddled with the buttons on his shirt and slid inside to touch his warm chest. His hands pressed against my back and slid under the waistband of my shorts. I sucked in air as his mouth slid against my neck and traveled lower. My knees trembled.

"Do you think we should interrupt them?"

"Maybe we should go outside and knock."

"I say we watch. I bet Rebecca has popcorn in the kitchen."

It took a second before I realized the voices I heard weren't coming from out on the street. They were inside my apartment.

I jumped back from Lionel and spun toward the door.

Halle Bury, Erica the Red, and Anna Phylaxis stood in my doorway.

Erica the Red took a very large step forward and dropped a suitcase at my feet. "Don't let us interrupt. Just tell us where we can dump our stuff and we'll be out of your hair."

I blinked. "What do you mean, dump your stuff?"

Erica frowned. "George told us about the disco ball. After what happened to Sherlene-n-Mean, we aren't going to take any chances on losing you, too. We're moving in."

Seven

Sean was right. I should have locked my door. Three very buff derby girls were inside my apartment, and I had no idea how to get them out.

Lionel was no help. He just kissed me on the cheek and said, "Looks like you're in safe hands, Becky. I have to get up early to visit some patients. I trust you ladies will keep her safe."

Before I could sputter a protest, he disappeared out of sight. Great. I blew a lock of red hair out of my eyes and turned to face the derby girls.

All three were derby Glamazons, which meant they were the giants of the team. Anna was the shortest, at five feet eight inches, and rail thin. Halle and Erica were five-ten and had more curves to throw around. I was scrappy, but there was no way I could shove all three out the door and live to tell about it.

Since brute force wasn't an option, I said, "I'm flattered you guys are concerned for me, but there's nothing to worry about. Honest."

Erica flung her magenta-dyed mane of hair back and forth. "Until Sherlene-n-Mean's killer is caught, the derby girls are your personal bodyguards. Someone might have tried to take you out tonight, and we wouldn't be able to live with losing another member of our team. Right, girls?"

Anna and Halle cheered, "Right."

Erica picked up her suitcase and headed past me into the apartment. "I'm going to change for bed. Don't worry about playing hostess. We can find everything we need. You'll never even notice we're here."

The other two grabbed their duffel bags and tromped after Erica, leaving me strangely touched that they included me in their team. Still, I had to wonder how I went from almost having the greatest sex of my life to the slumber party from hell.

While the girls unpacked in the spare bedroom, I grabbed a bottle of Motrin and headed for a hot bath. Drying off, I heard the sounds of the television and laughter coming from the living room. I put on a tank and a pair of sweatpants and went out to see what my guests were doing.

The three had changed for bed and had certainly made themselves at home. Anna Phylaxis was sitting cross-legged on the floor. Her blond hair was pulled into pigtails. She was swimming in an EstroGenocide team jersey designed to fit a sumo wrestler. Erica was sprawled on the couch. Her size-twelve body was jammed into a lacy pink nightgown that clashed mightily with her brightly hued hair. Halle was nowhere to be found.

"Hey, Rebecca."

I jumped at the voice behind me. A black-haired Halle smiled at me above a large bowl of popcorn. "Hope you don't mind us raiding the kitchen. We had the munchies."

"No problem." What else was I going to say? A buff chick with three visible bleeding-heart tattoos wanted my popcorn. Saying no seemed like a bad idea. "You guys sound like you're having fun."

Erica sat up and waved Halle and me over. "We were telling Sherlene-n-Mean stories, and I just came up with another. A couple of months ago, we were in Cleveland for a bout against the Buckeyed Beavers. After we mopped the floor with them, we all went to the afterparty. Some little dude got trashed and decided to stick his hand down Sherlene-n-Mean's pants. Guess he figured it'd be fun to party with a woman twice his size. Sherlene picked him up and launched him down the bar. His head was knocking over drinks like a bowling ball knocking down pins! The bartender thought it was so funny, he bought us all a round of drinks."

Chances were the bartender was as intimidated by these chicks as I was. Then again, the story was pretty funny. The girls all laughed at the memory. Halle sat down on the floor with the bowl of popcorn, shoved a fistful in her mouth, and patted the floor next to her, inviting me to join her.

I was tired. I needed to go to bed. On the other hand, the popcorn smelled really good, and I had never gotten around to eating dinner. I joined Halle and Anna on the carpet and started to munch.

"George said you were willing to host Sherlene's funeral." Anna's voice was soft and sad. "She would have been touched."

I swallowed while shaking my head. "Only if her family agrees. I promised George I'd try to find them."

"That's right." Erica leaned toward me. "George said you were a hotshot private investigator. Are you looking into Sherlene-n-Mean's murder, too?"

Anna's blue eyes grew wide. "Isn't tracking down a murderer dangerous?"

"Danger doesn't scare Rebecca." Halle clapped me on the back, sending me careening forward. "She's tough. Just like us."

"Which is why we are going to help you," Erica announced.

We all looked at her with a variety of baffled expressions.

"That's a great offer, but I'm okay with finding Sherlene's family on my own. I'm just going to go to her house tomorrow and see if anything there points me to them. Nothing dangerous or exciting about that."

I ate two more handfuls of popcorn and listened to more derby stories. By the time I went to bed, I was pleased at how I'd handled Erica's offer. The derby girls might be sleeping in my house, but I had set boundaries. I was in charge.

"You need a bigger vehicle, Rebecca," Erica said, climbing out of my compact Honda Civic. "The legroom in that thing sucks. Next time we should borrow your grandfather's ride. That's my kind of car."

My grandfather drove a maroon Lincoln Town Car with a white canvas top. When he was decked out in full Elvis gear, Pop looked like a pimp cruising around town looking for new talent. Not exactly the inconspicuous look I was going for on my visit to Sherlene's house. Then again, being accompanied by a Glamazon decked out in electric pink pants and a sparkly silver tank wasn't exactly keeping me under the radar.

"You really didn't need to come along."

Erica gave me a flat stare. "Team members always watch each

other's backs. That's the first rule we learn, and it's the only one we all follow. You're stuck with me."

Great.

"Funny," Erica said, casing the neighborhood. "I would never have pictured Sherlene-n-Mean in a place like this."

I was thinking the same thing. Sherlene lived a couple of blocks from Kandie Sutra, only Sherlene's place was a whole lot bigger and much nicer. The two-story colonial was painted a muted green. Bright white shutters framed each window. A sun-flower welcome mat and a milk can filled with almost lifelike silk sunflowers greeted our arrival. The neighboring houses all looked just as neat and clean. June Cleaver would feel at home on this block, but Sherlene-n-Mean? I had to wonder how the neighbors felt about their resident derby girl.

"Now what?" Erica the Red perched her hands on her hips and looked down at me. She was wearing four-inch silver heels, which put her well over the six-foot mark. "How do we get inside?"

Good question. "A lot of people hide a spare key just in case they get locked out." I'd run across this before and hoped Sher-lene was one of those people.

I crossed my fingers and flipped over the colorful welcome mat. Nothing. Nothing on the inside of the milk can. No hide-a-key fake rocks in the flower beds. Nothing in or near the mailbox.

Meanwhile, a smirking Erica watched me while leaning against the front door. Perfect. Not only did I not want a bodyguard, I was stuck with one who considered me entertainment.

"I'm going to see if there's a back door." I headed around the corner on the perfectly cut grass without waiting to see if Erica followed me. I hoped she'd get the hint and stay put.

She didn't. She stumbled along the side of the house, leaving a path of stiletto-sized divots in her wake. I waited for her to fall on her butt, but body-bashing people on skates had given her great balance. Damn.

Everything in the backyard looked like it belonged in a magazine. From the sparkling sliding glass doors and the white wicker patio furniture all the way to the green and white shed at the back of the lawn, everything was perfection. I was starting to wonder if we were at the wrong house.

I searched the inside of the grill, under a couple of potted plants, and anywhere else I could think of. No key.

"Now what do we do?" Erica tapped her heel on the concrete, sending dirt flying.

I had no idea, but I wasn't about to admit that. The Roller Derby girls were under the delusion that I was a brilliant investigator. "She might have left a spare key with a neighbor. People do that all the time."

Erica laughed. "Not Sherlene-n-Mean. She insisted the locker next to hers stay empty. She didn't like sharing her space. No way she'd ever let a neighbor have a key."

She was probably right. Which meant I was stumped.

"That means we head back to the rink. I'll do a little digging on the Internet and see if I can't find her fam—"

I jumped at the sound of glass shattering and spun around. Erica tossed aside a potted plant and brushed the dirt from her hands. She reached into a gaping hole in the glass door and gave me a big grin. "We're in."

"Are you crazy?" I had to fight to keep my voice down. If the cops caught us, I didn't want to add disturbing the peace to the breaking and entering charge. "A neighbor must have heard you. They're probably calling the cops right now."

"Look at this neighborhood." Erica perched one hand on her hip and gestured with the other. "No one is home. The kids are at school, the moms are weeping with Oprah, and the dads are at jobs they hate. Who's going to call the cops?"

I looked around. No gardeners were outside. No children were racing through the grass. No sirens in the distance. I hated that Erica was right again. I gave her what I hoped was a stern look. "Next time, before you break something, run it by me first. Okay?" Not that I was planning on there being a next time, but you never know.

I waited for Erica to give me attitude. Instead, she hung her head and said, "Sorry. I got a little carried away. This private investigator stuff is exciting."

Clearly, Erica had never been on a stakeout. I tried it once and had only a numb butt to show for it.

I walked to the door and canvassed the nearby backyards, just in case someone had decided to enjoy the seventy-degree weather. Not a soul was stirring. So I pushed back the sliding glass door, careful to avoid the broken glass. My legs had been stung by enough antiseptic.

The inside of Sherlene's house was tidier than the outside, probably because there was very little furniture. A single brown sofa sat against the side wall. Flanking the sofa were two end tables complete with lamps and coffee-table books. A wooden rocking chair sat in the corner, an afghan perfectly settled over one arm. That was it. No pictures, no television, and—more important—no clues.

The dining room set and the living room furniture looked like they had just arrived from the showroom. Weird. The kitchen told me Sherlene liked liverwurst sausage and skim milk. Yuck. If not for the EstroGenocide flyer lying on the counter, I really would have thought we were in the wrong house.

Erica dug through a cupboard and came up with an industrial-sized bag of Fritos. "Sherlene-n-Mean must have a maid. I roomed with her on the road, and she was a total slob." Erica opened the bag of chips. She grabbed a fistful and sent crumbs flying.

My stomach grumbled as the smell of corn chips filled the air. Eating a dead woman's food felt disrespectful. Then again, the chips were going to go to waste if someone didn't eat them. This was the kind of moral dilemma they never prepared you for in school. Erica ate another handful and waved the bag under my nose.

Damn. I couldn't help myself. I grabbed a chip and leaned against the counter. "How long ago did Sherlene join the team?"

Erica swallowed and said, "About three months ago. She joined up just before the team was forced into changing rinks. We normally make girls go through a lot of training before putting them on the squad."

"You need to make sure they can skate first and learn the game." Makes sense.

She nodded. "Those are important, but even if she knows how to skate, a girl might not make the team for a while. It takes lots of training before most chicks feel comfortable body-checking someone on wheels. Sherlene-n-Mean knew how to skate, and she had no problem using her body as a weapon. That takes talent."

I had never thought about it that way.

Erica took a drink of water from the tap and continued, "Two weeks after Sherlene-n-Mean asked to join, Typhoon Mary put her on the traveling squad. A few girls were pissed. They said Sherlene-n-Mean got special treatment. Hell, I thought so, too, but I wasn't stupid enough to say anything. Sherlene-n-Mean got wind of the gossip and knocked them on their respective asses during the next practice. No one complained after that."

No one could say derby girls were stupid.

"Come on." I rubbed my salty fingers on my jeans and pushed away from the counter. Time to check upstairs.

Erica followed behind me, still carrying the Frito bag. If the police did show up, they only had to follow the crumbs to find us. Sherlene-n-Mean wasn't the only sloppy roommate in the derby circuit.

At the top of the stairs was a hallway. There were three doors to the left and two to the right. I headed left since it had the most doors. The first was a bathroom that looked like it had never been used. No makeup in the drawers. Extra toilet paper and cleaning supplies under the sink.

We found a treadmill, free weights, and a television and DVD player in the next room. We walked across the hall, and I smiled. This was a room I could believe belonged to Sherlene-n-Mean. Derby posters hung from the walls, while leather bustiers and pink spandex team jerseys hung in the closet. Along the shelf were framed pictures of the EstroGenocide team next to dozens of artistic skating trophies.

Weird. Artistic skating was worlds away from Roller Derby. More often than not, artistic skaters turned their noses up at derby. The derby girls reciprocated the feelings. They wouldn't be caught dead skating in the cute little skirts and frilly costumes.

I picked up one of the trophies. First place, Great Lakes Region,

Women's Senior Figure Skating, 1992. Twenty years ago. The other trophies were either from around that time or years earlier. No wonder Sherlene could outskate most of the derby girls. By my calculations, she'd been skating since she was a tot. Artistic skating might be a galaxy away from derby, but learning to jump and spin on four wheels took skill. Clearly, she'd learned to channel that into her new roller sport.

"What the hell is that?" Erica dropped the bag of Fritos and snatched the trophy out of my hands. Luckily, she'd downed most of the chips, so the collateral damage was minimal. Then again, the greenish look on Erica's face said the chips might be making a return appearance. "Sherlene-n-Mean was a figure skater? I thought she was one of us."

I pried the trophy out of her white-knuckled hands and set it gently back into its place. "Sherlene was a derby girl. The fact she learned figure skating two decades ago doesn't change anything."

Erica still looked ready to hurl.

"Look, everyone has things in her past she might not be proud of. Right?" Personally, I thought Sherlene had every right to be proud of those trophies. My mom had tried to help me earn a first-place one for years. Needless to say, I never managed to get it. I was more than a little envious of Sherlene for succeeding where I failed.

While Erica recovered from her shock, I headed down the hall to the other two rooms. The one on the right was the master bedroom. I walked in and sighed. It felt like I'd entered a spa. Everything in the bedroom and attached bath was decorated in ice blue, pastel green, and a creamy yellow. The large sleigh bed was constructed of a lightly stained wood. At least eight pillows were perfectly placed at the top. A dresser and mirror sat on one side of the room. A cream-colored armchair and a side table were arranged on the other. Sitting on the table was a well-used Bible.

I hadn't figured Sherlene for the Bible-reading type. Then again, I was beginning to wonder if anyone on the team could really claim to know her.

A peek in the closet revealed a lot of conservative skirts, shirts, and dress pants. Nothing I'd ever seen her wearing. Many of the items still had dangling price tags.

In the last room I hit pay dirt. It was an office.

The room had a very big oak desk positioned under the back window. The desk was equipped with the requisite computer, printer, and keyboard. There was also a large desk calendar in the middle. Friday's date was circled in red with the words *Quad City Queens' stomping* written below. Nothing else. I flipped the page to October. Two derby meets were marked, along with a tournament.

I fired up the computer, sat down in the black leather office chair, and began opening drawers. Pens. Pencils. Sticky pads. Aha. In the back of the middle drawer, neatly stacked and tied together with a blue bow, were greeting cards. I slipped a card out of the pile. *To my daughter on her birthday.*

Eureka! I flipped the card open. Inside the card, Mom had written the date, April 24, 1999. I perused the rest of the stack. Sherlene had kept every birthday and holiday card from her mother over the years. Including several from this year. Unless tragedy had struck, Sherlene-n-Mean had a mother ready to start buying a Christmas card for her daughter. How sad.

Unfortunately, while Sherlene saved every card, she didn't save the envelopes. Each card was signed "Mom," which was accurate but gave me no insight into Mom's full name.

Nothing else in the desk drawers gave me any clues. No address book. No half-written letter home that had never been mailed. No pictures with any identifiable landmarks. Nothing. To top it off, the computer was password protected, and my attempts at breaking the code failed miserably.

Sighing, I went back down the hall to find Erica. Only she wasn't where I'd left her. Several artistic skating trophies were tipped onto their sides, and one had fallen to the floor. The fact that they weren't in pieces suggested Erica was over her snit, but the trophies gave me an idea. I slipped one of the first-place statues into my purse and headed in search of my stiletto-wearing sidekick.

I found her sitting at the kitchen table looking dejectedly into a glass. "Time to get out of here," I said, starting for the back door. After a quick sweep-up of the glass and a patch job of cardboard and tape, I headed out.

Erica caught up with me at the car. She folded her body into the passenger side and asked, "Did you find anything useful?"

"I know Sherlene's mother is alive."

"So you're going to call her about the funeral?"

Once I found her. "I have a few details to iron out before doing that."

"Like what?"

"Like talking to the police. They might have already tracked down Sherlene's mother, which means they might already know her wishes for the funeral. If they haven't, then I have to figure out how to break the news to her." Part of me was hoping Sean had won this particular foot race.

We drove back to Indian Falls while listening to Erica's iPod, which meant loud, fast, and lots of percussion. Normally, I would have objected. It *is* my car. However, the volume made it impossible to hold a conversation, which allowed me to ponder what I had learned about Sherlene. I still had no clue whether Sherlene was the intended murder victim, but I did know there was more to her life than met the eye. Too bad I had no idea if her secrets were enough to get her killed.

I pulled into the Indian Falls Police Department parking lot. Erica took an uncomfortable look at the building and volunteered to get doughnuts at the DiBelka Bakery next door. Guess Sherlene-n-Mean wasn't the only Roller Derby girl with secrets.

I stepped into the police station and was greeted by the smell of stale coffee and nail polish remover. The receptionist/dispatcher on duty, Roxy Moore, was busy at her desk behind the front counter giving her fake nails a new coat of shiny pink polish. She looked up as I approached and greeted me with an overly bright smile. "Good morning, Rebecca. I'm so surprised to see you here today."

For some reason, Roxy didn't like me. Her daughter said it had to do with her designs on Indian Falls's finest, Deputy Sean Holmes. Roxy was at least a decade older than Sean and had plucked her eyebrows so much that they stopped growing. I wasn't an expert on Sean's type, but I was pretty sure it wasn't a woman with penciled-in eyebrows.

I leaned on the front counter. "I was wondering if Deputy Holmes had contacted Sherlene's family about her death. The derby team has expressed an interest in being involved with the funeral service, and I told them I'd look into it."

The snide smile disappeared. "Tell the girls I send my condolences. I didn't know Sherlene personally. I only cheered for her during matches, but my heart hurt yesterday when Sean told me. I just broke down and cried all over him."

I didn't doubt Roxy was saddened by Sherlene's murder, but

something told me her breakdown had more to do with Sean's comforting arms than her overwhelming emotion. I waited for Roxy to dab at her eyes before asking, "So, did Sean track down Sherlene's family?"

"As a matter of fact, I didn't." Sean strode down the hall, a pair of handcuffs dangling from his uniform's belt. "There isn't any record of a Sherlene Patsy with the date of birth listed on her driver's license. I'm doing a title search on her house to see if that gives me a different name." His eyes narrowed. "Unless I don't need to. Did you find Sherlene's family? Is that why you're here?"

All things considered, it was a fair question. "No. No one on the team knows much about Sherlene."

"You're a seasoned police official, Sean." Roxy sent him a high-wattage smile and fluttered her eyelashes. "Rebecca might be good at sticking her nose into other people's business, but she's not going to find that kind of information. That takes skill."

Okay, I knew Roxy was bucking for a date with all the flattery, but I couldn't help but take her words as a challenge. Besides, I had an idea that would get quicker results than a title search. If I tweaked Roxy's nose in the process, so much the better.

I found Erica juggling three bakery boxes in the parking lot. Ten minutes later, I was back at the rink, sitting at my desk with Sherlene's figure skating trophy, an éclair, and two cinnamon swirl bagels. Devouring the first bagel, I flipped on my computer and watched it flicker to life. The sounds of classical music from a figure skating lesson accompanied my munching. I logged on to the Internet and went to work.

Roller skating is a small sport next to ice skating, especially since ice skating is in the Olympics and roller skating isn't. Even so, the USA Roller Sports Web site is just as good as its counterparts, if not better. I clicked on the Great Lakes Region and waited. Another click and I was in the archives. I scrolled down to 1992 and smiled. The winner of the Women's Senior Figure Skating title was Shirley Cline, age fifteen. Bingo.

Sherlene Patsy must actually be Shirley Cline. It made a warped kind of sense. Sherlene Patsy vs. Shirley Cline. Country music fans would approve.

Aha! According to the online white pages, a Joanne Cline was living in Moline, Illinois—the same city Sherlene listed as her hometown. Was I smart or was I smart?

Now what? I could tell Sean about my discovery. I'd get the chance to watch Roxy implode, and Sean would get the responsibility of breaking the bad news. Except I meant what I said to Typhoon Mary. Sherlene's family deserved to hear the news from a friend.

Taking a deep breath, I picked up the phone and dialed. A woman with a light, happy voice answered. "Hello. Joanne speaking."

"Hi, Joanne. My name is Rebecca Robbins. I own a roller rink in Indian Falls." A lame opening, but it was the best I could come up with.

"Oh, is this about my offer to volunteer for the next meet? I thought it was going to be in Peoria. Did it get moved?"

"No, this is about your daughter." I waited to see if she claimed not to have one. When she didn't, I continued. "I was fortunate to get to know her. She's been skating here at my rink with the derby team."

Air was sucked in on the other end of the phone. An indignant voice informed me, "My daughter would never skate in Roller Derby. She has too much talent for that sport." Sarcasm dripped from the word "sport." No wonder Sherlene didn't mention her new hobby to her mother. Joanne Cline took a breath and said in a pleasant but firm tone, "Besides, Shirley has an important career that would frown on that kind of behavior."

"What career is that?" I asked.

"My Shirley is a nun."

Eight

"A nun?" Maybe I had hallucinated. Sherlene-n-Mean wasn't the nun type. Then again, I had never had an in-depth conversation with a nun, so what did I know?

"Yes, a nun," Joanne confirmed in a satisfied voice. "She is a religious sister in Springfield. She teaches physical education and history at one of the local schools there."

Physical education sounded right up Sherlene's alley. "I think I do know your daughter, Mrs. Cline," I said. "She's over six feet tall, and her birthday is April twenty-fourth. Right?"

For a moment, Joanne said nothing. Finally, she sighed. "Yes. That sounds like my Shirley. You said she was there skating at your rink?"

Now that I'd convinced her of my legitimacy, I didn't know what to say. Breaking bad news wasn't my forte. "She was a member of the Roller Derby team that skates out of my rink."

"Well, I'm sure she had her reasons. I'm sure that kind of women could use contact with someone like my daughter." Joanne gave a loud sniff of disgust. "Since you used the past tense, I'm assuming she came to her senses and left the team?"

Swallowing hard, I closed my eyes and hoped I wouldn't botch this. "I'm sorry to be the one to tell you, but Sherlene, uh, Shirley passed on yesterday."

I braced myself for tears. Instead she said, "Passed on what?"

My throat tightened in sorrow and sympathy. This woman had lost her daughter. I was supposed to be a shoulder for her to cry on. That meant I shouldn't be the one crying.

I tried again. "Perhaps I used the wrong words. Sherlene passed away yesterday. I'm sorry. Your daughter is dead."

"What kind of person are you?" Joanne's voice screamed through the receiver. "First you slander my daughter by claiming she's a member of your horrible derby team. Now you're tying to convince me she's dead?" My eardrums rang. "What kind of fool do you think I am? I watch *60 Minutes*. I know how these scams are run. Well, I'm going to call her school to prove you're lying. Then I'm calling the cops. I can't wait to see you behind bars."

The phone went dead.

Well, that went well.

I grabbed a couple of aspirin from my desk drawer and popped them in my mouth. Too bad pills weren't going to make me feel better about my conversation with Joanne. I was hoping they'd do something about the headache building in the back of my head, though.

Closing my eyes, I leaned back in my chair and tried to pretend I hadn't gotten out of bed that morning. Comfy mattress. Soft pillow. Warm blankets.

"My reputation is ruined."

My eyes popped open to see an unhappy Pop standing in the

doorway. His white hair was gelled into a spiky do. His silver T-shirt was about a size too tight, which was almost normal-looking compared to his jeans. Those were purple and low-rise, with several professionally frayed holes. Thank goodness the jeans were also on the snug side. Pop's hips were so narrow that the low-ride waist would otherwise have ended up around his ankles.

"What happened, Pop?" I asked, rubbing my temples.

Pop sauntered into the room and propped against my desk. "Everyone at the center is talking about your disco ball incident."

Oops. "Sorry, Pop. I meant to call and tell you about that, but I forgot. I know you like to hear about those kinds of things."

Pop waved off my apology. "I figured you were busy with the cops and the paramedics. Agnes listens to the police scanner when her cable goes out. She needs to get a dish. Anyway, she rang me with the news and told me you were the one who called in the incident. I figured since you could talk, you were okay. Besides, Sean would have called me if anything really bad had happened." Pop smiled at me. I winced. His top row of teeth was pulling away from his gumline.

"Your teeth are coming loose," I said, trying not to appear creeped out.

"Damn. I was afraid of that." Pop reached into his back pocket and did a wiggly little dance. A moment later, he was holding a small tube of denture adhesive aloft like a trophy. Considering how tight his pants were, I was amazed he'd been able to fit anything extra in them. Pop had skills.

He did a little adhesive magic, smacked his lips together a couple of times, and smiled. "I was in a big hurry getting ready this morning. Your father wouldn't get out of the bathroom, so I put my teeth in without a mirror. Thank God they didn't come

81

out when I was at the center. It's hard to be sexy when your teeth are falling out."

Pop tried to jam the tube of denture glue back into his jeans pocket. No dice. Nothing was going back in there. Holding his breath, he sucked in his stomach and shoved the tube into a front pocket.

Once Pop was breathing again, I asked, "So, not knowing what happened here at the rink last night ruined your reputation?" Pop was famous at the center for being in the know. Not having the scoop must have upset him and his fellow gossips.

"Nah. I described the disco ball to them and said the rest was confidential because of the police investigation."

"Good plan. So what's the problem?"

"Your bodyguards are the problem." Pop gave me an injured look. "I mean, how does it look that my granddaughter asked three women to protect her instead of her grandfather?"

It looked like I was smart. Three buff, Amazonian women had a better chance against danger than my grandfather. Pop had a three-hundred-pound attitude trapped inside a body that weighed less than mine. In the intimidation department, Pop came up lacking.

"Look," I said, "the derby girls just showed up at my apartment. They wouldn't leave."

Pop wasn't convinced. "Agnes said she saw one of them getting in your car this morning. I bet she was helping you with your investigation. You replaced me."

"The girls insist they go wherever I go. They're not giving me much choice in the matter."

My grandfather stood up straight and flexed his almost nonexistent left bicep. "Do you want me to tell them to leave you alone? It might get physical, but I can handle it."

He'd probably end up flattened like a pancake, which I definitely didn't want on my conscience. I needed Pop alive and in one piece. Now that my father had thrown me over for some computer geek, Pop was the only real family I had.

I grasped for a way to distract Pop from the idea. "I have to go see one of the derby girls who fought with Sherlene before she died. Then I'm going to see Guy Caruso. He stopped by to talk to me last night, but I was out. You want to come along for the ride?"

"Hot damn!" Pop was positively giddy. I wasn't sure I shared the sentiment. Having Pop along during an investigation often caused more problems than it solved. Still, he was happy. I'd live with the fallout.

I grabbed my purse, and we exited the rink and headed toward my car. We were most of the way there when I realized someone was following us. Pop didn't seem to notice the sound of heavy footfalls. Instead, he was busy talking about his new plan for breaking the band into the big time.

I listened closely to the sounds behind me as Pop continued his monologue. I heaved a sigh of relief. The sounds were gone. I must have imagined—wait. There they were again, and they were moving faster.

I got a firm grip on my purse and prepared to wield it as a weapon. There wasn't much in there, but the buckle on the front could do some serious damage. Besides, it was all I had.

I turned, raised my arm, and stopped short of letting it fly. Halle Bury and Anna Phylaxis stood there with goofy smiles on their faces. Both were wearing black jeans, stretchy black button-down shirts, EstroGenocide ball caps, and shades.

"What are you two doing?" I lowered my purse, trying not to look as foolish as I felt.

83

Halle took off her sunglasses. "Erica had some work to do. So the two of us are on duty."

Pop walked over to Halle. "My granddaughter doesn't need bodyguards. She's got me."

The speech would have been impressive if he hadn't been on his tiptoes. Halle was only wearing three-inch heels, but next to Pop, she was a giant.

"Sorry." Anna walked to the other side of my grandfather and gave him one of her patented wide-eyed smiles. On the rink floor, that smile was typically followed by a hard ass bump. "We promised our team not to let her out of our sight. You don't want us to break a promise, do you?"

Direct hit.

Pop let out a heavy sigh. "I've always told Rebecca that breaking a promise is one of the worst things a person can do. I can't go back on that now." My grandfather turned to me. "Guess you don't need me tagging along after all."

Technically, I didn't need any of them. I was going to a bowling alley, not a crack house. Something told me my three would-be bodyguards wouldn't appreciate the difference.

Before I could express my opinion, Anna said, "Of course we need you. Halle and I don't know the people in this town very well. You do. Together we'll keep Rebecca safe. Right?"

Apparently, while Anna didn't mind dislocating shoulders and breaking bones, she wasn't into crushing Pop's ego.

Pop smiled up at Anna and winked. "Right. Let's go."

They did a fist bump and a high five and headed for my little yellow car. Never had it felt so little. To accommodate the derby girls' long legs, my seat was pulled up so far the steering wheel now had an intimate relationship with my chest. Pop had also pulled his seat up, but he didn't seem to mind the close quarters. Then again, anyone who wore his kind of clothes was used to feeling squeezed in.

First stop for my clown car was Laurel Loveless's place. She lived two towns over in a renovated barn. According to Anna, Laurel had two aging parents who needed help but didn't want the stigma of having a daughter live at home. So Laurel hired a team of carpenters to go to work on the barn. From what I could see of the outside, they did a bang-up job. The red barn had white shutters, three skylights, and two potted plants on either side of the front door. What it didn't have was a doorbell, so I knocked on the door and waited.

A moment later, the door swung open. Laurel took one look at the derby girls behind me and her purple-lined eyes went wide. "Did someone else die? Why are you guys here?" Her petite shoulders started to shake, and her lips quivered.

Oops. I'd forgotten that Laurel was one of the more emotional girls on the team. "No one else died," I said, hoping to prevent the flood of tears that looked to be forming. "I need to ask you a couple of questions."

"Thank God." Laurel sagged against the door frame and gave me a weak smile. "After Sherlene-n-Mean, well, you never know who could be next. I've been tempted to move back into the big house, but I don't want to put my parents in danger."

"That's really nice of you," I said, ignoring the snickers from Halle and Anna. Laurel's voice had taken on a melodramatic quality. Death and danger were high drama, and she was milking it for all it was worth. "Typhoon Mary mentioned you had a fight with Sherlene-n-Mean recently. Would you mind telling me what it was about?"

Laurel's eyes narrowed, and she crossed her arms over her chest. When Anna or Halle stood this way, they looked intimidating. Laurel was almost a head shorter. On her, the pose looked petulant. "Why do you want to know?"

"You're a suspect, chicky," Pop yelled from behind me. "You either answer our questions or the cops will haul you in."

Laurel flinched.

I sighed. "You're not a suspect." Maybe. I shot a glare behind me. Pop wasn't paying attention. He was busy exchanging high fives with the derby girls. Turning back to Laurel, I explained, "I'm just trying to figure out more about Sherlene and what she was up to before her death. You never know what information will help the cops."

Her eyes brightened. "George said you were a private detective. That's really exciting. I don't think my fight with Sherlene-n-Mean will help. I mean, it was all my fault. I overheard Sherlene telling Kandie Sutra not to skate full out. I thought she was trying to get Kandie to throw the match on Friday. So I waited until after practice and told her I was going to have her kicked off the team."

"Sherlene must have loved that," Anna quipped.

Laurel tugged on a lock of her dark hair. "She wasn't happy. If I'd asked about what I'd overheard, things might have gone better. Anyway, she forgave me after she realized what I'd thought I'd heard."

"And after she threw you in a cold shower," Halle said. Anna laughed.

Laurel frowned. "How do you know? You weren't there."

"No, but J. K. Fouling was leaving the locker room when Sherlene was shoving you in the shower."

"Oh." Laurel's cheeks turned a blotchy shade of pink. "Well, she apologized afterward and told me she wasn't trying to sabotage anything. Kandie's leg was sore. Sherlene just wanted Kandie to rest it for a few days so she'd be okay for the bout."

Made sense. Skating injured was something derby girls did all the time. They wore their wounds like badges of honor and pushed themselves beyond what most doctors would call good limits.

We were about to leave when Laurel added, "Hey, I don't know if it means anything, but I saw an old woman creeping around the back of the rink last night near the Dumpsters. I figured she was looking for Sherlene-n-Mean memorabilia to sell on eBay, but the cops might want to look into it. Our fans can be a little scary."

Next stop was Ten Little Pins, Indian Falls's answer to all things bowling. The bowling alley had occupied this spot since before I was born. Considering the animosity Guy felt for me, I found it ironic that the bowling alley used to be one of my favorite places.

Not that I had any delusions about my bowling skills. I sucked. Gutter all the way. During my childhood, though, there were two places to hold kids' birthday parties: Ten Little Pins and the Toe Stop Roller Rink. Since I hated being the only kid expected to practice spins and jumps during a party, I viewed a bowling alley event the same way most kids would view a no-school holiday. Today, visiting the alley was more like going for a root canal.

I walked through the dirt-spattered glass doors and was hit with the smell of stale smoke and wood oil. Illinois had a law against smoking in public places. Either Guy hadn't had the place cleaned in the past five years or he had decided to give the middle-finger salute to the smoking statute. From the haze coming from the bar area, I was pretty sure it was the latter.

The bowling alley had a bar and a glorified snack counter, which Guy called a restaurant, on one side and twenty lanes on the other. Two of those lanes were currently occupied. Two retired guys were on one. Zach Zettle, local mechanic and all-around nice guy, was bowling on the other. I gave Zach a wave. He smiled, raised an eyebrow, and pointed to my entourage. I shrugged. He chuckled. Zach was a close friend and poker buddy. He was used to my antics.

"You have some nerve coming in here," a shrill voice cackled from somewhere to our left.

I squinted through the cloud of cigarette smoke. A woman with long, frizzy white hair and lots of wrinkles peered out at me from her seat at the bar. "What do you think you're looking at?"

Pop plopped his hands on his hips. "We're looking at you, Fern. You got a problem with that?"

"Yeah." Fern took a drag on her cigarette and blew out a stream of smoke. We could no longer see her face, so I guess that problem was solved.

I nudged Pop. We moved away from the cloud of secondhand smoke and headed to the rental counter on the other side of the building. My two bodyguards' heels clomped behind us.

"Who was that woman?" I asked.

Pop hitched up his purple jeans and frowned. "Fern Caruso. Guy's mother."

"Why don't I know her? Is she a member at the center?"

I'd attended so many of Pop's Elvis concerts at the center that they had made me an honorary member. By default, I knew most of the members by sight if not by name.

Pop shook his head. "She was when she first moved back to town eight months ago. Turns out she cheats at cards. We caught her red-handed, palming an ace in order to win a big pot during a Friday poker night. She said she was framed. A couple more aces fell out of her pocket when she stormed out in a huff. The next day the board sent her a letter revoking her membership."

"You kicked her out for cheating at cards? Eleanor and Ethel cheat all the time." I would know. They were at my table the last time Pop roped me into card night. They bilked me out of a roll of dimes before I caught on.

"Nah. We kicked her out because she was a pain in our backside. According to our bylaws, that isn't a good enough reason. Cheating is."

Made sense.

We strode up to the wood-paneled counter and waited for someone from the office behind the counter to appear. No one did. A sign on the shelf of shoes behind the counter read RING FOR ASSISTANCE. I looked down and hit the little silver bell sitting atop the scratched Formica.

Ding. I doubted anyone could hear the tiny sound over the crash of bowling pins. Zach bowled a strike. He turned to see if I was watching. I gave him a thumbs-up and hit the bell again.

"Here, let me try." Halle Bury grabbed the bell and smashed it down against the counter. When no one appeared she stalked around the counter and yelled, "Hey, your bell system sucks."

That did it.

Guy Caruso came charging out of the office. His frizzy black hair was jutting in different directions. His oversized purple T-shirt was untucked, and his face was red. Which was actually an improvement. His complexion usually erred on the side of pasty

89

white. Guy wasn't the outdoorsy type. In fact, no one could actually remember seeing him standing outside in sunlight. A couple of kids had started the rumor that he was a vampire, only no one believed it. In movies, vampires wore stylish clothes and were cool. Guy fit into neither of those categories.

I waited for him to start yelling at me. Only he didn't. Instead of looking angry, Guy smiled. "Rebecca, I'm glad you came by. I wasn't sure George would give you my message. I'm certain he's aware of our differences."

I bit the inside of my lip to make sure I wasn't asleep. Ouch. Nope. I was wide awake and completely baffled. "Differences?" Guy had declared war on me and my rink, yet he was acting like we'd had an argument over who got the last slice of pizza. Weird.

Guy shrugged. "I know I've been difficult. Business has been a little slow, and I took it out on you. That's why I came by last night. To call a truce."

"A truce?" I felt like a parrot, but I couldn't help it.

He nodded. "I want to say how sorry I am about causing trouble with your renovations." His big brown eyes grew wide and sad. "After your friend died yesterday, I realized how much you were going through. You don't need me adding to your problems."

"Damn right, she doesn't." Pop slammed his fist down on the counter. "My granddaughter has been through enough without a blowhard like you coming around and making trouble for her."

A vein in Guy's left temple began to pulsate, but the smile didn't disappear. It got bigger. Guy might not be a cool vampire, but he was starting to look a lot like the Joker. Not a good look for him.

Guy held up his hands in mock surrender. "I apologize for going a little over the top. What do you say? Truce?"

He held out his hand. I stared at it for a moment, wondering if there was a hidden camera somewhere. The Guy I knew wasn't the apologetic type. Maybe he had tried to off me in the dunk tank and was now using this truce to avoid suspicion? If that was the case, it wasn't working. This was definitely suspicious.

Not seeing any reason not to, I stuck out my hand and made nice. Under the overzealous smile, Guy looked relieved.

"Are you still having your grand opening this week?" he asked, looking genuinely concerned. "Considering what's happened, people would understand if you postponed out of respect for . . ." He blinked. "What was her name again?"

Anna was at the counter in a flash. "Sherlene-n-Mean was her name. She would have considered canceling the bout a slap in the face. We aren't postponing nothing. Right, Rebecca?"

"Right," Pop cheered. He executed another fist bump with Anna and Halle. I just nodded. Anything else would have felt anticlimatic.

Guy tugged at the hem of his shirt and took a step backward. I didn't blame him for being nervous. Derby girls had that effect.

"Well, you knew her best," he said with another comic book smile. "I'm planning on closing the bowling alley for a few hours so I can be there. Us business owners need to support each other."

He ducked back into his office, leaving me stunned. A truce and now a show of support for the grand opening he protested? Either Guy was taking happy pills or he was plotting something.

I noticed Zach packing up his bowling bag, so I detoured over to his lane, leaving my bodyguards fighting over who got first dibs on the Ms. Pac-Man machine. I smiled as he pushed his hair away from his face only to have it fall right back. Zach was good-looking in a headbanger kind of way. He perpetually had oil under his nails and shaggy brown hair that was at least four inches too long for Indian Falls.

"I heard about the murder and the disco ball thing from Lionel." Zach wiped his hands with a towel. "How are you holding up?"

I shrugged. Zach nodded. Being a man of few words, he understood the unsaid. Besides, I wasn't sure I could talk about it without tears.

"Do you bowl here a lot?" I asked.

It was his turn to shrug. "At least once a week. I belong to a winter league. Things are just too busy in the summer to commit to a team." He smiled.

Made sense. "How well do you know the owner?"

"Not well. Fern just moved back to town not too long ago."

I blinked. "I thought Guy was the owner."

Zach flipped the towel into his bag. "Everyone does. I just happened to be hanging around in the bar last year when Guy found out his mother was moving back." He glanced around and lowered his voice. "Guy wasn't what you'd call overjoyed. With her gone, he might as well have owned the place. With her back?" Zach shrugged. "From the state of things, I'm guessing she's calling the shots and most of them are bad."

"Hey, it's my turn."

"No, it's not." Pop's voice echoed in the nearly empty building. "You got eaten by the ghosts fair and square."

"You bumped me," Anna pouted. "I would have gotten away clean."

"No dice, chicky. You were toast."

I sighed.

Zach chuckled. My life was amusing to everyone not living it.

"I should probably get out of here before they destroy that machine."

"Good idea." Zach nodded. "That's the only working video machine Guy has left."

I dragged a reluctant Pop, Anna, and Halle out of the bowling alley and, not without a little trouble, stuffed them back into my car.

Driving away, I tuned out the trio's plans for video game night and tried to decide if I'd learned anything important. Guy's war on the rink made a little more sense now. No doubt the return of his mother and the ensuing lack of control over his own business triggered his strange behavior. Still, I wasn't ready to cross his name off the suspect list yet.

I stopped at a light and heard a voice yell, "Rebecca!" Turning, I saw Danielle Martinez racing down the sidewalk in a blue wrap dress and four-inch stiletto heels. "Rebecca, hold up."

The light turned green. No one was behind me, so I waited for my friend to huff and puff her way over to my car. My passengers were so busy discussing the merits of Grand Theft Auto and Super Mario they never even noticed.

I rolled down the window. "What's with the heels? I thought you didn't need them anymore."

Danielle Martinez was a former Chicago stripper. She moved to Indian Falls in search of a different life. Dressed like a librarian, she caught the interest of St. Mark's Pastor Rich. She broke out the high heels and tight skirts when Rich wasn't showing a lot of interest. Now they were engaged and the heels had been relegated to the back of the closet. At least I thought they had.

Danielle sighed. "I needed a pick-me-up. Rich's mother is trying to take control of the wedding. She's coming to visit this weekend and is bringing her grandmother's lace wedding dress for me. Which means I have to find a dress before she arrives or I'm stuck."

"Is the lace dress so terrible?"

"Picture Scarlett O'Hara meets the Bride of Frankenstein."

Ouch.

"So can you help?"

I was the maid of honor. It was my job to say, "Of course."

Danielle smiled. "Great. Let's go."

She opened the back door.

"Right now?" I squeaked. "Do you see who's with me?"

She smiled and climbed onto Anna's lap. "The more opinions, the better."

Right.

A car beeped behind me. I pushed on the gas pedal and tried not to panic. I was taking my grandfather, a former stripper, and two Roller Derby chicks wedding-dress shopping.

Heaven help me!

Nine

Thank goodness the Nothing Borrowed Nothing Blue Bridal Boutique owned and operated by Tilly Ferguson was only a few blocks away. The boutique was on the north side of town right next to the local Jenny Craig franchise. Ballistic brides could cry over their waistlines in the full-length mirror and then trot right over to sign up for the newest diet plan. As if getting married weren't stressful enough.

I pried Danielle out of the backseat and headed into the store. The only time I'd ever been inside was dress shopping for my senior prom. I had been nominated for the prom court, and my mother was determined to make the experience one to remember. Mrs. Ferguson brought out every frothy, fluffy, gaudy dress in the place. Most of them were pink. Redheads shouldn't wear pink. The prom pictures of me and my date prove it.

A bell tinkled as we entered. The store still lived up to its name. Nothing in the store was blue. Muted gray carpet. Long glass counter with a variety of rhinestone and fake pearl accessories. A display of white veils and shoes. Racks and racks of dresses with exorbitant price tags, proving that nothing around here was ever going to be borrowed.

Pop and the derby girls rang the bell again. Pop made a bee-line for the couch in the middle of the room. The derby girls headed for the shoes.

"Oh, hello, Danielle," Tilly tittered as she appeared from the back room. Her salt-and-pepper hair was teased into a bouffant up-do. The style went perfectly with her long gray skirt and black and white sweater set. She was a bridal-selling Cruella De Vil. "I was wondering when you'd come in. You're not leaving yourself much time to plan."

Danielle and Pastor Rich were getting hitched over Thanks-giving weekend. Danielle already had the guy, the church, and the Elks Club. Two months should be more than enough time for the rest. Right?

"And Rebecca Robbins!" Tilly's voice took on a singsong quality. "I haven't seen you for years and years."

She'd seen me a year and a half ago at my mother's funeral, but I wasn't going to correct her. Talking about my mother's death made my throat tighten and my stomach clench, and it was a seri-ous downer. Depressing the bride wasn't on my agenda.

"I see you brought other friends will you." Tilly pursed her lips as she contemplated Halle and Anna. The two derby girls smiled. "Dare I ask if they are in the wedding party? If so, I'm not sure this is the boutique for you."

Halle balled up a fist, which Anna caught before it could have a chance to fly.

"No," Danielle stammered. "They're guarding Rebecca."

"I heard about the murder yesterday and the disco ball accident." Tilly's eyes swung back toward me, so she missed Halle's extended middle finger. "I guess you can't be too careful. Make sure they don't break anything."

Anna's finger matched Halle's.

Tilly turned back to Danielle and got down to business. "So, what did you have in mind for your wedding dress, dear?"

I waited for Danielle to answer Tilly. She didn't.

Danielle looked at me and asked, "What kind of dress do you think I should wear?" She turned back to Tilly. "Rebecca is my maid of honor."

I wasn't a wedding expert, but I was pretty sure picking out the bride's dress wasn't in the maid of honor handbook. Neither Tilly nor Danielle seemed to understand that, though. They both looked at me with unblinking eyes . . . waiting.

Not sure what to do, I said, "Danielle needs a dress that is appropriate for marrying a Lutheran minister." Whatever that might be.

"You are quite right, dear." Tilly nodded as though I'd imparted great wisdom. "Let me see what I can find." Off into the back she went, leaving Danielle chewing her bottom lip.

"Sorry," she said with a wince. "I really need help with the dress part. You grew up here. I figure you know exactly what I need to wear to impress the locals without looking too . . . you know."

I did know. Danielle had a figure even exotic dancers would envy. She oozed sensuality, which Pastor Rich probably loved— but the St. Mark's Women's Guild wouldn't. There was a fine line between making an impression and causing a scene. Unfortunately for Danielle, I'd never mastered the art.

Tilly returned flushed and excited. "I put three gowns in the first dressing room. Let's try them on, shall we?"

Leaving Pop and the derby girls reclining on the sofa, I followed Danielle into the dressing room. One look at the dresses and I started to laugh. Maybe this was a case of the dresses looking better on, but I didn't think so. All three were off-white with high necklines and zero shape.

Danielle sighed and reached for the first dress.

"What do you think you're doing?" I demanded. "There is no way you're wearing these."

She took the first dress off the hanger. Her eyes were sad but resigned. "Tilly has lived here all her life. If she thinks these dresses are appropriate for a pastor's wife, then that's what I should wear."

Suddenly, my Pepto-Bismol prom dress made perfect sense. I had let Tilly steer me to the appropriate dress. She was either a sewing sociopath or stylistically clueless. Regardless, I wasn't about to let her ruin Danielle's wedding. This maid of honor was about to kick some wedding boutique butt.

I snatched the dress from Danielle, grabbed the other two, and marched out of the dressing room. "Tilly, these dresses aren't going to work."

"What do you mean?" Tilly stiffened and pulled her cardigan tight against her body. "Those dresses are exactly what you described. I would stake my reputation on it."

I changed tactics. "I must not have explained myself clearly. Why don't you take these lovely garments back to their racks while Danielle and I look at the dresses out here. I'm sure the perfect dress is hanging somewhere."

Without waiting for Tilly's approval, I dumped the dresses into her arms, grabbed Danielle's arm, and headed for the showroom. Anna and Halle were sitting on one side of the sofa, discussing the addition of garters to the team's attire. Pop was sleeping on the other.

Out of the corner of my eye, I watched Tilly disappear into the back room. Once she was gone I announced, "Everyone needs to pull dresses that don't have tulle or ruffles or bows. We have to find Danielle a dress, pronto. Preferably before the owner of the store can object."

I'd like to think that Halle's and Anna's springing off the couch was due to a genuine desire to help Danielle. Only something told me it had more to do with annoying Tilly.

Within minutes, the front-of-store inventory was completely rearranged. Dresses that were possibilities were laid on the couch. The rest were discarded onto the counter or shoved onto the end of the racks. Halle accidentally, or not so accidentally, dropped one on Pop, which woke him up and added him to our workforce.

In those minutes, we'd found fourteen options. The girls and I gathered the dresses and left Pop behind to deal with Tilly's return.

The first few dresses weren't all that flattering on Danielle. However, once she was done with a dress, Anna and Halle tried it on. Turns out Anna was too thin for the samples and Halle a little too big. I tried to ignore the occasional ripping sound as Halle struggled to get the fabric over her hips. I hoped no serious damage was done. Too bad she hadn't tried on Tilly's choices. Destroying those would be a favor to all womankind.

Dress number nine was a winner. Danielle looked like a dream. Even Tilly agreed when Danielle modeled it in the showroom. In fact, Tilly was downright complimentary about the dress, which, with its fitted drop waist and two-inch shoulder straps, was the antithesis of her selections.

Danielle put down a deposit, scheduled her fittings, and even picked out her shoes. Tilly continued to act warm and solicitous through it all. She even smiled at Halle and Anna when they purchased several garters.

Once we hit the sidewalk, I turned to Pop. "What did you do to Tilly? She's never that nice. Did you give her drugs or something?"

"Worse." Pop winced. "I promised to go to dinner with her tomorrow night. Tilly's a big fan of the band. I thought about bringing her to rehearsal tonight, but I need to focus. The guys are working on helping me learn the songs in Spanish to broaden our appeal."

Pointing out that Pop had a hard time remembering all the words in English seemed counterproductive, so I turned to Danielle. "Feeling better?"

She beamed. "The dress is wonderful. Now I can tell Rich's mother I already have a dress. I only hope finding hotel rooms for the guests will be as easy. I've been striking out."

Strange. Indian Falls wasn't exactly a vacation destination. "Have you talked to the hotels near the highway?" I asked.

Danielle nodded. "And the motel here in town. They said that a bunch of archaeologists have booked up all the rooms for the next couple of months. I'm worried I'll have my entire family living in my apartment the week of the wedding."

Not to mention having her mother-in-law around on the honeymoon. "My father is helping out a kid whose family owns the Presidential Motel. Let me ask him about setting some rooms aside for your wedding."

It was my job to help. Besides, it gave me a great excuse to check out the place again and see what my father was really up to.

. . .

The Presidential Motel was located at the southernmost edge of Indian Falls. The last time I was here, the cobwebs and peeling linoleum made the place look like something out of a horror film. This time, the lobby was newly painted and spider-free. In fact, the place looked really nice. A soft blue carpet had been laid on the floor, two comfy armchairs were ready for guests, and the front counter setup looked completely professional. I was stunned. Maybe Dad really was helping Alan spiff up the place. The kid had gumption, but I didn't think he could have done all this himself.

The kid in question came out of the back office wearing a white button-down shirt and jeans. He spotted me and smiled. "Hey, Rebecca. Who are your friends?"

I looked behind me and sighed. I'd forgotten my entourage. What did it say about my life that I'd tuned out two Roller Derby Glamazons and my Elvis grandfather? Nothing good.

"Anna and Halle are members of the EstroGenocide Roller Derby team. They had some time to kill and decided to come along for the ride."

It sounded plausible. At least, Alan seemed to buy it. His cheeks turned three shades of pink as he gave the girls a little finger wave.

"The place looks great," I said before Alan embarrassed himself by speaking to them. "You've done a lot of work since the last time I was here."

Alan beamed. "I couldn't have done it without your father. There was so much to do. I didn't know where to start. Stan helped me prioritize the renovations and get a marketing plan in place. All the paint and new furniture in the world won't bring in guests, you know. They have to know about us in order to buy what we're selling."

Yikes. My father must have turned ventriloquist. I could swear his voice was coming out of Alan's mouth.

"That's why I'm here," I said, ignoring a strange feeling building in my chest. "There's a wedding coming up on Thanksgiving weekend for Danielle Martinez and Pastor Rich. They have a lot of guests coming in from out of town. I'd like to block off a bunch of rooms for them."

"Oh." Alan tugged at the collar of his shirt. "Um. I don't know if we have anything available. Your dad's marketing plan worked really well. Most of the rooms have been booked for the rest of this calendar year."

"Could you check for me?" I asked.

I no longer thought Indian Falls was the worst place on the planet, but it wasn't exactly Disneyland. Why the run on hotel rooms?

Alan ran a hand through his greasy black hair and nodded. His fingers flew over the keyboard. "Yep. We're pretty booked. There are two rooms we haven't committed yet, but that's because I wasn't sure we could renovate them in time."

Bad rooms were better than no rooms. Especially when mothers-in-law were involved. "Book them, and anything else that opens up, for Danielle."

Alan did some more typing and nodded. "Okay. I've got a note in the system that requests all rooms that open up for that weekend go automatically to the wedding party. I can't promise anything, though." The kid was sweating. Bad.

I leaned an arm on the counter and asked, "What gives? Why are all the hotels around here booked solid?"

"Maybe Johnny Higgins grew another religious vegetable." Pop moseyed up to the counter. "Four years back, one of his rutabagas looked like the Virgin Mary. Well, I thought it looked more like Barbra Streisand, but people still came from all over to take pictures of it. I couldn't get a seat at the diner for weeks. There were wackos everywhere."

Alan nodded. "I remember that. The hotels near the highway were full, so people actually stayed here."

"That rutabaga was a humdinger," Pop agreed. "I bet Johnny has another winner on his hands. The last one he sold on eBay so he could take his wife on a cruise to the Bahamas. Maybe this time he'll spring for a few of his friends to go along. I should call him. A guy needs to know who his real friends are in times of good fortune."

Pop tugged at his skintight jeans in an attempt to free his cell phone from his pocket. He looked kind of like a dog chasing his tail. Anna laughed. Halle offered to fetch the phone herself. Alan just looked worried.

He leaned over and said, "Mr. Higgins's vegetables aren't the reason the rooms are booked."

"No?" I ignored Halle grabbing at Pop's butt and asked, "What is?"

Alan shrugged, shuffled his feet, and sighed. "Well, there is this Indian thing that we . . . well, people are interested, you see, in the Indians that used to live here—"

"What Alan's trying to say is that new arrowheads have been discovered in what may be a burial mound," my father's voice boomed.

We all turned to see him standing in the doorway. He was wearing faded jeans and a white button-down shirt. I looked at

Alan and then back at my father. My mouth dropped open. The look-alike ensembles were creepy.

My father didn't notice my reaction to his fashion statement. Or he didn't care. He just continued, "So a large number of archaeologists, students, and curiosity seekers have come to town. Alan and I are lucky the renovations were started in time to capitalize on this historic event."

Alan didn't look like he was feeling lucky. He looked like he was ready to pass out.

"I haven't heard about new Indian arrowheads being found around here." Pop had stopped chasing his butt. His attention was firmly planted on my father.

Stan shrugged. "Guess the experts got wind of it first. Who knows how these things happen? You just have to take advantage of them when they do." For the first time, Stan seemed to notice me. "I heard about the disco ball incident. Too bad. Your mother loved that thing."

I waited for him to ask how I was doing. To alleviate the unhappiness he'd just caused to well up inside my chest. To do something dadlike.

He smiled and turned to Alan. "Come on, son. We have to file those permits before we get back to work. We'll pick up lunch on the way."

Alan couldn't shoo us out the door fast enough. I stood in the newly paved parking lot, watching Stan clap Alan on the shoulder and laugh at something the kid said. Poor kid. Stan would disappoint him someday soon. I should know.

I herded my bodyguard menagerie into the car. Pop started dialing to get the scoop on the arrowhead discovery. None of the senior gossips had heard a peep about it. Something was off about the whole thing.

Then again, maybe I wanted there to be a problem with my father's foray into mentoring. Maybe I was jealous.

When we got to the rink, a police cruiser was parked by the front door with its lights flashing. Pulse racing, I hurled my car into the nearest parking spot and hit the ground running, listening for the sound of an ambulance. There wasn't one. That was good, right?

I skidded to a stop as Sean Holmes stepped into view. "Has something happened?" I asked, trying to keep the fear from my voice. "Why are you here?"

My three cohorts pulled up behind me. Breathing hard, we all waited for his answer.

Sean's face darkened. He put one hand on his gun and sighed. "I'm here, Rebecca, to arrest you."

Ten

I swallowed hard and tried to stay calm. A neighbor must have reported the break-in at Sherlene-n-Mean's house. Sean must have put two and two together. Considering my involvement in the case, that wasn't hard to do. So now I was going to jail. This was definitely not my best day.

"If you want to arrest her, you're going to have to go through me." Halle Bury strutted in front of me. She crossed her arms in front of her chest and glared at Sean. Anna followed suit. The two stood back-to-back, creating a barrier between me and my would-be arresting officer.

Sean raised an eyebrow. To his credit, he didn't go for his gun. His restraint surprised me.

Not wanting to be left out, Pop called, "You'll have to go through me, too." He took his place in between the two derby girls and placed his hands on his hips. "No way are you throwing my granddaughter in the clink. *No mi pollo muerto.*"

Sean blinked. "What does a dead chicken have to do with this?"

"I said, 'Over my dead body.' " Pop sighed and shook his head in disgust. "Why would I talk about a dead chicken?"

I didn't understand Spanish, but I was pretty sure Sean had this one right. He'd won the Spanish Award his senior year of high school—a fact he was proud to inform me of a while back.

While Pop and Sean debated Spanish terminology, Anna turned toward me and whispered, "We've got him covered. Run."

For a split second, I considered it. Who wouldn't? Only, I wasn't going to run. I had illegally entered Sherlene's house. Yes, it was for a good cause, but I did it and I got caught. I might not be thrilled about the prospect of spending a night in jail—which, knowing the Indian Falls justice system, was all it would be—but I had earned it. On the upside, maybe if I went quietly, Sean would let me order a pizza. It was long past lunch, and I was hungry. Being a hunted felon worked up an appetite.

I stepped around Indian Falls's answer to Charlie's Angels. "I appreciate the support, but Sean is just here doing his job. Don't worry, I'll be fine."

Sean's expression said he was waiting for the punch line.

Extending my hands in front of me, I said, "Go ahead. Cuff me."

Sean's mouth twitched and then broke into a wide smile. "You have no idea how often I've dreamed of this."

I wasn't sure how I felt about being handcuffed in Sean's dreams. I certainly wasn't crazy about his getting a bang out of arresting me. During the past few months, we'd declared a minor truce in our war. We'd had a few relapses, but I'd assumed that our skirmishes now occurred out of a warped sense of fun rather than real malice. Guess I was wrong.

Sean reached for the handcuffs on his belt, stopped, and started to laugh. "I'm not really going to arrest you," he choked out between chuckles.

"You're not?"

He shook his head. "Nope. Not that I wasn't tempted to haul your ass in for kicks. You deserve it after the day I've had."

"Wait." Pop wagged a finger at Sean. "You said you were here to arrest Rebecca. My bladder might not be what it used to be, but my hearing is just fine."

"Okay, maybe I was having some fun telling Rebecca I was here to arrest her," Sean said, grinning at me, "but I didn't actually say I was going to do it. There's a difference."

There was also a difference between deliberately slapping a cop silly and accidentally hitting him in the head with your purse—a dichotomy I planned to explore as soon as the opportunity presented itself. For now I asked, "Who asked you to arrest me?"

"Does Joanne Cline ring any bells?" The expression on my face must have screamed yes, since Sean continued. "She claimed you besmirched her daughter's good name."

"Besmirched?"

Sean held up his hands. "Her word. Not mine."

Pop shook his fist. "My granddaughter never smirks."

"He said besmirch," Anna corrected. "Not smirk."

Pop cocked his head to one side. "What's the difference?"

"Besmirch is to tarnish someone's reputation," Anna explained. "To smirk is to smile in a manner that is smug or insolent. I agree that Rebecca doesn't smirk."

We all stared at Anna in amazement. Anna shrugged. "I teach middle school English."

"Shouldn't you be in school today?" I asked. It was Monday, after all.

"It's Yom Kippur."

I blinked. So far today I'd learned my Roller Derby team had a nun and a Jewish teacher on the roster. It felt like the makings of a bad bar joke.

Sean shook his head. "Anyway, first Joanne Cline asked that I arrest you for lying to her about knowing her daughter. Ten minutes later, she called back in tears, demanding that I arrest you for turning her daughter away from her calling and corrupting her with your wicked ways. It took me another ten minutes to figure out I was talking to Sherlene Patsy's mother." Sean's amused expression turned to annoyance. "You should have told me you found her."

I nodded to appease Sean, but I was processing the news that Sherlene was no longer a nun. Her former colleagues might not have appreciated her derby-girl lifestyle, but at least she wasn't leading a double life. "Did you tell her about Sherlene's death? I broke the news, but she wasn't inclined to believe me."

He nodded. "To tell you the truth, I'm not sure what upset Mrs. Cline more, her daughter's death or the fact her daughter was in Roller Derby. It was a strange conversation."

"Is Mrs. Cline planning on having the funeral in Moline?" I asked. "The team will want to know."

Sean shrugged. "I informed her that the autopsy will be performed today and that once it's complete she can claim the body. That's when we got disconnected. I tried calling back, but the line was busy. I'll try again later."

Odds were Joanne hung up. Not that I blamed her. Sean had that effect on me, too.

"Next time, I'd appreciate it if you tell me when you find the next of kin. Breaking the bad news isn't fun, but it's my job."

Sean started to walk away but then stopped. He turned and gave me a strange smile. "You might also want to tell me why you were so willing to let me cuff you and take you to jail. Something tells me there's a whole lot more that I don't know, but I plan to find out."

Sean winked and walked away, whistling.

Perfect. Well, if I was going to worry about potential jail time, I wasn't going to do it on an empty stomach.

I turned toward my entourage. "Pizza, anyone?"

Anna gave me her portion of the black olive and mushroom pizza. The Jewish holiday gave her the day off work but also meant she couldn't eat until the sun went down. I knew there had to be a catch.

Once we were done with our very late lunch, I opted to do rink work. My bodyguards wouldn't let me work the ticket booth up front. They thought my would-be assassin might come calling. So I took a turn at the rental counter, exchanging smelly shoes for skates. Not the most glamorous job, but one that required minimal focus. That left ninety percent of my brain free to contemplate Sherlene-n-Mean's murder and who might have done it.

By the time I'd given the last shoe back to its owner and locked the rink for the night, I'd come to one conclusion: I needed to be certain who the intended victim was. Otherwise, I was just spinning my wheels. Sherlene-n-Mean's autopsy had to have turned up something, and since Sean wasn't going to share the information, I had to go to a source who'd witnessed it. Lionel. He might not want to talk about Sherlene's autopsy, but I knew I could persuade him given half the chance. I just had to go see him.

Which in theory was no problem. Except I'd forgotten the tattooed team of women who had taken a pledge to guard me with their lives. They were waiting outside the rink's front door as I locked up for the night. Within seconds I was flanked by Erica the Red and Halle Bury. Anna took up the rear.

Rounding the corner, I was struck by a sense of déjà vu. I had seen these girls do this routine before in match after match. In derby, each team is allowed one jammer and four blockers on the floor. The jammer starts behind the pack of blockers. She has to fight her way up to the front and around the rink in order to score. The blockers help their jammer get to the front of the pack while also making sure the opposing jammer and blockers get beat to hell.

Erica and Halle were known for flanking their jammer and getting her safely to a scoring position. They were also known for bashing other blockers with their butts. Any assailant coming after me was going to have his or her hands full.

The trio escorted me safely to my apartment. They even made me wait in the living room while they walked through each room, just in case. That done, they settled in front of the television with six sodas, a large bag of potato chips, and a box of chocolate chip cookies they found in my cupboard. I had no idea how old the cookies were. In fact, I didn't even remember buying them. My sugar binges require fresh-from-the-oven bakery cookies. I'm a cookie snob. Besides, bakery cookies come with less guilt. You have to eat all the cookies in the box since they go stale by the next day.

Erica popped a cookie into her mouth before I could warn her about its dubious heritage. When she didn't gag or break a tooth, I said good night to the gang and headed to my room.

It was time to plan a jailbreak.

Easier said than done. The apartment had one exit. The derby girls were guarding it, and they weren't going to sleep anytime soon. Not with the sugar and caffeine they were consuming. I was going to have to find another way out.

When I was a kid, my mother was nervous about the lack of multiple entrances to our apartment. One always seemed like enough to me, but Mom didn't see it that way. One entrance meant one exit. Not great during a fire evacuation. We never did have a fire, so all that motherly worrying was wasted. Until now.

I dug into the depths of my closet, pulled out a heavy metal case, and flipped the lid. Eureka! A retractable ladder. The thing was old as the hills, but as of two years ago, it still worked. Mom made me haul the thing out and practice setting it up every time I came home from the city—just in case. For love of my mother, I humored her. Who knew I'd be thanking her now.

Opening my door, I listened to the sounds from the living room. Anna, Halle, and Erica were having a great time hurling insults at the local weatherman. I closed the door and locked it. If I did this right, the girls would never know I'd gone.

I opened the window, popped the screen, and attached the ladder hooks to the sill. Keeping my fingers crossed, I gave the ladder a fling and waited for it to unfurl.

The ancient fire ladder banged against the wall several times. I cringed and waited for charging derby divas.

Nothing. Huh. My bodyguards weren't exactly inspiring confidence. Well, I couldn't be upset. At this moment, their lack of skill worked to my advantage.

Purse and car keys in hand, I scanned the parking lot for any potential killers. Not seeing any, I swung one leg over the edge of the windowsill and shimmied down the ladder. Once my feet were on the ground, I made a dash for my car and sped off into the night.

Dr. Lionel Franklin's veterinary clinic and farm was located about fifteen miles north of town. The lights were off when I pulled into the driveway of his green and white farmhouse, which had a sign reading LARGE ANIMAL VETERINARY CLINIC. My cell phone clock said it was only nine forty-five. Lionel wasn't the early-to-bed type. I made my way down to the barn in case he was hanging with Elwood.

The sounds and smells of cows and sheep greeted me as I walked into the dimly lit structure. Animal stalls ran the length of both walls, although only half of them were occupied. Lionel only had three animals of his own, two horses and Elwood. From what I understood, the horses arrived a month after Elwood took up permanent residence. They were here to prevent Elwood from getting lonely. Lionel liked fixing problems. That made him a good doctor. It also made him a meddling boyfriend.

I heard a distinctive grunting from the back of the barn. Elwood trotted down the center aisle toward me. He nudged my hand and I scratched the side of his face, careful not to dislodge his Chicago Cubs baseball hat. The camel rolled his eyes and grunted with happiness.

Elwood was busy roaming the halls. That meant Lionel was lurking nearby.

The camel and I strolled to the back of the barn. Sure enough.

The sounds of baseball were emanating from the recreation room. The room had a leather sofa, chairs, a poker table, a television, and, most important, a refrigerator Lionel kept stocked with snacks and adult beverages.

Lionel was on the couch drinking a beer when I stepped over the threshold. A bottle of wine sat in a bucket on the poker table. Next to the wine were two long-stemmed glasses. Either I'd interrupted a hot date or Lionel was expecting me.

He looked up from the game. "What took you so long? I figured you'd be here hours ago."

I didn't like being predictable. Still, I was glad he was waiting for me and not some blond bimbette. "Had I known you wanted to see me, I would have snuck away from my bodyguards earlier."

A slow grin spread across his face. "The girls are still bunking with you?"

"Yep. They've made camp in my living room to make sure no bad guys come through the door."

"How'd you sneak away?" Lionel asked. Then he shook his head. "Never mind. I don't want to know." Lionel downed the rest of his beer, put it on the table, and stood. Actually, it took two tries for Lionel to get off the couch and onto his feet. Once there, he swayed slightly before walking slowly to the fridge for another beer.

I surveyed the room with surprise. An open pizza box sat on the coffee table. Only one piece was missing from the large Papa Dom's deluxe toppings pizza. An unopened bag of pretzels sat next to the couch, along with three empty beer bottles. Lionel was a guy who liked control. Heavy drinking wasn't part of his normal routine. Especially on an empty stomach. Something had pushed Lionel over the edge. I wanted to help pull him back.

114

"What's wrong with the pizza?" I asked for lack of a better opening.

Lionel shrugged. "Wasn't hungry."

For the first time he looked directly at me. I gasped. Dark circles around puffy eyes. Disheveled instead of perfectly combed hair. Lionel looked like hell.

I did the first thing I could think of. I wrapped my arms around him and hugged. Lionel tried to shake me loose, but I was scrappy. I hung on tight. Finally, he surrendered and rested his head on top of mine. After a few minutes of standing there listening to the Cubs broadcasters celebrate a late-season win, Lionel pulled away. "Thanks. I guess I needed that. Today really sucked."

"Sherlene-n-Mean's autopsy?" I asked.

He took a slug of beer. "I don't know how Doc does it."

"There aren't a lot of murders here. That probably helps." Sherlene's death was the second murder this year, which was as many as the town had in the preceding two decades. The movie actor blown up in a car explosion wasn't technically a murder, so I wasn't counting him.

Lionel flipped off the television and sank into the leather couch. "I see a lot of terrible things as a vet, but Sherlene's autopsy was way worse."

I sat down next to him and gave his hand a squeeze. "So, did they determine the cause of death?"

I knew asking about the autopsy wasn't the best form of therapy, but I thought it might help. Besides, I really needed to know what he'd learned.

My nosiness didn't annoy Lionel. Instead, he looked mildly amused. "Sherlene was electrocuted. Had it not been for all her metal jewelry, she might have survived."

"Really?"

"The source of electricity was a stripped down hair dryer. Those don't produce enough current to kill."

"I thought people died all the time from hair dryers in the bathtub." At least that's the way my mother made it sound while I was growing up. That was why I cut my hair short when I was ten. Or maybe I just liked playing with scissors and ran out of cool things to cut.

"No, I looked it up. The hair dryers in the seventies and eighties had flaws that could cause electrocution in water. The newer models fixed the problems. Only one hair dryer death was reported in the last four years."

Some of the anguish faded from Lionel's eyes as he talked. So I didn't feel as guilty asking, "Then why did she die? Sherlene-n-Mean was healthy and strong. Wasn't she?"

"Healthy as a horse." Lionel drained his beer and sighed. "The hair dryer's ground fault-circuit interruptor was disabled, which by itself shouldn't have killed her. However, there were burns on her wrists and on her torso. From what I can tell, she hit the electrical wires with her metal bracelets and closed the circuit. The closed circuit caused the electricity to flow directly through her body. That's what stopped her heart. If it weren't for the metal . . ."

Sherlene would be alive. Who knew fashion choices could kill more than your reputation? It made me glad I couldn't accessorize.

"If the electricity wouldn't have killed her without the bracelets, why would anyone bother to put wires in the tank?"

Lionel shrugged and leaned back against the sofa. "Maybe they were playing a prank. The person hitting the water would get a little jolt and everyone would laugh."

I thought hand buzzers were the lowest form of humor. This sank even lower.

"The salt makes sense under that theory," Lionel added in a sleepy, slightly slurred voice. "It's something a prankster would do."

"Salt?"

He yawned. "The water in the tank was salty. Someone must have added the salt to make sure the electricity had a better chance of zapping the victim. Minerals help conductivity. I'm sure you learned that in high school chem."

Maybe. All I remembered was the days I put into memorizing the periodic table for our first test. The exam was worth twenty percent of our grade, so I crammed hard. The day of the test, I walked into the classroom ready to blow everyone away with my periodic prowess. Only the decorative periodic table on the classroom wall hadn't been taken down. The teacher invoked the honor system for the test and asked everyone to ignore the chart. I think to this day she believed we all studied for dozens of hours and earned our perfect scores. After that, I never bothered to study for a test again. That I got an A in the class should demonstrate how little chemistry was actually learned.

Still, the salt in the water was making Sherlene's death sound more like a high school practical joke than a murder. And I employed lots of high school students.

Great. I had been hoping Lionel would give me evidence that put Sherlene or Jimmy at the top of the target list. Instead, I was now the obvious choice.

"Did you tell Sean about your theory?"

No answer. Lionel's eyes were closed. His mouth was open. A line of drool snaked from the left corner of his mouth to the middle of his neck. Not a sexy look for him. The guy had a hard day, so I wasn't about to count this against him. Anyone who had to perform an autopsy earned passing out.

Huh. I wasn't sure what to do now. Lionel didn't look all that comfortable sleeping upright, and the couch wasn't long enough to accommodate his six-foot-two frame. After the day he'd had, Lionel didn't deserve to wake up with back and neck pains.

I roused him to a semiconscious state, which—thank goodness—turned off the drool. Then I got him to his feet. One arm draped around my neck, Lionel leaned on me while shuffling slowly toward the door. It took us fifteen minutes to make it to the main room of the barn. At this rate, he'd be in bed by sunrise.

Elwood trotted over, butted Lionel with his head, and grunted. Instinctively, I petted the attention-seeking camel, which meant I let go of Lionel. He stumbled and sank to the hay with a thud. Damn.

I knelt down and tried to figure out how to best get Lionel to his feet. Elwood knelt down next to me with a snort. He was probably worried. He'd already lost one owner. I looked at the camel, then back at Lionel's inert body, and smiled. Elwood had let me ride him a couple of times. What were the chances he'd help get Lionel home?

"Okay," I said to the camel. "Sit there a minute while I get Lionel onto your back."

Elwood grunted but remained on the ground. I took that as a good sign. I tugged on Lionel's arm and pulled him to a seated position. Hay was stuck to the drool on the left side of his face. I stood up, grabbed his hands, and gave a yank.

Oof. My grip slipped, and I found myself back on the barn floor, covered in hay. Between Lionel's dead weight and my sweaty hands, things weren't going according to plan. Two more tries and I finally got Lionel to his feet with his eyes open. I guess tugging his arms out of their sockets had an awakening effect. Elwood sat still while I got Lionel seated. Success. Slowly, Elwood stood. He started walking down the aisle and out of the barn. I walked along beside him, keeping a slumping Lionel on board.

The cool fresh air and the bumpy ride roused Lionel enough that he was able to stumble, unassisted, up the stairs to his room. Once he was tucked in, I took Elwood back to the barn. I gave him a couple of carrots from the fridge and headed out with a new list of suspects: my employees.

I turned off my headlights before pulling into the rink, just in case my bodyguards were still awake. After crossing the lot, I reached my ladder and started climbing. I was three rungs up when something grabbed me around the waist and pulled. My feet hit the pavement, and I did what any self-respecting person would do. I opened my mouth and started to scream.

Eleven

A hand clamped over my mouth. I struggled against the arms squeezing the air from my lungs. The hand in front of my face slipped. I opened my mouth and chomped down on my attacker's skin.

"Ow!"

The arm let go. I spun around, ready to kick the heck out of whoever was behind me.

"You didn't have to bite me." Deputy Sean gave me an indignant stare.

I blinked. I didn't know who I expected to see in the dim streetlight, but Sean Holmes wasn't it. "What are you doing here? Did something happen to the derby girls?"

"Yeah. You." Sean shook his hand to get rid of the sting. "Your friends got worried when they knocked on your bedroom door and you didn't answer. They found the bedroom window open and called me. I didn't want you to scream and freak them out. They're wound pretty tight."

"How did they see my window was open? Did they come out-side?"

Sean smirked. "You're going to need a new door."

Crap. I should have left the door unlocked. Who would have guessed they'd break it down? They did Roller Derby, not demolition.

"So . . ." Sean reached over, picked a piece of hay out of my hair, and held it up. His eyes narrowed. "You were at Lionel's?"

I shrugged and tried not to squirm.

He flipped the straw to the ground. "Did you ask him about the autopsy?" He took one look at my face and sighed. "You didn't have to go behind my back. I would have given you the results."

Since when? "You never share information with me. When I try to ask you something, you threaten to arrest me."

Sean met my glare with one of his own. We stood there like that for a moment before he looked away. He blew a strand of hair off his forehead. "I'll admit that I haven't been thrilled with your interference. Police work should be done by professionals. This case is different, though."

"Since I was the intended victim."

My bluntness caught Sean off guard. He shifted his weight from his left foot to his right. "We don't know that for sure."

I put my hands on my hips and waited.

He frowned and launched into his cop impersonation. "We don't know anything for certain. However, given the current facts, you appear to be the most likely target."

"Well, when you put it that way, I feel much better." Before Sean could blow his top, I added, "Look, I get that this was probably a prank gone bad. The perpetrator is most likely a teenager now consumed with guilt over Sherlene's death. He or she will probably crack under pressure." I was hoping Sean would let me do the pressuring since the offender was most likely one of my employees. Committing manslaughter was going to scar the kid for life. Being grilled by the cops was only going to add to the therapy bills.

Sean shook his head. "I'm not so sure this was a prank. Look at the pieces. First the dunk tank. Then the falling disco ball. I think you're still a target."

I realized he was serious. "I thought you said the disco ball falling was an accident."

"I said there was no evidence of foul play. Technically, that's not the same thing."

It was after midnight, three derby girls were tearing apart my apartment upstairs, and Sean was playing the semantics game. Not my idea of fun.

"Listen," I said. "Someone thought it would be funny to knock my ass into the water and give me a jolt. Instead, someone got killed. I hate that this happened, but once we find the kid the case will be closed. I'll talk to my staff tomorrow and see if someone confesses. If they do, I'll let you know. Now I'm going upstairs before the derby girls break something else. Okay?"

Sean didn't say no, which for him was akin to agreement. I gave him a wave and headed up the stairs to whatever catastrophe awaited.

Turns out the catastrophe wasn't too bad. There were chip remnants on the living room floor and cookie crumbs doing the Hansel and Gretel thing down the hall. The only other casualty was my bedroom door. The broken lock could be replaced, but I had no idea how anyone would get the eleven assorted foot-shaped dents out of the door. Apparently, breaking down doors was harder in real life than it was in the movies.

The real loss was the girls' trust. Halle confiscated my ladder, and Erica insisted on sleeping on the floor next to my bed. I didn't protest. I was so tired I didn't care if the team held a speed skating drill in my room.

Anna and Halle were gone by the time I woke up, leaving Erica in charge. Since it was a weekday, I'd have to wait until late afternoon to start playing Grand Inquisitor. My high school labor was laboring in class. I didn't have much time to plan strategy, either. Today the Chippewa School's two third-grade classes were coming for a field trip. Chasing around forty hyperactive eight- and nine-year-olds required all my attention.

At noon, George and I waved good-bye to the kids with a sigh of relief. Even with seven chaperones and a less than enthusiastic Erica pressed into referee duty, the rink was showing signs of the peewee invasion. Pairs of discarded skates were strewn around the rental area, while napkins and chips were decorating the snack section's floor. Not to mention the mirror in the men's bathroom. It was in a thousand pieces.

George had unclogged a toilet in the bathroom yesterday and left the plunger to dry in the corner. Today, an industrious nine-year-old decided the rink was the perfect place to perform a new extreme sport—roller plunging. Apparently, it was possible to propel yourself along on skates by sticking a plunger to the floor and pulling. Sticking the plunger on the mirror was not so successful.

By the time Indian Falls High's final bell rang, the rink had been set to rights, a replacement mirror had been found in the back and installed (perhaps Mom had experienced the plunger problem before), and I had consumed two servings of corn chips and processed cheese to bolster my courage—not to mention my backside.

My first interviewee was Brittany, a high school senior and one of my assistant managers. Not that I believed she did anything. She wasn't the prank-playing type. Besides, she liked me. A couple of months back, I'd helped Brittany clear her name when a few local busybodies blamed her for disfiguring church property. She was into goth style back then and was the perfect scapegoat. I cleared her name and then gave her a job so she could save for college. If Brittany knew who tried to zap me for fun, she'd spill.

"George said you wanted to see me." Brittany poked her head into the office and smiled.

I smiled back. "I did. Have a seat."

Brittany's smile disappeared. "Am I in trouble?"

"No. I'm working on something, and I thought you might be able to help."

"Sherlene-n-Mean's murder?" Brittany sat down. "We've all been wondering if you'd figured out who killed her yet."

"Who's been wondering?" I asked.

"The whole staff. Everyone keeps asking me questions since I'm a manager." Aside from her black hair Brittany looked the part. She was wearing khaki pants and a pink sweater. She'd come a long way since the days of heavy eyeliner and oversized black goth clothes. Brittany had matured.

I was counting on that maturity. "Is anyone on staff acting worried or a little off? Having someone you know die can hit some people hard. I want to make sure everyone on the staff is coping well."

Okay, my cover story was lame, but it was the best I could come up with.

Brittany cocked her head to one side. "Jack is down, but I think he's having some trouble with his grades. Calculus is kicking his butt." Brittany smiled. I smiled back. Jack walked around talking about how smart he was. Brittany was taking calculus, too. She was acing it.

"Anyone else?"

Brittany stopped gloating. "Tommy has been acting weirder than normal."

I sat up in my chair. "Weird how?"

She shrugged. "He's been jumpy. He made me look behind the snack counter yesterday just in case someone was hiding back there. He's seen one too many zombie movies."

Or maybe he had reason to worry.

"Oh," Brittany continued, "and Brenda is moping around and crying, but I think that's because Rick told her he wasn't going to homecoming. Which really sucks. They've been a couple for two years. They were both nominated for the court, and she'd already ordered his boutonniere and everything. Makes me glad I always go to dances stag. The whole high school dating scene has way too much drama."

Normally, I would have told Brittany that the dating scene's drama quotient never went down. Right now I was too focused on Rick ditching homecoming. Rick was an all-American football guy. He never called in sick because he never wanted to look weak—as if being felled by a cold were a strike against his masculinity. If he bailed on the homecoming dance, he had a reason.

"Did Rick break up with Brenda?"

Brittany shook her head. "No, that's the part Brenda is freaking about. If they broke up, she could dig up another date, but they didn't, so she can't. Like I said, way too much drama."

"How'd you get so smart?" I smiled and sent Brittany back to work. With her help, I'd narrowed my potential suspect field from ten to two. Not too shabby.

Rick was at football practice today. I'd have to track him down later. So I headed over to the snack counter, where Tommy was making popcorn.

Tommy Corwin was a tall, lanky kid with large black glasses and auburn hair that never looked combed. I think it was the red hair that made me agree to his employment in the first place. It was definitely what kept Tommy employed. Tommy was sweet, smart, and a complete klutz. He managed to break more skates, CDs, and cash registers than everyone else combined. I cringed as he poured popcorn kernels into the machine and hit the switch.

"Hi, Tommy. How are you?"

The kid jumped, sending kernels flying. My fault. Experience should have warned me not to speak until the popcorn bag was safely on the counter.

Tommy scurried for a broom and dustpan. "I'm fine. How are you, Ms. Robbins?"

"Everyone else calls me Rebecca," I said for at least the twelfth time.

He bobbed his head up and down. "Right. Can I get you a drink or something?"

"No thanks." I watched Tommy sweep up the stray kernels. "I just wanted to make sure you were okay. You look a little jumpy."

Tommy rocketed upright, propelling the unpopped kernels forward. Right at me. Ouch. Direct hit to the nose.

The kid's eyes grew wide behind the black frames. "I'm sorry, Ms. Robbins."

"It's okay." I reached over, pried the dustpan from Tommy's white-knuckled hand, and did a fast cleanup. Then I put the pan away and asked, "Is there something you want to talk about?"

My high school principal used to ask that question all the time. Kids always spilled their guts, thinking he must know what they had been up to. I was hoping the technique would work for me.

"What do you mean?" Tommy developed a rapt interest in his sneakers.

I put my cards on the table. "Is Sherlene-n-Mean's death bothering you? Talking about it might help."

The color drained from the kid's face. His blue eyes darted from side to side, looking for an escape route. "How did you know?" he whispered.

Clearly, my shot in the dark had connected. Too bad I had no idea with what. Channeling the high school principal, I gave Tommy a reassuring smile and waited.

An old Journey tune accompanied the waiting. Halfway through "Don't Stop Believin'," I was about ready to call it quits.

White-faced, Tommy whispered, "You won't tell anyone about this, will you?"

"Not if you don't want me to." If Tommy confessed, I fully intended to spill the story to Sean, but sharing that fact wouldn't be helpful. Sue me.

Tommy's hand started to shake. "Look, I just found out the other day, and I didn't believe it. Technically, Sherlene's death isn't my fault."

Bingo. I reached for my cell phone. "But you feel responsible for Sherlene's death."

He nodded. "I should have listened, but it was just a stupid booth at the festival. It was supposed to be for fun."

In my mind, getting a jolt of electricity was never fun, but what did I know?

"I didn't believe Madame LeManski." Tommy shook his head with regret. "She told me I was cursed, and Sherlene-n-Mean died because of it."

I blinked. Who the hell was Madame LeManski? I took my finger off Sean's speed dial number. "Wait a minute. How does your being cursed have anything to do with Sherlene's death?"

He sighed. "A bunch of us went to get our cards read. Madame LeManski's been coming to the festival for years. She knows things. When it was my turn, she looked at my cards and said that a dark cloud was hanging over me and any that I touched."

"And you touched Sherlene?"

He nodded. "I bumped into her coming out of Madame Le-Manski's tent. A half hour later she was dead."

Two tears leaked from the corners of Tommy's eyes. I leaned over the counter and patted him on the shoulder. He really believed his encounter with a fake psychic led to Sherlene's death. For a smart guy, Tommy was awfully gullible.

"Look," I said. "Sherlene's death wasn't your fault. You didn't put the wires in the dunk tank or throw the switch. Give yourself a break."

Tommy sniffled. "But what about my being cursed? Madame LeManski said I should be careful or great tragedy would follow, and it did. I have to find a way to get rid of this curse or more people will die."

I blew a strand of hair off my forehead and sighed. "I don't think the curse is real. If it makes you feel better, though, I'll go talk to Madame LeManski and see if she can remove the curse."

Tommy's eyes blinked twice. A relieved smile spread across his face. "Really? That would be awesome, Ms. Robbins. You're the best."

I smiled and crinkled up my nose. Behind Tommy, a waft of black smoke wound its way from the popcorn machine to the ceiling.

"Oh no!" Tommy raced to the machine and pulled the plug.

Too late. The smoke detector blared to life. On the floor, George honked on his whistle and waved his arms in the air. Moments later, people were heading outside as the rink filled with smoke.

I yanked a protesting Tommy out of the rink as the Indian Falls fire truck arrived. He wanted to go back in and fix the problem. Considering his emotional state, I wasn't about to tell him that he *was* the problem.

The smell of burned popcorn hung heavy in the rink after the fire fighters gave the all clear. Every time I'd been involved in a call, which in my opinion was way too often, they'd seen action. I could tell the singed popcorn had filled the boys in yellow with disappointment.

As a result of the intense smell, George canceled that evening's open skate. The Roller Derby girls would still practice, which meant I'd have burned-smelling roommates tonight. I hung a CLOSED FOR AIRING sign on the front door, and while my bodyguards' senses were addled by popcorn fumes, I crept to my car. Football practice was over. It was time to pay Rick Shepard a visit.

The Shepard residence was a large, old-fashioned white farmhouse complete with wraparound porch. It was the style of house I sneered at as a kid but nowadays had a strange attraction to. Something I was sure would go away when I saw skyscrapers again.

I rang the bell and induced bedlam.

"Get the door, Rick!"

"I'm doing my homework! Maggie can get the door!"

"Why do I have to do it? This is my TV time!"

Meanwhile, dogs barked, a baby cried, and several other kids screamed. Finally, the door swung open. Rick's five-year-old brother stood in the doorway with a sucker jammed in his mouth.

"Hello." I smiled and hoped the kid wouldn't notice I'd forgotten his name. Rick had six brothers and sisters. On occasion, even Rick's parents forgot their names.

The kid gave me a purple-toothed smile. "Hi. Do you want to come in?"

Of course I wanted to come in, only the responsible adult side of me couldn't do it. The kid shouldn't be answering doors and inviting strangers into his house. I could have an ax behind my back. I didn't, but that was beside the point. Clearly, "stranger danger" wasn't enforced in this household.

I squatted to look the kid in the eye. "I'd love to, but you really shouldn't invite a stranger into the house without your mother's permission. Is she at home?"

"Mom's not wearing a bra." The kid licked his lollipop. "She won't come to the door. She says it's not polite."

She was right. Annie Shepard had breasts the size of watermelons. Unrestrained, they could do serious psychological damage. "Could you ask Rick to come to the door?"

The kid chomped on his sucker and headed back into the house. A few minutes later, a very sweaty Rick came into view.

He saw me and stopped in his tracks. "Rebecca, what are you doing here? I have today off. Football practice."

It looked like Rick had brought most of the football field home with him. His shirt, neck, and arms were streaked with mud and caked-on grass. His hands and his handsome, teen-idol face, however, were clean.

"I know. I wanted to talk to you about something and thought it would be best to do it here instead of at the rink."

"What do you want to talk about?"

Was it me, or had Rick just swallowed hard? I looked down and saw the five-year-old watching us with big eyes. Nodding at the kid, I said to Rick, "Why don't you come outside so we can talk in private."

Rick swallowed again and stepped onto the porch. He closed the door, leaving the five-year-old safely on the other side.

Smiling, I said, "I heard you decided not to go to homecoming. Are you and Brenda having problems?"

Rick blinked. Clearly, this was not the conversation he expected. "No. I just don't feel like going to another high school dance. I guess I've outgrown them."

Yeah, right. Rick loved being big man on campus. More like he wanted to stay out of sight just in case someone remembered him near the dunk tank. "I was worried Sherlene-n-Mean's death might have something to do with your decision."

Rick's eyes went wide. He crossed his arms in front of his chest, and his face took on a strange pasty yellow color. "No. I mean, why would you ask me about Sherlene-n-Mean's murder? It doesn't have anything to do with me."

The five-year-old was now peeking through the window at us. I decided to push for a confession before he decided to join us. The kid was going to be scarred enough from the combo of Sponge-Bob and his mother's breast issues. No reason to add to the therapy bills.

"Did you know water doesn't conduct electricity very well on its own? Did you learn that in chemistry? I think I did." Rick flinched. I kept talking. "Well, someone dumped salt in the dunk tank. Without the salt, the electricity wouldn't have been able to kill Sherlene-n-Mean. You wouldn't know anything about that, would you?"

"Don't tell my mom. Please."

Not the reaction I was expecting. Rick looked toward the house and back at me with a pleading expression.

"Rick, I think there are more important things to worry about than your mother finding out." Being arrested. Being convicted. Giving up football to bunk in a cell with a guy named Bubba.

He ran his hand through his hair. "My mom said if I stepped out of line again she'd make me quit the team. We're ranked number four in the state. Scouts are coming to the games. I can't get pulled from the team now."

Sherlene was dead and Rick was stressing about football? The kid needed a priority adjustment.

"Look, the salt was supposed to be funny. I'd hit the target. You'd fall into the tank and get a mouthful of saltwater. No big deal." Rick started to pace. "We do it to rookies all the time. It's funny. How was I supposed to know someone had put some kind of electrical wires in the tank and that adding salt to the water would cause someone to die?"

It took a minute before Rick's words slammed home. "You didn't put the electrical wires in the tank?"

Rick's eyes opened wide. "No." He took a step back. "No, that wasn't me. I would never . . . you've gotta believe me, Rebecca."

Damn it. I did believe him. The horror on his face was enough to convince me. Rick was behind the salt. Someone else set the wires, which meant the killer was still out there—and chances were good he or she was still coming for me.

Twelve

Sean took Rick's statement, all the while shooting me dirty looks. I don't know what he found more egregious, my nosing into his case or my bringing a football player into the station. Sean probably thought high school players were above the law. That was the way he was treated when he was quarterbacking the team to victory.

Rick explained the salt prank.

Sean nodded. "So you weren't trying to hurt Rebecca. You were just showing her you thought she was cool."

"Yeah." Rick smiled. "The freshman guys get a kick out of that kind of thing. It makes them feel special, you know."

I waited for Sean to say no, but his expression said Rick's reasoning made all the sense in the world. It was at moments like these that I understood how different the male and female races really were. Give a woman flowers or pay her a compliment and she'll feel special. You have to dunk a guy's head in ice cold saltwater to achieve the same effect. I hated pantyhose and menstrual cycles, but at this moment, I was really glad I was a girl.

The boys continued to talk football hazing while I looked around the room. I'd never actually set foot in Sean's sheriff's department office before. It definitely wouldn't make the cover of *Deputy Digest*. A metal desk occupied the middle of the boxlike room. Several black plastic bins sat on the desk, encouraging organization. Sean hadn't taken the hint. Paperwork was scattered on the desk, on one of the chairs, and atop the five-drawer filing cabinet near the door.

The only thing Sean knew how to file was trash, which was at the almost overflowing stage. Sean was leaning back in his chair behind the desk, laughing at Rick's football story. I was seated across the desk in a hard, uncomfortable wooden chair that was putting my butt to sleep.

"So is Rick free to go home?" I asked, cutting short Sean's trip down football glory lane. "His mother might start wondering where he is."

Rick jumped to his feet at the mention of his mother. "Rebecca's right. Mom is going to start looking for me. You don't need to tell her about this, do you?"

Sean raised an eyebrow. "I don't see any reason to tell her." Rick smiled, and Sean added, "For now. If I find out you've been pulling more pranks, I may change my mind."

Rick's smile disappeared. Clearly, I wasn't the only person Rick was making feel special.

I stood up and headed for the door.

"One second, Rebecca. We need to talk."

Rick and I turned. Sean stood. His arms crossed over his chest, and a half-smile twitched on his lips.

"I have to drive Rick home," I said, taking a couple of creeping steps toward the door. "I was his ride here."

"Don't worry about it," Rick said. "A couple of my teammates were going to the diner. They can give me a lift."

I looked at Sean and back at Rick. Rick had the Sean pose perfected down to the partial smile.

Creepy. In fact, the two of them kind of looked alike. They both had sandy hair, broad shoulders, and slightly crooked noses, which no doubt resulted from their football days. The only difference was that Rick's nose had a slight bend to the right. Sean's was to the left. Too bad neither of their nasal imperfections detracted from their looks. Both of them could use more external flaws to knock their egos down a few pegs.

"Don't get into any more trouble, Rick," Sean warned. "I don't want to be talking to your mother or your coach anytime soon."

Rick bolted out of the office.

"Would you actually talk to his coach?" His mother I understood, but the football coach seemed unnecessary.

He grinned. "The kid doesn't get fed if he pisses off his mother. He doesn't play if he gets in trouble with Coach. Which do you think will bother him more?"

Food was high on my priority list, but football was king for high school boys. There was no contest.

"Now what?" Sean perched one hip on the edge of his desk.

I blinked. "What do you mean?"

He raised an eyebrow. "We both know you aren't going to step aside and let me handle this. I figured I'd ask what your plans are so I don't run into you doing something . . . questionable."

I tried not to flinch. His tone suggested he knew about the break-in and suspected my part in it. "Questionable?" I tried to sound wide-eyed and naive.

"Don't worry." He put a hand on my shoulder and gave it a

squeeze. "I have plans for the jail cells in this place that don't involve you."

Good to know. Now that I was certain arrest wasn't in my immediate future I admitted, "I'm not sure what my plans are. Rick was my best suspect."

Guy had fallen pretty low on the probability scale, none of the derby girls had seen Kandie since Sunday, and my father—well, I had no idea what he was up to, but I was keeping my fingers crossed it wasn't murder.

Sean nodded. "I'm hoping the fingerprints we took and some forensic evidence will turn up some better ones. Taking the salt out of the equation will help narrow the focus. Our perp was looking to scare you, not fry you. That makes a difference."

I was about to agree with Sean when I realized something was very wrong. Sean was discussing a police case . . . with me. He hadn't taken his hand off my shoulder, either. My stomach began doing a strange somersaulting kind of thing.

I took a step back. Sean took his hand away, and I breathed a sigh of relief.

"I should get going," I said, making tracks toward the door. "The derby girls will be wondering where I am."

"That reminds me." Sean's voice stopped my retreat. "Joanne Cline called again. She's decided not to claim her daughter's body. She said her daughter wasn't the person she thought she was, and she didn't feel comfortable being in charge of laying her to rest."

My hand balled up into a fist. I wanted to hit something. Too bad Sean was being nice. Maybe I could convince him to make a pass so I could slap him silly. Sherlene might not have turned out to be the perfect nun Joanne wanted for a daughter, but still. Wasn't motherly love about getting past that? This sucked.

"What do I have to do to claim the body?" My voice trembled with rage. "The team and I will make sure Sherlene has a proper burial."

Sean's face tightened. For a second, I thought he was going to fight me on principle. Then he shocked me again, saying, "I figured you would. I let Eleanor at Dr. Truman's office know you'd be coming by the office tomorrow to make arrangements. The body should be returned to them by then."

"I appreciate it." Still annoyed by Joanne's lack of maternal instincts, I stormed out of the office and headed for the entrance, barely registering Roxy yelling a terse hello. I hit the streetlight-lit parking lot and found a reason to smile. A spandex-free Pop and my three derby bodyguards were milling around near my Civic. Anna spotted me and pointed, sending three heads turning in my direction.

"There she is." Pop grinned. "Didn't I tell you she'd talk her way out of trouble?"

"No." Erica shook her mane of hair. "You were too busy trying to figure out how to put a file in the cake you bought from the bakery. Halle said Rebecca wouldn't land in jail."

Pop harrumphed. "Well, what kind of grandfather would let his granddaughter spend time in jail? And now we have a cake to celebrate. From what I can see, this all worked just about right. *Se perfecto.*"

"Say what?" Erica asked.

"*Perfecto*. It means perfect in Spanish." Pop puffed up his chest. "I'm trying to work my new vocabulary into sentences. Eduardo says that using the language every day will help me sound like a natural Spanish speaker."

Right now Pop's accent made him sound a lot like Speedy Gonzales.

"Sean just gave me some news," I said, breaking up language class.

"Did they find Sherlene's killer?" Anna asked.

"No, but they've ruled out a few suspects. That's an important part of the process." There was no reason to tell them that Sean had no viable leads. It would only freak them out. I was already freaked enough for all of us.

"So what's the news?" Erica demanded.

I sighed. "Sherlene's mother decided that Sherlene's teammates knew her best. She's willing to step aside and let us take care of the memorial and funeral arrangements."

And pigs would fly once hell froze over. I just couldn't bring myself to tell them what Joanne Cline really said. Sherlene deserved having people think she had a mother who loved her.

Anna sniffled. "That's about the nicest thing I've ever heard. We should send her flowers or something."

"Go with a fruit basket," Pop said. "I'll even throw in one of my demo CDs. That'll cheer her up."

I listened to the four discuss floral arrangements with a grimace. Only the thought of the woman getting Pop's CD kept me from putting the kibosh on the whole process. Joanne Cline had earned a trip to hell and back. Pop's singing was a good start.

Halle turned to me. "So when should the memorial and funeral take place?"

I had no idea. "Soon, I guess."

"You have to do it pretty quick," Pop said with authority. "Most folks around here get buried pretty fast on account of there ain't nowhere good to store the bodies." In the dim streetlight, I could see the derby girls' faces go pale. Pop didn't notice. "You also don't want to lose the crowd. Quick funerals mean people are still interested in the person who dropped dead."

The girls considered that long enough for me to jump in. "Why don't we talk to Typhoon Mary and the rest of the team before picking a date?"

"They're at the rink practicing," Anna said. "We were there, too. Then Arthur said some lady named Ethel saw you being dragged into the police station in handcuffs. So George and Mary let us leave practice to rescue you."

The derby girls piled into a silver SUV and headed off to the rink. Pop and I followed in my car. "Did Ethel really say she saw me in handcuffs?"

Pop winked. "She saw you at the station. I added a little more zip to her story. Artists have to make things their own."

I counted myself lucky that the story hadn't had me shot or worse. Still, by the time the gossips were done with it, I might end up with dozens of get-well-soon cards and a couple of referrals for lawyers who specialize in police brutality.

The front doors were propped wide open when Pop and I pulled into the lot. One step into the rink had me gasping for fresh air. The burned-popcorn aroma was overwhelming. I looked around the zooming derby skaters at the emergency doors on the side of the rink. Damn. Those were open, too. There was no escaping the smell.

Typhoon Mary skated over to me. Not far behind was my trio of bodyguards and George. They were all beaming.

"The girls told me all about Sherlene's mother. What an amazing woman. We'll take up a collection after practice for flowers for her and also to pay for the service. I've never had to plan one, but I think a day or two should be enough time. If that's okay with you."

That put the service on Thursday or Friday. Friday was the grand reopening, which took that day out of play. "How about Thursday at seven? That should give people enough time to get here from work, right?"

Mary nodded. "Should be plenty of time. If not, the girls will find a way to get here. Don't worry."

At the moment I was more concerned about the rink smelling like a singed movie theater.

"What about the funeral?" Pop asked. "Around here the wake or memorial service is one day and the funeral is the next. You can't break with tradition."

"He's right," George said. At least, I thought that was what he said. George had a whistle in his mouth. The accompanying hooting made the words hard to understand. George spit the whistle out of his mouth and continued. "Folks around here won't understand if she's buried later than that. They'll believe it was because no one would perform the ceremony instead of our organizational issues. We don't want people raising eyebrows and tarnishing Sherlene's reputation."

"Friday it is." Mary looked around the group. They all nodded. She turned to me. "Who do we talk to about all of this?"

When my mom died, I talked to the funeral director. He filled out some paperwork, gave me books to look through for cards and verses, and basically took care of the rest. Since we weren't going the traditional route, I hadn't a clue how to begin.

Luckily, Pop did. "I'll talk to Midge and Fred Weddle. I just did a show for their fortieth wedding anniversary. I gave them a good deal on the band, so they owe me a favor. Their son is the funeral director over at Restful Repose Funeral Home. He'll be able to work out the details. We'll just have to pick the casket and come up with the color scheme for the flowers, a couple of Bible verses for the funeral, and something for her to wear."

Mary took responsibility for Sherlene's final attire. The girls said they'd handle food for the memorial service, and George took the rest. I breathed a sigh of relief. The thought of going to Restful Repose and picking out caskets brought back memories of Mom's funeral. A year and a half had passed and thinking about it still made me cry.

Just when I thought I'd gotten off scot-free, Mary said, "Of course, this only works if Mrs. Patsy can come. Will you ask her, Rebecca?"

I blinked. Who was Mrs. Patsy? Then it hit me. Sherlene's mom, Joanne Cline.

"Oh. Sure." What else could I say? "Although I don't know if she'll be up to traveling."

Anna looked ready to cry. "But she has to come so we can tell her how much we liked Sherlene."

"I'll do what I can," I said, resisting the urge to cross my fingers behind my back. Yes, I'd call the woman—but convincing Joanne Cline to show her mean-spirited face was the last thing I intended to do.

George looked at his watch and gave a yelp. "We don't have much time left for practice. Go get your skates and get on the floor. We want to do Sherlene proud on Friday."

George grabbed his whistle, shoved it back into his mouth, and darted back onto the floor. Mary followed, and Erica and Anna headed for the locker room.

Halle smacked her hands on her hips. "Crap."

"What's wrong?" Pop asked.

She blew a lock of hair off her face. "A couple of ball bearings came off my wheel at the end of practice yesterday. I never fixed it. George is going to ream me."

I looked down at Halle's feet. She was taller than me, but our feet looked close to the same size. "You can wear mine."

She brightened. "Do you think they'll fit? I'm a size nine."

I wore an eight and a half. Halle didn't strike me as the type who would let a little toe pinching slow her down. "Go ahead and try." I gave her my locker combination and watched her race off to the back of the rink.

George blew a whistle. Speed drills commenced. A few minutes later, my three bodyguards emerged from the locker room. Halle gave me a thumbs-up and began building up speed. George's whistle blew again, and the sound of whizzing skates and shouts of encouragement filled the air.

I was about to head to my office when Pop said, "Sherlene's mother must be a real piece of work."

"What do you mean?"

Pop grinned. "You might have the girls fooled, but they never had to watch you explain why Ollie Van Osterman's turkey was eating your grandmother's homemade bread in our bathtub. The donation-to-the-petting-zoo story was a good one."

"Mr. Van Osterman shouldn't have brought the turkey to visit the school if he was going to chop off its head."

My second-grade class told our teacher we wanted to adopt the turkey as our mascot. She, in turn, broke the news of the turkey's impending death sentence.

"He lost his head anyway, and you got grounded."

"Grandma believed me."

In fact, Grandma never spoke to Ollie again, which I would have felt worse about had she not disliked the farmer in the first place. To the day she died, my grandmother believed Ollie promised me he'd donate the turkey to the petting zoo only to go back on his word.

Pop nodded. "So did your mother. But your left hand twitches when you get creative with the truth. Which is how I know you want Sherlene's mother far away from the service."

Neptune wouldn't be far enough in my estimation. I was about to tell Pop about Joanne when a voice boomed, "Arthur, you need to teach your granddaughter some manners."

Pop and I turned to see Old Man Leerschen hobbling in our direction. He was called "Old Man" when I was a kid, and aside from a few extra wrinkles, he still looked the same. Old Man Leerschen was five and a half feet tall and clad in a brown flannel shirt and overalls; his steely, watchful eyes were edged on top with one long bushy gray unibrow. He walked with a limping gait, which might have been from a war wound or from a disagreement with a pitchfork. Gossips weren't sure which.

My grandfather plopped a hand on his hip. "My granddaughter has more manners than you, Harold. I don't think you've ever chewed with your mouth closed or washed your hands after using the urinal."

I made a mental note never to shake Harold's hand.

He just smiled. "That makes me colorful. Not responding to a message is just plain rude. Don't you think?"

With all the excitement of the past forty-eight hours, I'd forgotten George had mentioned Old Man Leerschen dropping by.

"I'm sorry, Mr. Leerschen," I said, before Pop could dig up an appropriate insult. "Things have been a little crazy around here."

His eyes twinkled under the unibrow. "What the hell did you do to this place? It smells like my sock drawer. Or maybe my underwear drawer. I'm old. I get those things confused."

If I ever got that old, someone needed to shoot me.

"The popcorn machine overheated. We're working on airing the place out."

"You need to wash the place down with tomato juice," Mr. Leerschen offered. "If it gets the smell of skunk out of my collie, it can fix burnt popcorn."

"Thanks for the tip." If the smell was this strong in the morning, I might actually try it. Sherlene deserved better than a memorial service that reeked. "What did you want to talk to me about?"

His smile disappeared, and his eyes narrowed. "I don't want to talk, young lady. I want to yell. You ruined my chance to see Jimmy Bakersfield light up like a Christmas tree. What did you have to go and take his place for?"

Stunned, I looked at Old Man Leerschen for a minute while I tried to keep my jaw from hitting the floor. "Did you rig the dunk tank with electrical wires?"

He blinked at me and then let out a cackling laugh. "Hell no. I just noticed someone doing it. I figured Jimmy must have stepped out with his girl, too. Jimmy needs to be taught a lesson."

"If a woman doesn't have a ring, Jimmy considers her fair game," Pop agreed. "He doesn't understand the niceties of dating etiquette."

For a moment I wasn't sure which was stranger, my love-'em-and-leave-'em grandfather preaching dating dos and don'ts or

Jimmy being in the position to break those rules. The Jimmy I knew wore plaid pants, dirty tube socks, and holey T-shirts. The fact that he could dig up a date did not leave me optimistic about my septuagenarian years.

I pulled my focus back to the real issue. "You saw the person tampering with the tank? What did the person look like?"

He shrugged. "I wasn't wearing my glasses, so I didn't get a good look. Not even sure if it was a man or a woman. Kind of scrawny. Although the sun was in my eyes, so that might have been my squinting. My late wife always squinted when she looked in the mirror. She said squinting took off fifteen pounds."

Before my grandfather could comment, I asked, "What was the person wearing?"

"A black shirt and a white baseball hat. Or maybe it was blue. Or the hat could have been blue and the shirt was white. Hard to say. I wasn't paying too much attention, seeing as how the Miss Native American Days contestants were walking by."

Great. An eyewitness who didn't see anything. The murderer could be any sex, age, weight, or size. Still, he was able to place the time of the tampering. The Miss Native American Days contestants were required to attend a lunch hosted by the Women's Guild. Almost every year a couple of the contestants came down with food poisoning due to some poorly cooked potluck creation. It was as much a part of the festival's tradition as was the time the luncheon was held. The Women's Guild all attended early mass then went to set up the event. That meant the murderer was playing electrician sometime before noon.

I flipped open my cell phone and hit Sean's number. The phone started to ring as a terrified cry echoed though the rink. I turned

146

just as Halle Bury hit the back wall facefirst and slid slowly to the floor.

I waited for Halle to get up. The girls used that kind of stunt in exhibitions to wow the crowd. It worked every time.

Only Halle was still on the ground.

I raced onto the floor as George blew the whistle and ordered everyone to stop skating. I knelt down beside a motionless Halle. Her eyes were closed. A stream of blood trickled across them from a source I couldn't see.

"Someone call 911," I yelled, trying to decide whether or not to remove her helmet and look for the wound. I didn't want to move her if that would cause more damage. That was when I noticed her skates. The front two wheels were lying next to the left boot.

My left boot.

I swallowed hard and looked closer. The kingpin had scratches around the section where it had snapped. It looked like someone had filed through the kingpin so it would break with enough pressure. Someone wanted to hurt the person wearing those skates. I had no doubt who they intended to hurt.

Me.

Thirteen

"Are you okay?" Lionel put a hand on my shoulder as I watched two paramedics load Halle into the ambulance. Halle had regained consciousness about the time Lionel and Sean Holmes arrived. I don't know if she was more pissed about the concussion and sprained ankle Lionel thought she had or about the fact that she'd probably miss Friday's match. Both had her pretty riled.

Seeing Halle angry was way better than seeing her still and apparently lifeless on the floor. I was beginning to wish that whoever wanted me dead would take better aim. Not that I had a death wish, but watching my friends get hurt really sucked.

Anna climbed into the ambulance next to Halle. She gave me a sad wave before the doors closed. Lights flashing, the ambulance did a U-turn and sped off with a delighted Robbie at the wheel.

"The hospital will probably keep her overnight for observation. It's lucky she had her helmet on or this could have been a lot worse."

Lionel was trying to make me feel better. I was open to the

idea, but it just wasn't happening. Standing on the sidelines watching Halle hit the wall had made me feel useless. I was scared and angry. Since scared wasn't useful, I shoved it aside and focused on being mad. Mad felt powerful. It was time to put that emotion to good use.

I turned on my heel and marched into my rink. Pop and Old Man Leerschen were sitting on a bench, ogling the remaining derby girls. I scanned the rink and found what I was looking for against the rink's far wall.

"Sean," I yelled. "Could you come over here?"

Sean looked over and frowned. He said something to Sheriff Jackson and stalked my way.

"I'm in the middle of something right now." Sean glanced over his shoulder. Sheriff Jackson was kneeling down next to where Halle had hit the wall. He stood, backed up a few steps, and began running at the wall as though reenacting the crime. "I'll be back to take your statement later."

I understood Sean's desire to get back to the crime scene. Sheriff Jackson was a great guy, but his mind wasn't always focused. Everyone in Indian Falls knew he had his forgetful moments, but year after year they elected him to office. I couldn't say I blamed them. When he was coherent, Sheriff Jackson was a really nice person. How do you kick someone like that out of his job? No one around Indian Falls was willing to run against him for that reason.

Instead of hitting the wall, Sheriff Jackson pulled up from his run. Shaking his head, he backed up and started running again.

"Wait," I said as Sean started back toward the sheriff. "Old Man Leerschen witnessed the murderer tampering with the dunk tank. You need to take his statement. Now."

Sean stared at me. I guess I looked serious, because he nodded and took out his little cop book.

"You were at the park on Sunday, Mr. Leerschen?"

Our witness frowned at me and grumbled, "Yes. Is that a crime?"

"No, but I am interested in what Rebecca here says you witnessed. Did you see the person who killed Sherlene Patsy?" Sean's pen hovered over the notebook as Sean waited for Harold's reply.

Old Man Leerschen cocked his head to one side and pursed his lips. Finally, he said, "I think Rebecca heard me wrong. I was telling Arthur that I was at the park on Sunday and witnessed something important, but I was referring to the girls parading around in short skirts. Their legs might cause heart attacks, but they didn't do anyone in on Sunday. I would have heard about it. Not a bad way to die, if you ask me."

Sean's book closed with a sharp snap. He gave me a look that could melt Pop's false teeth and stormed off toward the other end of the rink.

"Wait." I caught up to him. "Mr. Leerschen told me he saw somebody tampering with the dunk tank. He didn't tell anyone about it because he figured someone was trying to teach Jimmy Bakersfield a lesson."

Sean stopped and gave me an icy stare.

I crossed my arms in front of my chest and stared back. Righteous anger zipped through my veins. I was handing Sean a legitimate lead to Sherlene-n-Mean's killer, and he was looking at me as though a mutant zit had taken up residence on my nose. "Pop was right there when he said it. Ask him."

The dare hung in the air. Sean let out a loud sigh and brushed past me. Moments later, he was deep in conversation with the sheriff, who was now sporting a derby helmet and a set of knee pads.

I stormed back to where Harold Leerschen and my grandfather were seated. "Why didn't you tell Sean what you told me? I thought you were trying to help track down Sherlene's killer."

Old Man Leerschen nodded. "I am."

"Then why didn't you talk to Sean? He's in charge of the police investigation."

"I don't like him."

I blinked. "So?" There were days I didn't like Sean, but I still called him when things were blowing up or people were dying.

"So, almost twenty years ago Sean Holmes lit a bag of dog shit on fire and threw it onto my porch for me to stomp on. You can't trust a man who does something like that."

Pop stroked his chin and agreed. "He's got a point, Rebecca. The dog-crap-bag trick is just mean-spirited." He turned to Harold. "Did you step on it?"

"Hell no." His eyes glittered under his gray unibrow. "I knew what he and his football buddies were up to. I dumped my beer on it. Waste of a fine beer, but I didn't need to shine my shoes the next day."

Before the conversation could get any more out of hand, I asked, "Why did you tell me? You had to know I was going to tell the cops."

He shrugged. "Everyone says you're the real investigator in this town. Besides, you have a stake in the outcome. It seemed like the proper thing to do." He stood up and hitched up his overalls. "Better be getting home. I'll let you know if I remember anything else about the guy at the dunk tank. Seems to me there was something I should remember." With that, he limped across the carpet and out the front door.

"Now what?" I asked no one in particular.

"You investigate." Pop gave me a look that he reserved for my particularly dense moments. "Harold's right. This town thinks you're a detective, and everyone knows you have skin in the game. They'll answer your questions. Now you just have to figure out who to talk to and which questions to ask."

Sean was still annoyed with what he assumed was my bogus witness claim, which meant Sheriff Jackson took my statement. The sheriff had some trouble remembering what questions he wanted to ask, so it took longer. He was nice to me, though, which counted for a lot. He even let me point out that anyone could have gotten inside the rink tonight with no trouble. All the doors were opened in order to get rid of the popcorn smell.

By the time all the statements were taken, it was midnight. Pop had left an hour before. He had a big gig tomorrow at the Elks Club, and he needed his beauty sleep. George and Erica had left just after that, hoping to sneak into the hospital and check on Halle. None of them had checked with the others to see if someone was staying behind to play bodyguard. Which left me alone to lock up.

Normally, I was fine closing up the rink on my own. In fact, I liked it. More often than not, I laced up my skates, threw in a Chicago CD, and burned off some energy before heading to bed.

Not today. Everywhere I looked there were shadows. I turned off the office computer and hit the light switch. The floor creaked behind me, and I spun around ready to do battle with . . . nothing.

Grabbing my purse and keys, I checked the locks on the emergency doors and headed to the front before I could freak myself out any more. Outside, the air was crisp and everything was quiet. I turned my key in the rink's door, tested the lock, hurried around the corner to my apartment, and oof—ran headfirst into a male chest and let out a yelp.

"Hey, it's just me."

Lionel. He pulled me into his arms and held tight.

"Are you crazy?" I pushed him away despite the warmth he provided. I'd forgotten my jacket, and the fall breeze was cold. "You shouldn't be skulking around in the shadows. I could have taken your head off." The sudden trend of men accosting me in the parking lot had gotten on my nerves.

"But you didn't. Problem solved." Lionel's tone was the one he used when a rabid llama was ready to bite his hand. "George and Erica were worried about leaving you alone for the night. They asked if I'd play bodyguard."

I smiled. Hearing that my best skating instructor and my breaking-and-entering derby girl were worried about me made me feel better.

"Come on inside," I said, heading for the stairs. I wasn't sure if I wanted to be annoyed with Lionel. If we were going to fight, we could do it upstairs where it was warm.

Lionel followed me into the apartment. I flipped on the over-head light and all three living room lamps and threw the dead bolt on the front door. For a minute, I contemplated dragging the end table in front of the door. Nope. It might make me feel safer, but it would make me look wimpy. A bastion of courage I wasn't, but no way was I going to let Lionel see that.

"Do you want a drink?" Lionel asked.

I shook my head. "I need a clear head in order to think things through."

"I meant water or a soda."

Oh. "Water would be good."

Lionel disappeared into the kitchen and returned with two glasses of Indian Falls Tap. He handed me one. I sat on the sofa and drained half of it.

"I think I had enough to drink for both of us last night," Lionel said. He sat down next to me and put his glass on the coffee table. "I'm sorry about that. Yesterday was kind of rough."

"I know." I had been trying not to think about Lionel's experience. The idea of cutting open a body, dead or alive, made me weak in the knees. "Don't worry about it." Translation: Let's change the subject.

Lionel missed the hint. "The entire time I was working on Sherlene, I kept thinking how it could have been you." He wound his fingers through mine. "It made me realize how important you've become to me."

The look on his face said this conversation was turning romantic. Not good. Talking about "us" in the context of cutting up bodies made me want to jump out of my skin.

"Speaking of Sherlene," I said, before Lionel could completely wig me out, "Old Man Leerschen said he witnessed the murderer tinkering with the dunk tank. Only he was too busy admiring the pageant contestants to remember any pertinent details."

"Did he tell Sean?"

"He refuses to talk to him."

"Why?"

"They have . . . personal differences." I wasn't about to repeat the poop-on-the-porch anecdote. "Were you around during the pageant girls' entrance?"

"Yeah." Lionel frowned. The lines on his forehead scrunched together. "Annette was packing up her mobile massage parlor around then. Sammy and Mabel ran back and forth a couple of times while getting things ready for the Women's Guild lunch. Doreen was passing out business cards and selling raffle tickets for St. Mark's. I bought one when she came by to say hello to Elwood."

"Thanks. That gives me a place to start in the morning." I hoped one of those people would have a better memory than Old Man Leerschen. "I guess I should get some sleep."

I stood up and waited for Lionel to head for the door. Instead, he said, "Good idea. I have an early appointment with some sheep. Erica said she'd be here by six to take over guard duty."

Lionel was staying over. My shoulders tensed. Had the derby girls not interrupted us on Sunday, we would have already slept together and this wouldn't have been a big deal. We didn't, though, and now I wasn't sure if Lionel just assumed we would pick up where we left off.

Lionel shut off the living room lights and took me by the hand. Butterflies tickled my stomach as we walked down the hallways to my bedroom. I led Lionel inside without bothering to turn on the light. He leaned down. I closed my eyes, waiting for a kiss to sweep away my indecision. Instead, it barely grazed my lips.

"I'll be down the hall if you need me," he whispered. I opened my eyes and he was gone.

Well, crap. I hopped into bed and tried to ignore the sexual frustration. There were more important things than sex. Staying alive was definitely at the top of the list.

Lionel was gone by the time I dragged myself out of bed. I pulled on a black turtleneck, black jeans, and a pair of calf-high black boots. Black made me feel tough. I needed the boost.

Erica greeted me in the living room with a "Hey, great outfit." Aside from her black sneakers, we were wearing the same thing. I grabbed a piece of raisin bread and a Diet Pepsi from the fridge. It was hard to be tough on an empty stomach. Balancing my breakfast and my purse, I headed down the stairs with Erica following behind.

"Where to?" she asked, strapping herself into my yellow car.

"Shear Highlights. I'm going to get a haircut." Plus a new list of suspects, both from my friend Annette.

Erica gave me an update on Halle as we drove down Main Street. Halle indeed had a mild concussion and a sprained ankle. She was out of commission for Friday's bout, but with a little rest and some heavy-duty Tylenol, she'd be feeling good as new in no time.

I parallel parked in front of Annette's salon, walked in, and smiled. The place was hopping. Annette was nowhere in sight, but three different stylists were working on clients. Several of the Indian Falls Senior Center ladies were paging through books and magazines. They were tapping their toes to bad eighties music while waiting for their turn.

Annette opened the place when I was in high school. Mom and I worried she'd have to shut down after the first week. The salon caused a scandal by providing not only haircuts, perms, and manicures but full body massages as well. The St. Mark's Women's Guild protested by marching up and down Main Street carrying signs reading MASSAGES ARE THE DEVIL'S WORK and KEEP YOUR HANDS TO YOURSELF. The Elks Club walked the other side with signs reading RELAX AND YOU'LL LIVE LONGER. Since Annette's salon was still rubbing people down to this day, I'd say the Elks and Annette were the winners.

Annette emerged from the back room, spotted me, and smiled. Annette and I were a lot alike in the physical department—average height and lots of hair. Hers was a lovely chestnut brown, unlike my Orphan Annie red, and her blue eyes sparkled with perpetual laughter. Seeing Annette made me feel better than I had in days.

"Are you here for a cut?"

"If you have time," I said, nodding at the lineup of clients seated near the door.

"Of course I have time." She waved at me to follow and headed down the aisle of hairstyling stations. "You have an appointment."

I left Erica filling out a *Cosmo* sex compatibility test and hurried to the back of the salon where Annette was setting up her stuff. "I don't really have an appointment, Annette," I confessed.

She raised one perfectly shaped eyebrow and said, "They don't know that. Now let's get you shampooed so I can give you a sensational cut."

A few minutes later, draped with a red plastic cape, I was in Annette's styling chair, hair dripping. She brandished her scissors, ready to get down to business.

My eyes met hers in the mirror. "Do you mind if I ask you a few questions while you work?"

"I figured as much." She grabbed a comb and started pulling, twisting, and pinning sections of hair. "That's why I set up back here. The old biddies up front won't be able to hear us."

Between the distance, the radio, and the gossip, the women from the center might not notice an entrance by the Indian Falls High School marching band.

"Lionel said he saw you at the park on Sunday."

She pursed her lips, studied my hair, and began to snip. "I was there in the morning doing free neck massages."

157

A bunch of hair fell onto the floor. It occurred to me that Annette and I had not consulted on a style. I'd assumed she was going to give me a trim to cover up my real reason for sitting in her chair. Another two-inch hair cutting landed on my smock. Clearly, I'd assumed wrong.

"Don't cut it too short."

Her blue eyes sparkled with excitement, and she spun my chair to face away from the mirror. "Don't worry. I know what I'm doing."

That's what I was afraid of. Normally, I was very specific about what I wanted done to my hair, and, because Annette was a pro, she let me have what I wanted. However, given carte blanche, Annette was known to be a bit avant-garde. Attending Sherlene's memorial with a Mohawk wasn't what I had in mind.

Trying not to cringe, I asked, "Did you happen to see anyone walking near the dunk tank before noon?"

The scissors stopped. "I would have been packing up around then. I made sure only to give massages while church was in session to avoid confrontation."

Good plan. "So did you notice anyone in the area? I have an eyewitness who puts the murderer there around that time."

"Really?" Annette's voice rose an octave. I was glad Annette hadn't resumed cutting. Otherwise, in her excitement, I might have been scalped. "I didn't know there was a witness."

Decision time. I could tell Annette to keep the witness news to herself. She would do it. Option two was to board the Indian Falls Gossip Train and wait to see where it headed. I'd used the town's gossips to help me in the past. Would it help me again?

"The witness came forward yesterday. Sean thinks this will break the investigation wide open." I crossed my fingers underneath the cape. It might be juvenile, but it made me feel less guilty about lying to Annette. Even if it was for a good cause.

The scissors started clipping again. "I ran into Doreen and Mabel while I was packing up. Lionel was there, but you already know that."

I started to nod and stopped myself. Movement of any kind during a haircut was bad. "Anyone else?" So far, none of the names was a surprise.

Annette continued working. "Guy Caruso stopped by as I was leaving. He looked tense. I told him to come by the shop later and I'd give him a discount on a massage."

Guy was there? I sat up a little straighter as Annette grabbed a bottle of styling stuff and rubbed some into my hair. I was about to ask if she'd seen anyone else when she turned on the hair dryer and cut off any hope of communication.

A few minutes later, Annette turned off the dryer. She spritzed my hair with something that smelled like fabric softener and spun me around to face the mirror.

"Ta-da," she said with a smile.

I tried to smile, too, but the corners of my mouth were frozen in shock. Was that me? I squinted at the reflection. The eyes in the mirror squinted back. Yep. It was me, and I had a bob.

"This cut brings out your best features."

I shook my head to see what happened. A lock of hair fell across my eyes. Apparently, they were not one of my best features.

"You're not happy." Annette frowned.

"It's nice," I said, hoping I'd start believing it. "I appreciate it and the information."

She studied me for a moment and shook her head. "You definitely didn't inherit your father's talent for lying. Years might have passed, but some things stay the same. His ability to stretch the truth is still second to none."

Heat crept into my cheeks. "When did you see Stan?"

"He was in the park getting lunch on Sunday. I said hello. He hit on me. I turned him down. No big deal."

Actually, it was a very big deal. Annette's encounter meant one thing: Stan had lied about his alibi.

Fourteen

"Nice haircut. I like the way your hair falls across your eyes. Very sexy." Erica matched my stride beside me as I booked down the sidewalk.

I glanced over. She didn't look like she was joking about the hair.

"Where to now?" she asked.

I stopped walking. I wasn't sure where I was going. Confronting my dad was on the list. Only in my shock, I'd forgotten to ask Annette an important question: What was my father wearing Sunday? While Mr. Leerschen's description was sketchy, it was what I had to go on. I could either go back inside the salon and ask Annette for a rundown of my father's wardrobe, or I could find someone else who saw him at the park.

"We're going to see my Realtor," I decided.

No one was manning the desk at Nelson's Realty. Doreen and her husband had run the business together until he passed away in a tragic bass fishing accident. At least, that was the public story.

Pop never believed it since their office secretary happened to leave town on the very same day Mr. Nelson "died." Despite the whispers and innuendo, Doreen stuck to the widow story. She even kept a picture of her husband on the wall next to the front door. I wasn't sure which story to believe, but if her husband wasn't actually dead, I commended her ingenuity. If nothing else, her kids didn't have to wonder why their dad bailed. Trust me, being the child of a runaway father sucked. That I was here to ask about him was proof enough.

"Rebecca, I love your new haircut," Doreen's voice tittered as she appeared from a doorway in the back. Her eyes narrowed. "Did we have an appointment?"

"No. I just thought I'd stop by and see if there were any new prospective buyers for the rink." This was a great cover story, since it was true. Still, my stomach performed an uncomfortable flip.

Erica grunted and plopped herself into an industrial gray office chair. She and the rest of the team weren't fans of a rink sale.

Doreen glanced at Erica, adjusted her rhinestone-trimmed glasses, and let out a small "tsk." Turning back to me, she said, "Nothing at the moment. I thought I was meeting a prospective buyer on Sunday, but she missed the meeting. She's going to try to stop by next week. I'll know more then."

"I thought Annette said she ran into you at the park on Sunday." Not a great segue, but it was what I had.

She nodded. "She did. The prospective buyer said she was considering relocating to town and was interested in any business that might be available. We decided the festival was a good place to meet since it showcased many of Indian Falls's local establishments."

"So she isn't specifically interested in the Toe Stop?"

Doreen sighed. "Well, no."

Erica smiled at me from behind a home improvement magazine. Sticking out my tongue felt like an appropriate response, but I wasn't sure Doreen would feel that way.

"Too bad," I said, not feeling all that upset. "Annette and Lionel mentioned you were waiting near the dunk tank before noon. Did you happen to see anyone else hanging around that area?"

"Most people were just getting out of church, so there weren't many people around. I went to service on Saturday night." She puffed out her shoulders with pride at her own forethought. Suddenly, her eyes went wide behind her black, sparkly rims. "Wait. This is about that roller person's murder, isn't it? Does Sean Holmes know you're investigating?"

"Sean knows."

"Good. I'm glad that the two of you have settled your differences." She put her hands on her hips and nodded. "Okay. I know I saw Mabel and Sam. Mabel stopped to tell me she had pulled pork and sweet potato fries on special for Monday. I have a weakness for sweet potato fries."

Mabel and Sam made incredible pulled pork. I kicked myself for not going into the diner to do my spy thing on Monday. "Anyone else?"

"Guy Caruso was making eyes at Annette. So was your father, come to think of it." Doreen rolled her eyes. "Annette is too smart to fall for his lines. Still, if he really wanted to have a chance with her, you would think he would have dressed better."

"Did he have paint on his clothes?"

She shook her head. "Mud. All over his pants and shoes. He might have even had some on his hat. I didn't get close enough to be certain."

My knees had also been covered with mud—after tripping near the dunk tank. The rest of the park had been perfectly dry.

Ignoring the cold sweat on the back of my neck, I asked, "Do you remember the color of his shirt and hat?"

"White shirt. Chicago Cubs hat." She tsked. "Personally, I'm amazed the shirt was still white considering the state of his pants. Your father isn't my favorite person, but he's usually a good dresser. One has to wonder what that man was up to."

I was worried that I might already know.

Erica didn't say much on the way to our next stop. The look on my face must not have encouraged chat. The Hunger Paynes Diner was located on the north end of downtown. Because we were in between the lunch and the dinner crowd, only two tables were occupied.

Mabel and Sam Pezzopayne had run the diner ever since I could remember, and while their menus were reprinted every de-cade, I don't think the content was altered. Greasy burgers, enor-mous sandwiches, crispy fries, and at least a dozen different ice cream creations were perpetually in demand. While living in the city, I regularly found myself craving Mabel's famous meat loaf sandwich. Today, I couldn't choke it down if you paid me.

Erica didn't have my eating issues. The minute we plopped down at the counter, she hailed Mabel and ordered the breakfast special, eggs over easy, a side order of pancakes, and a glass of orange juice. I asked for coffee. My life was coming apart at the seams, but holding a coffee cup made me feel like things were al-most normal.

"Can I bring you some Seven-Up or toast, Rebecca?" Mabel asked, pouring my coffee. "You look pale."

The sympathy in Mabel's wrinkled face and deep-set eyes made me want to cry. Kindness unraveled me.

"It's been a tough week."

"Ain't that the truth." Mabel shook her head. "That young lady dying at the park has me locking my doors at night. It's hard to feel safe when a killer is walking around free."

"Actually, that's why I'm here."

Mabel nodded. "I thought you might show up asking questions. Sammy always says your nosy nature is the best thing to happen to this town. Sheriff Jackson and Deputy Holmes try their best, but murder and exploding cars are crimes that happen in cities. You're a city person. You understand those things."

I felt a twinge of annoyance at her description of me as a city person. Lionel had referred to me as such when I first came back to town. It bothered me then, and it irked me now. I'd spent the first eighteen years of my life in Indian Falls, as well as the next four summers and a great deal of holidays. In most towns, that was enough to count me among the locals. Here, I was considered a friendly outsider. The distinction rankled.

Shaking off my irritation, I said, "A witness saw a suspicious person lurking around the dunk tank before noon on Sunday. Lionel and Doreen mentioned you were around during that time."

Mabel set the coffeepot on the faded Formica countertop with a thudding slosh. "You don't think I had anything to do with that poor girl's death?"

"Not at all," I assured her. While age might not be a deterrent to murder, I was pretty sure seventy-year-old Mabel wasn't interested in hacking apart hair dryers. She could cause plenty of chaos just by hanging the GONE ON VACATION sign in the diner's front

165

door. "Actually, I was hoping you and Sammy would tell me who you saw in that area. It might help narrow down the suspect list."

"Hang on a second." Mabel walked over to the window between the counter and the kitchen and yelled, "How's that breakfast order coming?"

A gruff voice yelled back, "Hold your britches, Mabel."

Mabel returned the coffeepot to the warmer, tapped her toe, and peered back through the window. Moments later, two large plates of food appeared, followed by Sammy's head. "What's the hurry? Someone starving to death out here?" He spotted me at the counter and smiled. "You didn't order your usual."

With a practiced hand, Mabel whisked the two plates off the ledge and put them in front of Erica. Erica grabbed a fork and dug in.

"Rebecca wants to ask us some questions about Sunday." Mabel's whisper was loud enough for everyone to hear. The three customers lingering over coffee looked at Mabel, then at me.

Sammy nodded. "I figured you might be doing something like that." His weathered face disappeared from behind the window. Moments later he walked through the kitchen door. "What do you want to know?"

I could feel three sets of ears straining to hear our every word. Erica was the only one in the place not paying attention. She just shoveled eggs, toast, sausage, and pancakes into her mouth with focused intensity. Almost half the food was already packed away, and she wasn't slowing down. With a little training, Erica could eat competitively.

Before I could answer, Mabel said, "She wants to know if we remember who was in the dunk-tank area just before lunch. Doreen was there. So was Lionel."

Sammy nodded. "I talked to Doreen, Felix, and Guy. Doreen wanted to know the special. Felix was donating the plates and silverware to the luncheon. Guy was looking upset. I saw his mother a while later and guessed she might have something to do with his mood."

After meeting Guy's mother, I was pretty sure Sammy was right.

"Oh." Sammy snapped his fingers. "Your father was there making eyes at Annette." I must have frowned, because Sammy was quick to add, "None of us think Stan's behavior is a reflection on you. That man has always been looking for the next big thing, whether it be business or women. He's been in here a lot with that young man, talking his big talk. Poor kid has dollar signs in his eyes. He doesn't have your smarts to stay away from your father's shenanigans."

The kid also didn't have a father who ditched her before puberty and now might be trying to kill her in the hope of inheriting her money. A sick sense of dread settled into my chest. Ignoring it, I asked, "Did you see anyone else?"

Mabel started to shake her head, then stopped. "One of the pageant girls' mothers was standing near the dunk tank."

"How did you know it was one of the mothers?"

She smiled. "Big, bleach-blond hair, fake eyelashes, and lots of mascara that wasn't the waterproof kind. Her daughter must have lost, because she looked sad and angry all at the same time. You see it every year with a couple of those mothers. They tell their daughters they should be gracious even if they lose. The girls behave, and the mothers start Armageddon. At least this one was keeping her distance from the tent. Otherwise, there might have been another murder."

Sammy and Mabel couldn't come up with anyone else, which was a bummer. I now had Felix Slaughter, owner of Slaughter's Market, as a suspect, but he didn't have a motive. Felix and his wife were upstanding citizens. Not to mention members of the gourmet club I'd started. I might not be a four-star chef, but none of the food I'd concocted was ever bad enough to warrant death. I planned on asking Felix some questions, but in my gut I knew it wasn't him.

Taking a deep breath, I thanked Sammy and Mabel, threw a five-dollar bill on the counter, and headed for the door. It was time to go see my father.

"Did you find out anything important back there?" Erica asked, folding herself into my car. "You already knew that stuff, right?"

"Most of it." I was amazed she'd heard anything in her gastronomic frenzy. "Confirmation is important."

I stopped by Pop's house. Empty. No Stan. The Presidential Motel was another bust. Alan was doing a brisk business answering phones at the front desk. When I asked if my father was around, he gave me a pout and shook his head. Alan looked like he was going through Stan withdrawal.

"Now what?" Erica asked as I climbed back in the car.

I pulled out my cell phone and dialed Pop. He might know where I could find Stan. Damn. Voice mail. Pop and Stan were both missing in action. Perhaps they were together? Suddenly, I had an idea.

The senior center parking lot was packed. After five minutes of circling, I parked in a dubiously legal spot on the street. I hoped Sean was too busy running down leads to give me a ticket.

The sounds of an off-key "Shake, Rattle, and Roll" greeted Erica and me the minute we stepped inside. I'd know that singing anywhere. Pop was in the building. The hallways were deserted, so we followed the music. Turns out everyone was watching a purple-and-gold-clad Pop gyrate and wail to a karaoke track. The gig must not have paid much; otherwise, Pop would have brought the band.

A big sign over the stage read HAPPY ONE HUNDREDTH BIRTHDAY, RUTH. Pop reached for the final high note and missed. I winced. The crowd went wild.

The karaoke track changed, and a cheesy synthesized intro for "Can't Help Falling in Love" echoed in the large recreation hall/dining room. Pop strutted over to a white-haired woman in a wheelchair. He unzipped his shirt, revealing tufts of gray hair, and slid a sweat-soaked scarf off his neck. He kissed the scarf and, with a flourish, handed the swath of purple fabric to the woman. Everyone in the room sighed. I shook my head. I loved Pop, even roomed with him for a time when I first came back to town, but I wasn't interested in anything wet with his perspiration. Judging by the way the lady in the chair clutched the scarf to her chest, she felt differently.

Trying to tune out Pop's less-than-romantic-sounding vocals, I scanned the room. Bingo. Leaning against the far right wall, wearing an I LOVE ELVIS shirt and a sport coat, was my father.

I scooted around the folks standing along the wall and made a beeline for Stan. Behind me I heard people yell, "Watch out," and "Get out of my way." Erica must be following.

Stan was only a few feet away. Now that I had found him, what was I going to say? "Are you trying to kill me?" would send Stan running for the exit. Even if he stayed and had something to confess, Stan was smart enough not to do it in front of a hundred witnesses.

I was considering going back the way I came when Pop spotted me from the stage. He waved. Everyone in the room looked in my direction. What else could I do? I waved back. Everyone smiled. Including my father.

He walked over. "It's nice of you to come out and support your grandfather."

Pop hit the final note, performed a spin into a pelvic thrust, and went down on one knee. The women went nuts. The men smiled and applauded. Pop smiled wide and started throwing scarves from one knee. The music stopped, and Pop slowly rose to his feet. Waving, he gingerly walked off the stage and over to Stan, Erica, and me.

Before I could even say hello, a dozen female fans surrounded him. The smell of perfume and Ben-Gay almost knocked me off my feet.

Pop didn't seem to have any issues with the smell. He signed autographs, took pictures, and handed out more scarves. Why not? He'd purchased thousands of them online for almost nothing. Then he announced, "Check out the new T-shirts. My manager would be happy to sell you one for fifteen dollars. If you buy two, I'll throw in an autographed picture of me. Why don't you show them, Stan?"

My father smiled at Pop. It was a tense smile that said he was cheerfully contemplating strangling my grandfather. Stan took off his blazer, handed it to me, and turned around. A woman I recognized from other Aging Elvis concerts applauded.

"Ethel did a good job on the picture. It looks just like me. Don't you think?" Pop puffed out his chest and grinned. I gaped.

The back of the T-shirt featured a line drawing of someone in Elvis attire. If you squinted real hard and turned your head sideways, it sort of looked like Pop. It also looked like Larry King on a bad hair day.

Pop's fans didn't complain about Ethel's artwork. They dove into their bras and came up with cash for two T-shirts apiece. They all wanted a signed eight-by-ten glossy photograph. Pop brandished his Sharpie. After fifteen minutes of Pop selling shirts and signing photos, the staff asked the crowd to leave. They needed to clean up so the Scrabble tournament could begin promptly at three.

"Good show, Arthur." My father clapped Pop on the back. The impact sent Pop reeling forward. Erica stuck out an arm and caught him before he hit the deck.

"Thanks." Pop got his feet under him and gave Erica a smack on the rear. She looked ready to deck him. He winked. She laughed, and the threat of violence was over. Hands on his bony hips, Pop surveyed the room. "Good turnout, but I thought we decided to do less of these small-time gigs. We need events with exposure. Something the radio guys or the newspapers will cover. This is small potatoes."

Stan held up his hands. "You gotta be patient. Even Elvis took these gigs before he hit it big. You pay your dues while I'm working the phones, talking you up. Besides, you need to keep your loyal fan base happy. They're the reason you've gotten this far."

"You're right." Pop waved at a woman batting her eyelashes at him from a doorway. He blew her a kiss, and she looked ready to pass out. "Fans are important. Still, I hate doing gigs without the band. It feels disloyal."

"They won't be upset." Stan waved off my grandfather's

grumbles. "You're doing what you need to do to get ahead. That's the way the world works."

Something about my father's condescending tone set me off. "That's not the way the world works." I dropped his blazer onto the table next to us. "It's the way you work. Pop isn't willing to sell out his band to get ahead. He knows the difference between right and wrong."

"And I don't?" Stan asked. He arched a perfectly plucked eyebrow. I blinked. Until this moment, I hadn't realized he plucked his eyebrows. I glanced down at his hands. They were manicured. "Look," my father continued. "I may not have made the best choices while you were growing up, but I've learned from my mistakes. I've turned over a new leaf."

"Is that why you lied about being at the park on Sunday morning?"

Pop looked surprised.

Erica made a huffing sound behind me.

I held my breath, waiting for Stan to deny it or turn red.

Only he didn't. He just stood there looking at me.

"You told us that you were with Alan all morning on Sunday, but you weren't. Why did you lie?" I insisted.

"I didn't want your grandfather to know I'd stopped by the park. My schedule didn't permit me to play manager, and I knew he'd be upset." His clipped words told me anger was sizzling under the surface. He'd used the same tone when I was five. I borrowed his shaving cream to turn the green walls in the bathroom white.

"You finked out on my gig." Pop scrunched up his face. His two bushy gray eyebrows almost touched. "The fact that you were at the park earlier wouldn't have changed anything."

"I was trying not to make this worse." Stan shrugged. "Sue me."

My father was trying to look casual, but the muscles in his neck were twitching. They did that when he lied. Mom pointed them out to me when I was eight. I tried to ignore those twitches when he said he was going on a business trip and would be back in two days, just in time to see me play Anne in our elementary school production of *The Diary of Anne Frank*. He never came home, and I learned my lesson.

"You're lying."

My father flinched. "I have no reason to lie."

"You do." My heart thudded. My gut heaved, and I said, "Someone put electrical wires in the dunk tank right around the time you were spotted near that area."

Stan laughed. "You think I killed that woman? Why would I try to kill her? I didn't even know her."

"I don't think you wanted to kill her." I tried to ignore the blood pounding in my head and the tilting of my stomach. "I think you were trying to kill me."

Fifteen

That got a reaction. Dad's neck muscles bulged, his eyes bugged out, and his face turned several shades of white. For a moment he looked like he was having a heart attack. Finally, he yelled, "You what? Why would I kill my own daughter? I came back to town for you."

He came back to town to outrun an angry mariachi mob. I hadn't forgotten that I was a side note in the drama. Neither had Pop.

"That's a pile of horse crap." My grandfather poked a gnarled finger at my father. "You wouldn't have come back if you weren't in trouble, and you're only here now because you owe me money. You're going to owe me a whole lot more if you're trying to hurt my granddaughter."

My father looked from me to Pop and back at me. Taking a deep breath, he said, "I know I hurt you years ago, but I'm doing my best to make that up to you. I'm not a killer, and I didn't do anything to the dunk tank."

My father's eyes begged me to believe him. His shoulders slumped as though I had hurt him. I felt myself caving. Before I lost my nerve, I asked, "Then what were you doing in the park?"

He looked into my eyes for what felt like forever, searching for something. Finally, he straightened his shoulders and said, "I now realize how badly I must have hurt you all those years ago. I hope it helps to know you've done the same to me."

Stan grabbed the box of unsold T-shirts, shook his head, and walked out the side door. Pop, Erica, and I just watched him go.

Damn. My throat clenched. My eyes burned, and my lungs were having trouble sucking in air. That really didn't go well.

"I'm going to follow him." Erica's voice echoed in the empty space.

Pop and I looked at her.

"What?" she asked, crossing her arms. "You think it's a bad idea?"

Pop shrugged. "Couldn't hurt. He's hiding something. I just don't think he's hiding what you think he's hiding. The man's a menace, but he isn't a murderer."

Wait a minute. "You were the first one to suggest he was a suspect."

"Yeah, but I meant it in a hypothetical way." Pop patted my shoulder. "Your father loves you. Hell, he loved your mother. He just doesn't know how to show it, and he does such stupid things that it's easy to forget that he cares about more than money."

"But money comes first for him." My voice sounded pathetic and whiny. I hated it.

"Not necessarily," Pop countered. "He could have skipped town on the loan I gave him. I figured he would. Instead of leaving, he's hunkered in and put down roots. He wants to make things right with you. He's just too set in his ways to actually do it. I think he's hoping you'll do it for him."

Not until those winged pigs started serving ice cream sandwiches in hell. Still, I wanted Pop to be right. What girl doesn't want her father to love her and not want to do her in? Only I couldn't bring myself to take the leap of faith. If I did and I was wrong, my heart wouldn't survive.

Changing the subject, I said, "Following Stan might be a good idea. Just make sure he doesn't see you doing it."

Erica rolled her eyes. "What do you take me for? An amateur?"

Yes, but pointing that out wouldn't get us anywhere. "Just be careful."

Erica laughed. "I'll call you if I find out anything." She turned to Pop. "Do you have her back? I promised the team I wouldn't leave her alone."

"I got it covered." Pop held up his fist, and Erica bumped hers against it. Then out the door she went to spy on my father. "Now what?"

I had no idea. I should probably talk to Guy in case I'd missed something the first time, but I wasn't in any hurry to meet his mother again. My emotional equilibrium needed time to recover before facing her unpleasant disposition. Which left one option.

"Let's go get some groceries. I have a couple of questions for Felix."

Slaughter's Market was the only full-service grocery store within seven miles. There were a few convenience stores near the highway and one just outside of town, but those were only good for a bad cup of coffee and a bag of pork rinds. During the summer and fall, Slaughter's carried locally grown produce and milk products and had a full selection of everything else. Indian Falls didn't have any chain stores, and people liked it that way.

A couple of years before, my mother mentioned that a national chain grocery store was looking to build a franchise a few blocks away. The promise of lower prices normally brought out the welcome wagon. Instead, the chain store folks were greeted by twenty-two members of the Elks Club, who promptly unsnapped their pants and hung out their butts for public viewing. The chain store people demanded the men be arrested for public indecency. Sheriff Jackson refused due to lack of evidence, even though he was right there snapping pictures. Pop sent me the article about the store's decision to pass over Indian Falls for their new site. He also included one of Sheriff Jackson's pictures with Pop's tush featured in the center. Ick.

Pop grabbed a cart and zoomed off to do some serious shopping. I headed toward the checkout counter in search of Felix. I found him bagging a bunch of bananas for Eleanor Schaffer. Eleanor had dyed black hair, wore stretchy shirts at least one size too small to cover her ample chest, and had a personality to match her impressive physique.

Eleanor spotted me and smiled. "Rebecca! Great haircut. Felix and I were just talking about you."

Felix's narrow face turned a light shade of pink. He gave me a half-wave and went back to bagging. With anyone else, I might think he was embarrassed by the topic of their conversation, but Felix blushed at just about everything, including his own name. I wasn't worried.

"I was just telling Felix how wonderful you were to hold a memorial service for that poor girl." Eleanor gave my arm a squeeze.

"Sean called the office to let us know we could release the body to the team. A woman named Mary came by just after to ask about making arrangements. She even invited me to the service tomorrow night."

With everything going on, I'd almost forgotten the memorial for Sherlene. Thank God Mary and George were on the ball. Sherlene deserved better than a haphazard event. Damn. I remembered my promise to talk to Sherlene's mother. That would really cap off my day.

"Thanks for helping, Eleanor. I know you've been busy with Doc on vacation."

Eleanor covered Doc's office hours when he was out of town. Everyone was so used to her taking temperatures and having them say "ah" that the lack of *MD* next to her name didn't much matter. Especially when they had a cold or needed a reassuring voice. It had been that way since I was a kid. Of course, everyone also knew Eleanor would send them to the hospital if they needed a prescription or had a problem out of her comfort zone. Eleanor was careful, and she was smart. She also had the major hots for my grandfather.

The minute she spotted Pop zipping down an aisle, she said, "Here's my credit card. Just ring it up when you're done. I'll be back to collect the bags."

We watched her hurry after Pop. Once she was out of earshot, I got down to business. "I was talking to Sammy and Mabel. They mentioned you were in the park just before lunch on Sunday."

He shrugged. "The Girl Scouts ran out of popcorn and oil for their booth. I had to close down the store for fifteen minutes while I ran it over."

"Where was the rest of your staff?" There were eight employees at the market, including Felix. That made it one of the larger employers in town. As far as I knew, only three or four of them ever worked at one time. It seemed like there should have been plenty of help on hand on Sunday.

Felix blushed again. "I normally have Nigel helping out on Sundays. The others attend Sunday services. Barbara and I always go to mass on Saturday so I can cover the store."

"So where was Nigel?"

Felix smiled. "His hearing aid was on the blink. I figured it was better to close the store than let him wait on customers. Things can get a little dicey when Nigel can't hear."

Tell me about it. I'd run into Nigel and his temperamental hearing aid in the past.

"So, did you see anyone interesting at the park during your delivery?"

Felix chewed his bottom lip. "I saw Lionel getting Elwood unloaded from his carrier, and I ran into Sammy and Mabel."

Nothing new. "Anyone else?"

His face went from pink to bright red. Felix had definitely seen someone.

I braced myself for another diatribe about my father. Instead, Felix lowered his voice and said, "A blonde."

I blinked. "A blonde?"

"Shhh." He looked around the store as though waiting for the FBI to storm the front doors. "There was a blond woman in distress. I saw her on my way to the Girl Scouts. She was so upset I offered her my handkerchief."

"Why are we whispering about this?"

Felix blanched. He did the fervent store scan again and confided, "Barbara doesn't like me fraternizing with women. Customers are okay, but talking to a woman in the park wouldn't go over very well."

"Does Barbara have a problem with us talking?"

He gave me a small smile. "You're not blond. My wife thinks I have a thing for blondes."

Barbara was blond, so I could understand her assumption. She also had more chest and hips than I did. Both were probably points in my favor.

"I didn't know she was so jealous."

"She wasn't." He finished bagging the last of Eleanor's groceries and swiped her card. "I think it's the guilt. She's having an affair, so she thinks I must be having one, too. You know."

I didn't know. I gasped and started to cough. Felix leaned over and whacked me on the back.

"You didn't know?"

I shook my head and coughed again.

He shrugged. "I didn't either. I mean, I just figured she was dressing up to go out with friends or to make herself feel good. I like to dress nice when I'm in a bad mood. It cheers me up."

"Are you sure about this?" I asked. "I mean, have you talked to her?"

He paled. "I can't talk to Barbara about this. Besides, I don't think it's all bad. She wanted a divorce until she started having the affair. Now she doesn't. We're talking more than we have in years. In a strange way, we now have a much happier marriage."

Wow. If I ever got married and my husband had an affair, I'd go looking for a shotgun. Before I could frame a response, Pop and Eleanor appeared. Felix handed Eleanor her credit card and her groceries. She turned back to Pop, batted her eyelashes, and said, "I'll see you tomorrow, Arthur." Then off she went.

"Are you taking Eleanor on a date?" I asked, helping Pop load his groceries onto the belt.

"Nah. I promised I'd sit next to her at the memorial service tomorrow." Pop threw a box of Cap'n Crunch on the counter. "Eleanor gets weepy at sad events."

I could relate. I reached into the cart and came up with a box of Cookie Crisp. "I thought you ate oatmeal or shredded wheat for breakfast. What's with the sugared cereals?" Personally, I'd take a bowl of the sugared kind over oatmeal any day, but this was Pop.

"You father loves them. I like to put them in the cabinet where he can see them and then hide them before breakfast the next morning." Pop grinned. "It drives him wild."

"Oh, that reminds me," Felix said as he scanned bar codes. "Your father was at the park on Sunday. I almost forgot about that."

I wished I could. I thanked Felix for the information and drove Pop home, where I helped him unpack his groceries. Then I borrowed his phone. Since I was already in a bad mood, I decided to call Joanne Cline. I might as well get the unpleasantness with parental figures over and done with. Mine was lying about murder or something else, and Sherlene's refused even to bury her daughter. Maybe I should introduce them. They'd probably hit it off.

Pop grabbed a soda and some cold cuts out of the fridge and started assembling lunch. I sat down at the kitchen table and started dialing. After two rings a weary voice answered, "Hello. This is Joanne."

She sounded terrible. My throat constricted. She might not be Mother of the Year, but she didn't deserve to suffer this kind of hurt. No one did. "Hi, Joanne. This is Rebecca Robbins. We spoke a couple of days ago."

"Are you going to harass me, too?" She sighed. "I can't come for my Shirley's body. I told the annoying police officer that."

The words "my Shirley" made my heart lurch. "I'm not calling to harass you. I just wanted to let you know that Sherlene's friends—" Oops. "I mean, Shirley's friends are taking care of the funeral. They're also holding a memorial service tomorrow night. We hoped you might be able to make it."

"I don't think so." The belligerent tone from our past conversation returned. There was also a catch in her breath and two sniffles.

"Let me give you the information just in case you change your mind," I offered, then gave her the address of the rink and the numbers to the office and my cell before she could turn me down. "Shirley's friends want to get everyone who loved her together to celebrate her life. I believe it was a life worth celebrating."

Another sniffle, and the phone went dead. Joanne had hung up on me—again.

"How'd it go?" Pop set a plate in front of me. Roast beef and provolone sandwich on wheat and a pile of Parmesan potato chips. "Is she going to come?"

"The conversation could have gone worse," I said, picking up a chip. I wasn't hungry, but the combination of salt and potato was calling me. "I think she wants to come to the memorial, but who knows if she will. Sherlene and her mother had a bunch of unresolved issues."

"Everyone has unresolved issues after someone dies. It's the way it goes." Pop looked at my sandwich and then at me. I got the hint and took a bite. He smiled and said, "Your mother died thinking I was disappointed in her for marrying your father. I wasn't. It's kind of like you thinking your mother was disappointed you didn't stay in town."

I swallowed hard. "She was. She said more than once that she wished I liked Indian Falls more. Then I'd come home more often."

"You came home enough, and she liked visiting you in the city." Pop grinned. "She got a bang out of telling everyone about your adventures. Made it sound like you were living in the middle of an action movie."

"Mom was exaggerating. Living there wasn't a lot different from living here," I admitted. "There were more people, bigger buildings, a lot more cars and takeout." Of all those things, I missed takeout the most.

"Your mom was proud that you put together the life you wanted."

I pushed the chips around on my plate. "Mom wouldn't be proud of me selling the rink."

"The rink was your mother's dream." Pop reached over and laid his wrinkled hand on top of mine. "She loved every minute of running that place. If you love what you do with your life, your mother will be proud. Trust me."

I did trust Pop, and he was right. Mom would want me to live out my dreams. The problem was, I had no idea what those dreams were. I liked the city when I was there, mostly because it wasn't filled with the baggage I'd left behind in Indian Falls. Only things had changed, and I had absolutely no idea what to do about it.

Since I wasn't about to solve my personal problems anytime soon, I decided to take another whack at questioning Guy. The man didn't give off "killer" vibes, but he had turned suspiciously nice after Sherlene's murder. That bugged me.

Pop tagged along to the bowling alley. He'd changed out of his performance garb and into a slightly less conspicuous pair of brown leather pants, a stretchy deep blue sweater, and a pair of blue suede loafers.

Lots of cars were in the parking lot, and the bowling alley was hopping inside. The sound of pins crashing echoed through the building. High school kids were laughing. Business was looking up.

"Hey, Rebecca." Brittany waved from the lane closest to the door. The guy with her looked around with an angry frown, then saw me waving back and smiled.

I walked over to Brittany and her friend. "Hey. I didn't know you liked to bowl."

Brittany shrugged. "I normally don't. I can't make the ball go all the way down the alley. But Mike promised he could teach me."

The boy in question had blond hair and lots of freckles and was about six feet tall and rail thin. I wasn't sure how well he'd do throwing a heavy ball down the lane. If his thumb got stuck, the weight of the ball would take him with it. Well, that was one way to get a strike.

Brittany frowned. "George told me I had the day off. That you were airing out the rink after yesterday."

"We are, and you do."

She let out a relieved puff of air. "Good. I wouldn't want to look for another job. Aside from the rink, this is one of the only places in town hiring people my age." She shivered at the thought.

I looked around. "I always have at least three or four kids a week coming to the rink looking for a job. Why aren't the jobs here filled?" Was working at a roller rink the way to climb the

Indian Falls High School social ladder? It didn't do anything for me when I was that age.

Brittany shrugged. "No one wants to work here with the dragon lady. I know eight kids who have quit because of her."

The dragon lady must be Guy's mother. "Why? What does she do?"

"She 'accidentally' hurts them." This from Mike. His face was flushed and his eyes wide with excitement.

I looked to Brittany for clarification. She nodded. "Mostly she yells and smokes a lot. Except when a kid stands up to her. Then she gets even. I've never seen it, but a couple of kids say she trips them with her cane. Barbara broke her wrist, and Jeff ended up with a huge bruise on his face when he fell into the counter. Mrs. Caruso likes being in charge, and she lets people know it. Definitely not my kind of boss. You know?"

I did know. I spotted Guy handing out shoes, said good-bye to the kids, and headed over to the front counter. Pop trailed behind me.

"Looks like business is going well." I leaned on the counter while Guy made change for a pimply-faced kid wearing a shirt that read SET PHASERS FOR AWESOME. Any kid that age who owned *Star Trek* apparel had to be hurting for a social life.

Guy finished the transaction and rubbed his forehead with the back of his hand. "I need to get more help around here for days like this. Of course, your rink would have to be closed more often to have more of these days."

I rolled the words over in my head to see if they disguised a threat. Nope. Guy looked overworked and really stressed. Not homicidal. I smiled. "I'll see if I can't get one of my staff members to torch the popcorn machine at least once a week. Just for you."

Guy grinned. "I heard about that. You've had a tough week. Things are bound to get better, right?" His smile got even wider, but his eyes looked freaked. The combination made the hair on my neck stand on end.

"Why are you being so nice?" I asked. "Let's be honest. The whole businesspeople-should-stick-together routine doesn't really make a whole lot of sense to me."

His smile faltered, and his sweat glands began to work overtime. "You have every right to doubt me. I was under a lot of pressure. I still am." His eyes darted over to the bar doorway and back at me. I thought I saw a pleading look on Guy's face, but I could have been wrong. I knew his mean, threatening-to-put-me-out-of-business face. This one was new. He looked scared, and after talking to Brittany, I had an idea why.

"I can't help noticing that you started causing problems for me after your mother came back to town."

"Look," Guy sighed. "I love my mother, but she can be . . . difficult."

"And dangerous," Pop quipped. "We heard all about her killer cane."

Guy swallowed hard. "I called the cops and reported the incidents, but they couldn't do anything. She claims not to see well and says she has poor muscle control. She's seventy-three years old, so she might be telling the truth. The cops can't prove she's lying."

"But you think she is?" I really didn't need to ask the question. The answer was written all over Guy's panic-stricken face. "So what? You got frustrated with your mom and took it out on me?"

Another sigh. "She thought the business should be doing better and threatened to cut me out of the will if I didn't start driving up profits."

Made sense. "So why the change of heart this week?"

"Last week Mother decided I was better at day-to-day opera-
tions than at looking at the big picture. She decided I should do
what I do best and leave the rest of it to her. Whatever that means."

I had a feeling I knew exactly what that meant. Mrs. Caruso
wanted me dead.

Sixteen

Three kids dumped their rental shoes on the counter, sending Guy racing for their real ones. That gave me time to connect the dots. The rink was taking business from the bowling alley. Mrs. Caruso was mean and smart enough to know her profits would improve without me in the picture. The rink would be without an owner to run the place. Pop could do it—he'd done it in the past—but his emphatic retirement was the reason I ended up back in Indian Falls in the first place. Without me, the rink would limp along for a while and then, if it didn't sell, close. That was a perfect motive for a woman who used violence to torment high school employees. Electrocuting me was probably her idea of fun.

Once Guy finished waiting on his customers, I asked, "Would you mind if I talked to your mom? I have a couple of questions for her."

His smile was beatific. "I took her to Aunt Edna's earlier today. She won't be back here until tomorrow. Every Sunday and Wednesday, Aunt Edna gives me a break. I owe her a great Christmas gift this year. Maybe I could get her and my mother tickets on a cruise. What do you think?"

I thought it was a bad idea. Aunt Edna would probably push Mrs. Caruso overboard. Come to think of it, that might be just what Guy had in mind.

Pop and I said good-bye and headed out to the parking lot. I was bummed. If Mrs. Caruso was out of town on Sundays, I'd lost my newest and most attractive suspect. This was definitely not my day.

I was trying to decide what to do next when my cell rang.

"This job is boring." Erica was checking in.

"What's my father doing?"

"He's in the motel office with some kid, working on the computer."

"That's it? Does he look upset or anything?" I figured if Stan was innocent he'd be a little perturbed at being accused of murder.

"Nope. He actually looks pretty happy. A couple of guys with a lot of equipment checked into the motel, and your father looked like he'd won the Publishers Clearing House Sweepstakes. My mom always wanted to win that. One birthday, we made a fake check and bought a bunch of balloons and flowers and crap and pretended to be the Prize Patrol. Mom's expression was just like your dad's."

Stan was probably celebrating his and Alan's business success. "You don't have to stay there and watch him if you don't want to."

"I'll stay for a while longer," Erica assured me. "This is a great place to do my nails. I don't have time to go to the salon and have them done before tomorrow night."

Nails.

Wait a minute. My father's nails were manicured and his eyebrows sculpted to perfection. There was only one place in this town you could have those services performed. I needed to pay another visit to Annette.

Annette is a great poker player. She can bluff with the best of them. However, once she knows she's been busted, she has the grace and wisdom to fold. The minute she saw Pop and me walk into the salon, it was clear she knew the jig was up.

"To what do I owe the pleasure?" she asked with a wary smile.

"I need some sprucing up," Pop announced. "I have a hot date tonight."

Annette grinned. "Who's the lucky lady?"

"Tilly Ferguson."

Annette raised one eyebrow.

"Pop helped distract Tilly while I helped Danielle pick out a wedding dress," I explained.

"She's not normally my type," Pop added, "but you never know."

As far as I could tell, Pop's type was any female over the age of fifty-five. Having a date who qualified for the senior discount at the diner was important to Pop. He felt it gave them common ground. Something every relationship required.

"Let's see about getting you dolled up." Annette led Pop over to one of the stylists. The three conferred for several minutes. When they were done, Annette caught my eye and motioned for me to follow. We walked down the salon's center aisle into the back room. Annette made a beeline for the coffeepot. She poured two mugs of steaming coffee and set them down on the small wooden table next to the back wall.

"You talked to your father." She took a seat at the table and slid one mug toward the other seat.

I sat down. "You gave him a great manicure."

Annette stared into her coffee as her cheeks heated with color. "Stan started coming into the salon about six weeks ago. He had a falling-out with the barber and needed someone to cut his hair."

"And pluck his eyebrows?" Okay, my tone might have been a touch sarcastic, but I couldn't help it. She was acting like something embarrassing had happened between the two of them. Annette and my father? Ick!

Her head snapped up. "I don't know what your father told you, but I'm sure it wasn't the truth. You know him."

I thought I did, but I didn't. This week had taught me that much.

I leaned back with my coffee and said, "So tell me your side of things."

She sighed. "The first time he came in here it was almost closing. I started to throw him out, but he just needed a quick haircut. He was polite and said please. It was a word I'd never heard him say before, so I gave in."

I'd watched my father use the "please" routine. He looked humble, a bit sad, and completely sincere. He could win an Oscar with that performance. Annette should have known better. Being my mother's best friend and my godmother should have taught her something.

Annette didn't wait for me to comment. "I gave him a haircut, and he left. No big deal. Two weeks later he was back. I didn't see any harm in taking his money. I was finishing up his cut when he asked if I'd talked to you recently. If I thought you were doing okay since your mother's death."

Annette looked up at me. Tears glistened in her eyes. "Hearing Stan mention you and your mother in the same breath made me mad. I told him he had a lot of nerve caring after all this time."

"And he told you that he regretted the time away. That once he left he couldn't figure out a way to come back."

Direct hit. Annette bit her lip and nodded.

"He's used that routine on me." Always before hitting me up for money. "Did he pay you?"

"Yes," she said. "That time."

I wanted to roll my eyes, but I didn't. Annette was my friend. She had been taken in by the best con man in the Midwest. I felt sorry for her. "Then what?"

"He stopped in a couple of times a week. First he brought old pictures by. There was one of me and your mom and one of you and me at your christening. He had them framed so I could put them on my station and remember. It was such a nice gesture. I figured maybe the years had changed him. So the next time he asked about you and how you were handling your mother's death, I answered."

A chill went through me. I took a sip of hot coffee, but it didn't do anything to chase the chill. "What did you say?"

"I told him I was worried about you. Especially when you first came to town."

True enough. Annette had tried to get me to go see her shrink. I'd actually considered it once or twice since Dad came back into my life.

"But," she added, "I said I thought you had turned a corner. He said he was worried about your financial situation. He thought you might have gone into debt getting the rink back on its feet after the explosion, but I assured him the insurance covered everything. I said you were doing great things with the rink that your mother had never thought of and were bringing in new business. I might have even mentioned that I thought you were thinking twice about selling the rink and leaving town."

A few months ago, the idea of staying in Indian Falls would have sent me screaming from the room. Today, I had other concerns. "What did Stan say?"

"He said it was nice to know you had grown into a strong, capable woman like your mother and he hoped you would stay here. He wanted the chance to get to know you better."

That didn't seem too bad.

"We went back to my place for coffee and talked for hours about lots of things." Annette rambled on about memories of Mom and questions my father asked about life after he left. They'd talked about the changes in the town like the coffee shop and the new but yet-to-be-finished fountain in the park. Listening to her made me uncomfortable, but I let her continue since I was certain she was leading up to something important.

Finally, she looked down at her hands and said, "We were sad after talking about your mom. I couldn't help it. I let him kiss me." Her eyes begged me to understand. "That was it. One kiss. You have to believe that."

"I do." I meant it, too.

Annette finished off her coffee and set the mug down with a thud. "Saturday, Stan showed up and asked for the works. He had a big business venture launching Sunday, and he needed to look his best. This new deal was going to put Indian Falls on the map and secure his financial future." She shook her head. "When I finished his manicure, he gave me a peck on the cheek and said he'd settle up after his ship came in. Watching his butt sashay out the door, I knew I'd been had."

. . .

Once Annette pulled herself together, we went back to the front of the salon. Annette gasped. I gaped. Pop beamed. The sides of his hair were buzzed short while the top had been styled in a messy, spiked do . . . and it was platinum blond. We'd only been in the back for forty-five minutes. How did anyone manage to get that color that fast?

"What do you think?" Pop preened. "Pretty snazzy, huh? Melissa thought this cut would take ten years off me."

I know it took a couple years off me. I looked closer. The shorter sides did have a strange, youthful effect on Pop's face. The wrinkles weren't as prominent. Then again, I might not have been the best judge. My eyes were beginning to blur after looking at the iridescent color. I was pretty sure Pop was going to glow in the dark.

"You look like a rock star, Arthur." Annette flashed a tense smile. "Although I think you might want to tone down the color. Women should notice your handsome face first, not the color of your hair."

Pop looked in the mirror and frowned. "You might be right. I try to keep a low profile when I'm not onstage. It might be hard to blend in with this color. I don't want a mob scene everywhere I go."

"Why don't we save the town from the mobs?" Annette escorted Pop to a chair. As soon as Pop's head was in a sink, she shot a censorious look at the blond stylist sweeping nearby.

I took a seat and ignored the magazine sitting in my lap. My father was up to something. He put that something into motion on Sunday because he thought it would rake in cash. The majority of

Sunday, Stan also helped Alan paint. No matter how I tried, I couldn't come up with a way for Stan to cash in on sprucing up a motel. If Alan was paying him for painting, it would have to be a lot more than the going rate to make it worth Stan's time.

I glanced at the clock and called George.

"Hey. Did you catch the killer yet?" he asked.

"No. I think I may need Sean to step up and take this one."

He laughed. "Sean's good at breaking up fights and busting kids for joyriding. He's more of an action kind of guy. You're more the ask-questions-until-you-figure-it-out type. I'm betting you find the murderer first."

Personally, I didn't care which one of us figured it out as long as the perp was caught and behind bars before he or she could do me in. Death wasn't on my agenda for the week.

"How's the rink doing? Did leaving the doors open help air it out?"

"It might have helped, but it was hard to tell the difference."

Great. Maybe I should ask Lionel and a few of his paramedic friends to show up at tomorrow night's memorial. Typhoon Mary was bound to go overboard with the flowers. The smell of blackened popcorn and stargazer lilies might cause more than a few people to pass out.

"Don't worry," George said. "We've figured out how to lick it. Old Man Leerschen suggested a remedy. We've been implementing it over the past couple of hours. So far so good. I'll let you know when we're done." George disconnected the call.

Uh-oh.

I shoved my cell phone back into my purse and stood up. Mr. Leerschen wasn't serious about using tomato juice to take the smell out of the rink. Was he?

I walked down to the shampoo area. Annette was busy rinsing out Pop's newly dyed hair.

I must have looked tense, since Annette asked, "Problem?"

"There's a minor crisis at the rink. I just wanted to tell Pop I'm leaving."

"You're not supposed to go anywhere without me," Pop called, trying to pull his head out of the black basin. Annette firmly grabbed his forehead and pushed him back.

"I'm not done yet," she said, spraying water at the left side of Pop's head, "and I'm not letting you run out of here without blow-drying your hair. You'll catch your death of cold, and I'm not going to be the one responsible for it."

Pop sputtered. Before he had a chance to regroup, I yelled, "Good-bye," and bolted out the door.

I hit both stoplights on the way to the rink. Figures. I parked and raced through the front doors, sniffing the air. I detected a faint scent of burned popcorn coupled with the overwhelming smell of tomatoes with a hint of garlic.

Oh God. They had used tomato sauce.

I looked down at the blue and dove gray carpet. No red stains. The rink floor also looked fine. Actually, it looked better than fine. The oak floor shimmered as though it had just been waxed.

Suspicious, I got down on my hands and knees and sniffed. The floor smelled like spaghetti. My stomach growled even as it performed a panicked flip.

"What do you think?"

I jumped at the sound of George's voice and spun around. He looked like a kid who had just eaten his first cookie. "I wasn't sure Old Man Leerschen was right, but I was desperate. The tomato thing worked like a charm. I should give the old guy more credit."

"You put tomato juice on the wood floor?" I looked down again to assure myself it was okay.

George's smile disappeared. His eyes grew wide, and his mouth began to tremble. "Do you think I'm that irresponsible? Your mother would have never forgiven me if I harmed this floor."

"But you said you used tomatoes."

"Tomato-soup-scented air fresheners." He crossed his arms in front of his chest. "I bought a bunch of them and mixed the essence in with some floor wax. We also mixed a little in the carpet cleaner solution."

The tension in my shoulders disappeared. The popcorn smell was almost gone. Nothing was damaged in the process. This was good.

I smiled. "I apologize for worrying, but Mr. Leerschen had mentioned his tomato juice remedy to me and I panicked. I should have known you wouldn't use actual tomato juice to clean the rink."

George's cheeks flushed, and he began to fidget.

"What?" I asked. The flush grew deeper. "Where?"

He reluctantly pointed to the girl's bathroom. I walked over, swung open the door, and freaked. Red streaks covered the floor, the mirror, and the stalls. It looked like someone had been killed in there. Which was almost funny, because it didn't look that way four months ago when someone actually was murdered.

"What happened?"

George shrugged. "A couple of our high school employees helped out today. They were overenthusiastic in their spreading of the tomato sauce. The three of them had to go home for dinner, so they didn't get a chance to clean."

If George believed the home-for-dinner routine, I had a bridge to sell him. Teenaged boys would love creating tomato graffiti. Cleaning it up was a different story.

I sniffed the air again. "Smells like my grandmother's spaghetti sauce." Heavy on the oregano and basil.

"Slaughter's Market was out of tomato juice. We went with Ragu instead." George peered into the bathroom and sighed. "I should probably start cleaning up."

"I'll help. It'll go quicker."

We grabbed two buckets, mops, sponges, and lots of soap. Then we rolled up our sleeves and went to work. After several buckets of water and lots of suds, all evidence of the spaghetti massacre was gone.

"What are you both doing in here?" Pop asked from the doorway. His hair was no longer iridescent blond. Now it was more of a light silver. The spiked hair on top had also been toned down. Instead of looking like an aging boy band member, Pop now bore a strange resemblance to Bob Barker. Pop's smile made me think he was ready to give away a new car, too.

"George and I were cleaning up the bathrooms for tomorrow's service." Pop was known for burning bacon and toast whenever he cooked. I didn't want him to get any ideas about how best to get rid of the smell.

Pop nodded. "You should add a few boxes of Kleenex and some fancy soaps in here. The funeral parlor has lots of that stuff in the bathrooms. I've been to enough wakes to know."

"Good idea." George pulled a notepad out of his back pocket. He crossed *clean rink* off and added tissues to the bottom. "Nice haircut, Arthur."

"Thanks." Pop grinned into one of the sparkling mirrors.

"Annette did a nice job with the color. Although I kind of liked being a blond."

George looked confused. He looked ready to ask, but a high-pitched voice calling, "Where is my hunk of burning love?" ruined his chance.

"That must be Tilly," Pop said, grimacing. "I told her to meet me here." He took a deep breath, adjusted his tight leather pants, and walked out of the bathroom.

George and I followed.

Tilly spotted Pop, clapped her hands together with delight, and rushed over. Her salt-and-pepper hair was caught up in a ponytail tied with a sapphire blue scarf. She was wearing a matching blue sweater and a gray skirt so tight she could only move a few inches with each step. It wasn't surprising that Tilly was panting hard when she finally reached my grandfather's side. A hundred quick, birdlike steps requires a lot of effort.

"I'm sorry I'm late, Arthur," Tilly panted. "The traffic on Main Street is just terrible."

I tried not to laugh. Chicago had bad traffic on weeknights. Indian Falls didn't. Sunday was the only traffic day here, and that was because the two churches in town had parking lots facing each other. Patrons took it as their obligation to leave their parking lots first. This resulted in a lot of near-accidents and lots of angry shouts that seemed highly inappropriate considering where everyone had just been. On any other day, the only traffic congestion occurred when Doc Truman's wife took her car out for a spin. The woman thought going the speed limit was too dangerous.

"Is Mrs. Truman back in town?" I asked.

"Oh, goodness. I don't think so." Tilly shook her head, sending her ponytail wagging back and forth. "Then again, with all those people, it's hard to tell."

Okay, now I was curious. I excused myself from Tilly's gushing about Pop's new hairstyle and headed outside. I walked to the corner, looked down Main Street, and stopped in my tracks.

There were cars traveling up the street. Lots of them. I was so stunned to see traffic on Main Street that I almost missed one important detail. Most of the cars were vans—news vans. The last time news vans cruised through Indian Falls, there was a massive hole in my rink and a bomb-happy moviemaker being thrown behind bars. This couldn't be good.

Seventeen

My shoulder muscles tightened as I hurried down the sidewalk. We'd already had one murder this week. I hoped the appearance of the news crews didn't signal another. A serial killer running around town would really suck.

After power-walking several blocks, I rounded the corner and spotted where all the vans were headed. The park, where only days ago Sherlene-n-Mean was killed, was pandemonium. I counted seven large news vans parked on the street. Some were from the Quad Cities. One was from Springfield. Another two were from Rockford, and the last had come all the way from Chicago. The news had to be serial-killer big to rank a city crew coming all this way.

As the news crews jockeyed for space to set up their lights, I wrapped my arms around my torso and headed into the park. The late-September temperature had taken a dip. The thin sweater I was wearing felt fine during my hurried trek over here. Now, between the weather and a growing sense of dread, I was getting cold.

Thanks to the stylish lampposts the mayor added to the park last spring, I spotted Sean Holmes, Sheriff Jackson, and the mayor to my right, along with a cluster of other people. They were standing near the large hole where the commemorative centennial fountain would eventually sit. Yellow police tape had been strung around the hole. That was never a good sign. Sean was eating a doughnut, which made my stomach turn. Rubbing my arms, I hurried over.

Sean saw me coming and shoved the last piece of doughnut into his mouth. "I should have known you'd end up here."

I considered telling him not to talk with his mouth full but decided against it. "My grandfather's date mentioned the activity. I thought I'd check it out." I peered around Sean to the pit of dirt, trying to see the reason for the police tape. Nothing but shadows. "What's going on? Has someone . . ." I swallowed hard. "Has someone else been killed?"

Sean's eyes narrowed, and his mouth tightened. I braced myself for the bad news. Then he started to laugh. The sound started as a small chuckle. Then it got louder, and more irritating. I had asked a perfectly logical question, and instead of answering, Sean was laughing in my face.

"What's so funny?"

"You are." Sean shook his head and brushed a few doughnut crumbs off his jacket. Still smiling, he said, "No one died here. At least, not today."

Now I was confused. "Then what's with the police tape and the news crews?"

"Archaeological discovery."

I blinked. "What?" I had to have heard wrong.

Sean shrugged. "The sheriff and I were called in to help protect a major archaeological discovery. Turns out a large deposit of Native American arrowheads and other artifacts was discovered here in the park. The news crews are here to cover the story."

Don't get me wrong, I think history is great. When I lived in the city, I visited the Field Museum more than once. But seven news crews for a couple of arrowheads? Sherlene-n-Mean's murder didn't rate one. Today had to be a slow news day. Right?

I shifted from foot to foot, trying to keep warm, and looked around for the guys on the fountain construction crew. I'd gone to high school with a few of them. They didn't seem to be lurking in the shadows, though. "Who made this discovery?"

"A couple of college professors." Sean frowned, took off his coat, and wrapped it around my shoulders. "Why aren't you wearing a jacket?"

"I forgot." Sean's bulky Indian Falls Police Department coat was warm from body heat. It also smelled like chocolate and powdered sugar. I reveled in the warmth and bakery smells for a moment, then said, "Thanks, but you'll need this. It looks like you'll be out here for a while."

I started to remove the coat. Sean stopped me. "I've got another one in my car if I need it. Besides, I actually listen to the weather and dress accordingly."

The snide comment combined with his thick, fleece-hooded pullover helped alleviate my guilt.

"Good to see you, Rebecca." Sheriff Jackson wandered over with a very large box of doughnuts in his hands. A telltale spray of powdered sugar decorated the front of his sweatshirt. "Gloria

DiBelka saw us out here and brought coffee and doughnuts. Want one?"

There were at least a dozen different kinds to choose from. Normally, I wasn't much of a doughnut girl. Bagels were my pastry of choice, or an éclair if I was feeling particularly depressed. However, I wasn't usually engulfed in the lingering doughnut aromas that permeated Sean's clothes. They made me crave sugar. I snagged a Boston cream donut and savored the first bite.

"So, what are you doing out here?" Sheriff Jackson's brows knit together with concern. "Did something else happen at the rink?"

I shook my head and swallowed a mouthful of chocolate. "I saw the news vans and worried someone else might have been killed."

The sheriff leaned forward and looked around to make sure the coast was clear. In a covert voice he said, "No, but Mayor Poste might want to kill his wife before this is all over. These Indian artifacts wouldn't have been found if it weren't for the fuss she created about the fountain's design. You can't find something in the dirt if there's concrete sitting on top of it. These professors are saying this area is going to be the focus of a lot of attention and digging. The fountain's construction is going to have to wait until they're done, and from what I'm hearing, that might take a while."

"Isn't next year an election year?" I asked, hoping I was wrong. The mayor having to halt construction because of his wife made for amusing gossip, but if the fountain didn't get completed on time, people would stop gossiping and start talking about political challengers. Small-town politics had a way of getting personal, fast.

"Yep." Sean grinned big. Sean had personally given the mayor three speeding tickets this year.

I swallowed the last of my doughnut. The sheriff held out the box to tempt me with another. I ignored the siren call of the chocolate cake doughnut and took a step back. The sheriff shrugged, grabbed the object of my desire, and bit into it. In between chews he mentioned, "You should stick around for the press conference." Little bits of chocolate cake shot out from between his lips.

I dodged the spray.

Sean slapped his forehead and looked up at the sky.

Sheriff Jackson didn't notice. "The conference should start anytime now. The professors say they're going to put on quite a show."

Call me crazy, but after everything that had happened this week, I had a hard time mustering big enthusiasm for a press conference about events hundreds of years old. However, the reporters intrigued me. Cops on television often leaked details about their cases to journalists in the hope they'd get a reliable tip or provoke the murderer into showing himself. It couldn't hurt to chat up the press and tell them about Sherlene's death. Right?

"I think I will stick around." I eyed the box of doughnuts in his hand and looked back at the reporters milling around. "The press look like they're getting a little antsy. Got any extra doughnuts I can give them?" Bribery never hurt, either.

"Good idea." The sheriff grinned and passed over the box. "Hungry reporters can turn nasty. We don't want them leaving town with a negative impression of our hospitality. The mayor's going to have enough trouble as it is."

Armed with sugar-laced fried dough, I walked over to a cameraman and offered him the box. He grabbed a doughnut, shoved it in his mouth, and went back to whatever he was doing. The male reporter next to him did the same. The next three reporters all took my doughnuts but weren't interesting in engaging in conversation.

Feeling a bit dejected, I walked over to a tiny, dark-haired girl who seemed more like a college coed than a serious news reporter. She was holding a microphone and appeared more than a little annoyed.

"Hi," I said, with what I hoped was a friendly, agenda-free smile. "I thought you might like a doughnut while you wait for the press conference to begin."

"Haven't you heard that the camera adds ten pounds? I can't eat doughnuts if I want to get into a bigger market than Moline." Her eyes shot daggers in my direction. Then she looked at the jacket and her scowl morphed into a pleasant smile. "Oops. Sorry. I didn't mean to snap at you, Officer."

Huh? I looked down and smiled. I was still wearing Sean's sheriff's department jacket. I was about to correct the woman, but she kept talking. "It's not that I don't appreciate the gesture. Actually, it's very hospitable of you. I'm sure your department has more important things to do than feed all of us."

"The Indian Falls Sheriff's Department makes a point of being involved in any events that impact the town." I felt a tug of guilt for not correcting her assumption, and shoved it to the side. This was the only reporter willing to talk to me. If she heard I was a roller rink owner that willingness might change.

She got out a piece of paper and a pen and asked, "Do you mind if I quote you on that?"

Busted. If Sean heard the quote, he'd hit the roof. Landing in jail for impersonating law enforcement personnel wasn't on my agenda. "Actually," I said, trying to sound nonchalant, "you should interview Sheriff Jackson. He's been watching over this town since I was a little girl. I know he'll be happy to give you a quote. He might even do an entire interview."

Her eyes followed my outstretched finger to where Sheriff Jackson was standing. I tried to see him the way the reporter would. Broad shoulders, shiny bald head, and a laughing smile. From here, he looked like a trusted, wise enforcer of authority. It was this appearance that got him elected every time, despite his bouts of forgetfulness.

The reporter agreed. "Great idea. I'll make sure to find him after the press conference for a little local color."

"Just make sure you don't ask him about the murder investigation going on right now." I pretended not to notice her widening eyes. "We're happy to have a positive event occur in this park, considering what happened here on Sunday."

Her body vibrated with barely suppressed excitement. I could almost see the gears turning in her head. An archaeological discovery would get a lot more attention from her producers if it was paired with a grisly murder.

"I didn't know the murder happened at this park." Her breathy words almost tripped over one another. "Where in the park did it take place? It wasn't here, was it?"

"It was over there." I pointed across the park to where the dunk tank stood days before.

"Excuse me, everyone," a timid male voice called over a loud-speaker. The girl reporter and I turned toward the hastily erected podium. A tall, skinny blond man in a tweed three-piece suit and wire-rim glasses held the microphone. He pushed up his glasses and gave a nervous, hiccuping laugh. "Thank you for coming out to share this moment with us."

A large, dark-haired, burly man with a lopsided grin and an untucked dress shirt took his place next to the skinny professor. He grabbed the microphone from his friend and said, "Today is an historic day. Hundreds of years ago, this land was populated by Native American tribes. Over the years, we have found artifacts that teach us about their way of life and their culture. In this very park, we have discovered a number of Native American artifacts that consist thus far of three stone arrowheads, a pipe bowl, a bone tool, and what looks to be several pieces of pottery. We believe in upcoming days we will find much, much more." The man took a deep breath and flashed a smile at the cameras.

The skinny guy took his friend's mugging as an opportunity to get in the game. He grabbed the microphone and cleared his throat. "This area was thought mainly to be occupied by the Illini tribe. However, today we have embarked on a new era of study. The markings on the arrowheads give us reason to believe the Chippewa tribe might have also occupied this region."

The man stopped talking and gave us all an expectant look. I wasn't sure what he was waiting for, but confused silence probably wasn't it.

The big guy grabbed the mike. "The Chippewa tribe's territory has previously been thought to be what is now Minnesota and Wisconsin. Now that these artifacts have been located here in Illinois, historians will have to reevaluate everything we know about the Chippewa and Illini tribes." The man stood up straight and his voice grew louder. "Not everyone will appreciate the task, but we owe it to history to truly understand the lives of the original Americans. I personally am happy to do whatever I can to shed light on their lives and their struggles. I hope all Americans will join with me in appreciating this discovery and the ones that we will make at this site in the future."

A few audience members applauded. Several reporters hurried to capture his words on paper. The rest started asking questions. I yawned. I was about to leave when someone asked, "How long do you think the excavation will take?"

From ten yards away, I could hear the mayor suck in air.

Unaware of the political nightmare he was causing, the scrawny professor smiled at the crowd and answered, "These things can't be rushed. We have both taken a leave of absence from our respective universities so we can give this project the time and consideration it deserves. History demands that respect."

The mayor started coughing. The reporters didn't notice. They fired more questions. Meanwhile, the mayor continued to choke. Sheriff Jackson thwacked him on the back, sending him staggering backward into Sean. The mayor regained his balance, but Sean lost his. His feet flew up in the air, and he landed with a thump on his ass. Sheriff Jackson started to laugh. So did the mayor. I didn't dare.

Before Sean had the chance to take his annoyance out on me, I left the park and walked back to the rink. Pop and Tilly were gone, but George and the derby girls were there in full force, including Halle Bury. Halle was seated next to the rink, yelling instructions to teammates whizzing by. The pair of crutches on the ground next to her chair and a large bruise on her forehead were the only outward signs of her run-in with the wall.

I started to walk over, but then I stopped. Halle might not want to see me. After all, she sprang a trap that someone meant for me. Now she was missing a much-anticipated derby match as a result. I wouldn't blame her for being seriously put out.

George gave three quick blows on his whistle and called out the next practice item on the agenda. Erica the Red zoomed by. She grabbed the hand of one of her team members and used the trajectory of her body and her upper-arm strength to perform a whip, sending the other girl flying fast down the length of the floor.

"Yeah!" Halle yelled from her sedentary perch. "The Quad City Queens won't know what hit them. You guys rock." Halle spotted me and waved. "Hey, Rebecca!"

I dodged a derby girl careening toward me and walked over to Halle. "How are you feeling?"

Eyes glued to the rink, Halle shrugged. "This is nothing. Last spring, I dislocated my shoulder during an exhibition bout. That hurt big-time. A wobbly ankle and a headache aren't even worth a mention on our Web site."

I grinned. EstroGenocide had a Web site that told you everything you wanted to know about the team, including their worst, or in some minds best, injuries. They even had a photo gallery for colorful bruises, the most swollen joints, and a variety of breaks and sprains. The award for the most terrible injury went to Kandie Sutra. According to the site, she flipped over an opposing team member's back at top speed and crashed into the wall. The protruding leg bone put her injury over the top. Looking at the pictures made me slightly ill and more than a bit baffled. When I dislocated my knee, the last thing on my mind was taking a picture of the black-and-blue puffiness. In fact, I didn't want to look at it at all. Considering the sometimes bloody nature of the photos on the site, I concluded my team had a different set of priorities.

I grabbed a chair and dragged it next to Halle. "I was worried you might be mad at me."

Halle pulled her attention away from the action. "Why would I be mad?" She shook her head and let out a throaty laugh. "If anything, I'm pissed at myself. George always tells us to check our equipment before going onto the floor. I was in such a hurry to start practice that I didn't check the skate. Thank God I remembered to put on my helmet or I'd really be sorry."

"I'm not sure you would have noticed the sabotaged assembly even if you had checked. Whoever did it was careful and knew what they were doing."

"Good." She blew a hair out of her face. "I hate feeling stupid. So, do the cops have a suspect or are they waiting for this idiot to strike again?"

"The sheriff and Sean are trying to find the perp, but I don't think they have any real leads."

"But you do." Halle's smile was grim. "Erica told me she shadowed you this morning. She also staked out your dad this afternoon. The dad thing must really suck."

It did suck. Big-time.

"Are you going to turn your dad in?"

I was trying to decide how to answer that when Halle screamed at the top of her lungs, sending me up and out of my seat. Halle was too busy cheering a hard hip check to notice.

When I was seated again, Halle said, "Look, Erica the Red, Anna Phylaxis, and I were talking about your parental issues. We decided we'd be happy to flex our muscles around your father, but only if you want us to. Three angry derby girls should rouse some fear in him."

Yeah, something would rise in my dad, but it wouldn't be fear. "I appreciate the offer. Let me sleep on it."

Halle nodded. "Sure thing. I couldn't do anything tonight, anyway. I need sleep. For what they charge for a one-night hospital stay, you'd think there'd be rules about people coming in and out of your room in the middle of the night." She cheered a great blocking move and then said, "That reminds me. Erica, Anna, and I can't stay over tonight."

My stomach clenched. "That's okay," I assured her. "I can stay by myself." With the sofa pushed in front of the door and all the windows locked. Until this moment, I'd considered my bodyguard team to be a quirky annoyance. Now I was panicked at the thought of being without them.

"No way in hell." Halle gave her head an emphatic shake. "There's a killer on the loose, and he's after you. Staying alone isn't an option."

"Okay. I guess I can ask Pop to bunk at my place." Staying at his place meant sleeping under the same roof as my primary murder suspect. There was also the possibility of sharing breakfast the next morning with Pop's date. I was hard-pressed to say which option was worse.

"We have it covered," she said. "A professional always finds her own replacement, and the girls and I are professionals."

Professional what? I wasn't sure. Also, while I really liked my three self-appointed bodyguards, I wasn't certain I wanted to trust their replacement, whoever that might be.

"There's our replacement now. I hope you approve."

I followed Halle's eyes and smiled wide. Lionel stood in the rink's entryway, looking windblown and really sexy. He spotted Halle and me on the sidelines and started in our direction.

Halle's eyes twinkled with mischief. "We figured he was the perfect person to guard your body."

I had to agree. Until Lionel's face darkened and his eyes narrowed.

"Why are you wearing Sean Holmes's jacket?"

Huh? I looked down. Oops. I'd forgotten to give it back. "There was a press conference at the park earlier, and I forgot to bring my jacket."

"About Sherlene-n-Mean?" Halle sat up straight in her chair.

I shook my head. "Indian artifacts. Although I might have gotten one reporter interested in Sherlene's story."

George blew his whistle, and the team skated toward the center of the rink for a powwow. Halle grabbed her crutches, hefted herself up, and hopped over to the meeting, leaving Lionel and me alone.

He looked at the jacket one more time and sighed. "Sean is going to hit the roof if your reporter friend does a story on the murder. His anger's going to be directed at you."

I shrugged. The balance of the universe felt out of whack if Sean wasn't angry at me at least once a week. When he was nice, it was time to get nervous.

Lionel reached out and tucked a wayward strand of hair behind my ear. "Cute haircut. Annette's work?"

Reaching up, I touched my shortened hair. I'd forgotten about the new style. Now that I remembered, I couldn't help feeling a little silly. "I was too busy asking questions about my father to pay attention to what she was doing."

"You look sexy. I like it." The gleam in his deep green eyes made me suspect he was telling the truth. Huh. Maybe doing something new wasn't so bad.

"So you're my bodyguard for the night?" My voice sounded a little husky, but who could blame me.

Lionel grinned. "I tried to call you after Halle asked me to fill in, but your phone went to voice mail. I figured I'd just come over and see if you were okay with the plan."

"I'm glad you did," I said, diving into my purse for my phone. "Oops. I forgot to turn it back on after leaving the press conference." I was one of those rare people who turned off her phone at an event without being asked. Beeps, buzzes, and arcade noises during movies annoyed the hell out of me.

I pushed the ON button. A few seconds later, my phone beeped. I had a message. Danielle needed wedding help again, and I was the only one she could turn to. This time it was flowers.

"Something wrong?"

I shoved the phone back into my purse with a sigh. "Danielle needs my help tomorrow morning. She has to pick out flowers and wants me to do it for her. I thought being maid of honor involved showing up to the wedding wearing a tacky dress. This wedding-planner stuff isn't what I had in mind."

"Well, I hope poker is what you had in mind for tonight." Lionel looped his arm around my shoulder and led me toward the front door. "The guys want a shot at winning back their money."

During last week's poker game, I pulled four aces and cleaned everyone out. Doing the same tonight would go a long way toward making me feel better about life.

Lionel and I made small talk during the fifteen-minute drive to his farm and veterinary clinic. Poker night at Lionel's was a weekly tradition that started years before I returned to town. I'd managed to crash the party back in May while looking for murder suspects. A couple of players had been replaced over the past few months due to a murder and an arrest, but that hadn't kept the tradition from continuing. By the looks of Lionel's driveway, several of the players were already here.

We hopped out of Lionel's black monster truck and headed down to the barn. Elwood butted his head against my shoulder and greeted us with a couple of happy camel grunts. He was wearing a pink and white EstroGenocide poker visor I'd given him after his other visor had fallen into a visiting goat's pen. The goat had eaten the hat.

I gave Elwood a few pats, and we headed back into the rec room. Zach had his head in the fridge. Sean was sitting at the poker table, munching a cookie. He was the most recent addition to our poker game. Surprisingly, he didn't rub it in when he won, and he lost with class.

Sean spotted me and stopped chewing. It took a lot to come between Sean and his blissful enjoyment of bakery products, so this was not a good sign.

"Sorry we're late." Lionel grabbed two beers from Zach's hands and set them on the table.

Zach plopped down on a folding chair. "No problem. We already ordered the pizza."

Damn. Zach loved anchovies. No matter how carefully I picked them off, I could still taste the tiny, oversalted fish. Zach swore I would grow to love the flavor. Zach was insane.

Lionel doled out the poker chips. Sean shuffled the cards, all the while watching me out of the corner of his eye. I stuffed some chips into my mouth and pretended not to notice.

"So, Rebecca." Sean started dealing, but his eyes never left mine. "I had a reporter at the press conference ask about the murder from earlier this week. She said she had a sheriff's department source that confirmed where and when the murder took place." I tried to look wide-eyed. Inside, I winced. Sean kept dealing. "She even cornered the mayor about the danger lurking in Indian Falls. The mayor almost had a heart attack, and her cameraman caught it all on film." He flipped one final card onto his stack and set the remaining cards down in front of him.

I tried not to freak. Pissing off the mayor wasn't part of my grand plan.

Sean leaned toward me. "You wouldn't happen to know anything about any of that, would you?"

Who, me?

"What press conference?" Zach asked, chowing down on a fistful of pretzels. Sean stopped glaring at me long enough to explain Indian Falls's newest claim to fame.

When he was finished, he turned back toward me. "You were talking to this reporter just before the press conference started."

"I'm not a sheriff's department source." Tension built in the back of my skull as Sean continued to stare me down.

"You were wearing my jacket."

Sean's powers of deduction had improved since the first murder investigation. Good for the town. Bad for me.

"I was handing out doughnuts. She didn't want any. Said they'd make her look fat on camera." I threw a blue chip on the pile. My hand gave a slight tremble. So much for thinking I was immune to Sean's anger.

"I raise ten." Lionel tried to shift the subject back to poker.

Sean wasn't biting. "Are you saying you didn't mention Sherlene's murder?"

Saying no was a lie. I was bad at outright lying. My face turned red. My left hand twitched. The only people I could lie to were ones who didn't know me. Sean didn't qualify. Besides, he might already know the answer. I was stuck.

"Isn't there any onion dip?" Zach gave the chip in his hand a forlorn look.

Lionel pushed back his chair. "I have some up at the house."

Eureka! I was saved.

I leaped out of my chair and yelled, "I'll get it. You guys play without me," as I bolted out the door.

Almost dancing with relief, I walked with Elwood through the hay-strewn barn to the front entrance, all the while trying to come up with a way to distract Sean from talking about the reporter. Burning down the barn would do it. Only that seemed a trifle extreme, and it would make Elwood and his furry friends homeless. Nope. That wasn't an option.

I promised an attention-seeking Elwood I'd bring him back a carrot and headed out into the cold night. Maybe I could call George and ask him to report a prowler around the rink. Sean would get called away and—

I jumped as a loud pop rang though the night. I spun around and heard a louder pop and a thunk into the tree to my left.

Holy crap. Someone was shooting at me.

Eighteen

Another shot. I sucked in air as a clump of dirt went flying several feet to my left. Either the shooter forgot his glasses or he needed lots of practice. I didn't care which. My attacker's bad aim was the only reason I was still alive. I tried to see where the gunman was shooting from, but beyond the barn lights and the lit sidewalk, everything was awash in darkness.

Heart thudding, I looked toward the barn, then back at the house. The house was closer. My feet started trucking as another shot rang out. Somewhere behind me I heard a male voice yell, "What the hell is going on?" It sounded like Lionel, but I couldn't be sure. I was too busy saving my butt to focus.

Scrambling up onto the porch, I tipped over two potted plants as I raced to the front door. The window a foot to my right exploded. Yikes! Blood pounded in my ears as I grabbed the doorknob, twisted, and pushed. Locked. Shit! Who locked their doors in the middle of the country?

I jumped as another shot rang through the quiet evening. A potted plant on the porch steps bit the dust, and I hit the deck. My breath caught in my throat as I looked around. What now?

The next shot made my decision for me. A bullet lodged in the front door just above my head. I scrambled to my feet and vaulted off the porch, around the side of the house, and right into a large evergreen bush.

Several branches and a bunch of needles scraped my skin during my descent until I finally hit the ground with a thud. I pushed myself up to my feet. My left knee throbbed, but I didn't have time for first aid. Willing my legs to move, I limped as quickly as I could to the back of Lionel's farmhouse.

Leaning against the cool aluminum siding, I held my breath and listened for my attacker giving chase. No hurried footsteps in my direction. That was good. I took a deep, searing breath and flinched as a shot rang out. Then another.

"Stop!" Sean's voice echoed. "Police!"

Three more shots cut through the night, followed by the distant sound of a car door slamming and tires making tracks. Finally, silence.

"Rebecca?" Lionel's voice yelled.

It was followed by an angry Sean. "Rebecca, where are you, damn it?"

Heart still pumping hard, I limped back around the house. Lionel was twenty feet away. Zach and Sean were nowhere in sight. "Here I am," I tried to say, only the words stuck in my dry throat.

Swallowing hard, I yelled, "Over here."

Lionel swung around. A relieved smile spread across his face.

"Sean! She's up here, and she's okay." Lionel kept smiling, which made me feel better. I almost didn't need to hobble as I headed across the grass.

He gave me a hard, quick hug. I wanted to go limp against him, but he had other ideas. He pushed me away and knelt down to look at my knee, which I'd almost forgotten about. Although, now that he'd reminded me, my knee really hurt.

Lionel led me toward the house's front steps. I reached the top as Sean raced up the path, brandishing his gun and his cell phone.

"Where's Zach?" I asked, trying not to freak at the sight of the gun. Guns didn't usually bother me, but tonight's shooting-gallery experience had me jumpy.

"Zach went running after the car, trying to get the license plate number." Sean looked at my face and then down at the gun in his hand. Without a word, he holstered it and zipped up his jacket, making it disappear from sight. "I called the incident in to the sheriff. Did you see who was doing the shooting?"

"I tried, but it was too dark." I took a seat on the porch and winced at the sight of my knee. The fabric was ripped, and the skin underneath was torn and bleeding. Between the falling disco ball and this adventure, I wasn't going to be wearing skirts anytime soon. Lionel whipped out his first-aid kit and started working. Yeow! Trying to distract myself from the pain, I added, "Under the lights, I had to have been a clear target. The shooter must be someone who doesn't handle guns very often." Lucky for me.

Zach came running up the driveway, panting hard. He stopped, took several gulps of air, and said, "They headed toward town."

"They?" There was more than one?

Zach nodded. "I think so. It looked like two people in the car, but I couldn't get close enough to be sure."

Damn.

"But," Zach panted, "I would recognize the car again if I saw it. They were driving a maroon 2004 Ford Freestar minivan limited model with a gray undercarriage. I've worked on a few around here, but none of them are maroon, and nobody I've met shelled out the extra cash for a limited model. The bells and whistles don't mean much to folks around here."

Sean pulled his notepad out and flipped it open. "You're sure it was a Ford Freestar?"

Zach nodded. "It's a pretty quiet vehicle, but it sounds like Lionel's truck revving up when someone punches the accelerator. Trust me."

I did. Zach might not have graduated at the top of his high school class, but he founded the car shop club and managed to disassemble and reassemble several faculty members' cars during homecoming each year. If anyone could positively identify a car in stressful conditions and low light, it was Zach. So now I knew my would-be killer drove a fancy minivan. I wasn't sure if that made me feel better or worse.

The pizza guy arrived as Sean was doing his cop paperwork. We took the pizza down to the barn and righted the chairs that had been flipped during the boys' abrupt departure. With pizza and beer at hand, we sat down to go over the details of the shooting.

I was less interested in the details and more interested in the food. It's amazing how a little brush with death can make a person ravenously hungry. Of course, it didn't hurt that the pizza guy got the order wrong. Instead of anchovies, the pizza was covered with pepperoni and onions. I took this as a sign that better things were coming. I also chose to eat as much as possible just in case I was wrong. Being able to zip my jeans didn't seem very important after facing death. I'd probably feel different in the morning, but I'd deal with it then.

Sean grilled me on where and when each shot was fired. He did the same to Lionel and Zach. Lionel paled during his questioning, which may or may not have had something to do with my grabbing a fifth slice of pizza. Lionel hadn't eaten any.

Once the pizza and the questions were finished, Sean and Zach helped put away the unused poker chips and empty beer bottles. Then they hit the road. I hit the proverbial wall. The adrenaline rush was over, and the reality of being tired and scared had returned.

"I think I've changed my mind." Lionel's voice penetrated the fuzz around my brain.

"About what?"

"You staying in this town." Lionel stood up and raked a hand through his already disheveled hair. "Maybe you should go back to Chicago. It's what you plan on doing. Why wait?"

Three months ago I would have cheerfully agreed and started packing. Today, I wasn't so eager to bail. As a matter of fact, the idea of leaving made me mad. "This is my hometown, Lionel. I might not always like it, but there is no way I'm going to let some psychopath chase me away." Staying or going was going to be my choice.

Lionel wasn't backing down. "Be reasonable. The only thing keeping you here is the rink. George can run it for you while you wait for it to sell—back in the city."

His voice sounded flat and emotionless. Like he couldn't care less that he had just ordered me to move nearly two hundred miles away. That was a big deal. Or it should have been. Right? The whole guy/girl thing wasn't my strong suit, but hearing your boy-friend tell you to get out of town couldn't be a good sign.

"What about us?" I realized the faint, sad voice was mine. Yikes, I was pitiful.

Lionel's mouth curved into a sad smile. "As far as I know, there isn't an us. We keep skipping that conversation."

"It feels like there is," I said, pleased that my voice sounded less pathetic. Crossing toward him, I asked, "Do you really want me to move back to Chicago without knowing for sure?"

He looked like he was going to say yes. Then he stopped. Sigh-ing, he put his arm around my shoulders and kissed the top of my head. "Becky, when you're around I have no idea what I want. I think it's time to go to bed."

Maybe I was just glad to be alive, but both things sounded damn good to me.

I woke up in Lionel's guest bedroom disoriented and a little nau-seated. The next time I faced a near-death experience, I'd celebrate with salad. Pizza hangovers weren't much fun.

Still wearing a borrowed oversized T-shirt and a pair of box-ers, I hopped out of bed and went in search of Lionel. The jeans I'd been wearing yesterday were ripped and stained and brought back too many scary memories. They'd require serious cleaning and maybe even exorcizing before I put them on again.

He was gone. The note on the kitchen table told me he'd been called away on a cow emergency. He instructed me not to worry and gave me directions to the cupboard containing breakfast items. I ignored the food options and made a beeline for the cof-feepot.

Armed with a hot mug of caffeine, I padded into the blue and white country living room in search of the newspaper.

"Good morning."

I jumped at the sound of a female voice, sending a stream of coffee over the edge of the cup and onto my hand. "Ow." I put down the cup, wiped my hands on my shirt, and shook my hand in the air while looking for the intruder.

Erica the Red got up from where she was reading and asked, "Can I get you some ice?"

My hand was tinted a pale pink, but the stinging had already started to subside. "I'll be okay," I said. "I was just surprised."

Erica smiled. "Sorry. I guess by now I figured you expected to see me." She pointed to a bag next to the doorway. "I stopped by the rink and picked up some clothes for you. Your grandfather was nice enough to drive over and let me in. I think I caught him in the middle of something."

Ugh. I was pretty sure what Pop had been in the middle of and with whom. My already delicate stomach did a flip.

"Thanks." I said, hoping the coffee would wipe the icky taste out of my mouth. Morning breath and my grandfather's sex life wasn't a good combo. I took another caffeine hit and added, "I never said thank you for making time in your life to watch out for me."

"No big deal. I work out of the house, so my schedule is pretty flexible. Besides, I'm in between projects and am looking for inspiration."

"What do you do?" I asked.

She gave me a considering look. After a moment, she said, "I'm a romance writer."

I almost spit out my coffee. Erica was tall, broad shouldered, and drop-dead beautiful in a challenging sort of way. I pictured her as a truck driver or a construction foreman. Writing had never been one of my guesses, let alone romance writing. The romances I read back in high school were sweeping tales of tragic love that made you weep and laugh all while sighing. Of course, as a high school freshman, I was mostly interested in the sex scenes. Although the guaranteed happy ending was a big plus, too. My high school friends and I would read a book and then scope the halls for the male student who best fit the hero's description. There weren't many Viking warrior types hanging around Indian Falls then. Later, as an adult, I learned that sex wasn't quite what the books described. For some reason no one ever got an accidental kick to the shin or an elbow resting on her hair in fictitious sex.

Erica looked tense at my lack of response, so I said, "That's great. I don't think you'll find much inspiration in my life for your books, but you can try." Erica laughed. I drained my coffee, grabbed my bag, and headed off to get dressed.

Ten minutes later, I was back downstairs in stretchy brown pants, a deep blue cowl-neck sweater, and Sean's oversized IFSD jacket. Erica had packed my high-heeled brown boots, but I'd opted for last night's scuffed, dirty sneakers. What they lacked in style they made up for in speed. After last night, speed was a necessity.

"Where to?" Erica asked as we locked up.

Good question. "The rink." I needed to check in with George.

Erica steered her deep blue SUV toward town. "Thanks for not acting weird when I mentioned my job. Some people hear that I write romances and start acting strange."

"You probably get a lot of people who want your autograph."

She flashed me a smile. "Those are the fun ones. All writers get those, but some people make snide comments when I tell them what I write."

"Really?"

"That's why I don't broadcast what I do anymore. I wasn't always so careful, but I learned my lesson." She took a hard right onto Main Street, sending me flying into the door. "The owner of our team's last home rink acted normal until he heard about my books. All of a sudden, Jay started making passes at me. He figured I must be addicted to sex since I wrote about it. He also thought I'd be interested in having an affair."

"That must have been . . ." Terrible. Horrifying. Nightmarish. I settled on "Uncomfortable."

She nodded. "His wife, Linda, caught him making one of his passes. That's when things got really bad. She'd had me autograph a couple of my books and knew the kind of sex scenes I write. I guess that sent her imagination into high gear. Linda Salkin is not a woman you want to piss off. While screaming at me to get out of the building, she grabbed the gun they kept in the back office and started firing into the air. Thank God it was the end of the night and no one but the team was around. A kid could have gotten hurt, or worse."

Before last night, that story might have made me laugh. Now that I had been shot at, I was angry. "Did you call the cops?"

"The team asked me not to." She shrugged and hung a hard left into the rink's lot, sending me careening back against the door. "We didn't have any other place to skate. Linda avoided me but kept a close eye on her husband from then on. That's how she caught Kandie and Jay getting it on in the stockroom. She went ballistic, throwing plungers and buckets at Kandie. The next thing we knew, our team had been booted from the rink. I didn't mind the change. Having a semisane rink owner is a big plus in my book."

That was a compliment. I think.

The soothing sounds of Mozart greeted us as we walked into the Toe Stop. George was teaching a private lesson to one of our newer students, Nan Thain. Nan was seventy years old, with stylishly short gray hair and a wicked sense of humor. I'd seen her at some of Pop's senior center gigs and was surprised when she walked into the rink a month ago and signed up for private lessons. She had even purchased her own pair of skates. They were purple and red. So was everything else she wore.

Nan spotted me standing on the sidelines. She waved and zipped over on her purple wheels. She was going fast, and she didn't show signs of slowing. Her eyes grew wide. Oh God. Unless I was mistaken, Nan had no idea how to stop.

George raced to catch up with his wayward student. He grabbed her from behind and jammed his toe stop into the floor as she plowed into me. The three of us fell to the floor with a thud.

"Please get up," I squeaked, barely able to breathe from the bottom of the pile. The weight on top of me shifted, and I took a big gulp of air.

George held out his hand and helped me to my feet. "You should have jumped out of the way."

I should have, but I wasn't sure if George would catch Nan in time. We'd already had one person crash into a wall this week, and she had a helmet. Watching another one go splat wasn't my idea of fun.

"Thanks for catching me, dear," Nan said, in a quiet, high-pitched voice. Her cheeks were the same color as her vibrant red velour workout suit. "George and I were just practicing how to come to a stop. I guess I need a touch more practice."

"Practice makes perfect," George said, doing his best cheerleader impression. "Why don't you go back to practicing while I take a moment to talk to Rebecca?"

Nan gave me a sweet smile. "Rebecca, dear, you should come over next week for dinner so I can thank you for breaking my fall. I'll make turkey. Tell your grandfather to come, too."

She pushed off, almost fell over, and regained her balance. With a victorious smile, she zipped off to practice.

"Take it slow," George yelled, not that it did any good. It was obvious that Nan liked speed. From her invitation, I would say she also liked my grandfather. That explained her interest in lessons. Pop enjoyed hanging out at the rink. Most of the senior center women weren't interested in skating or coming to the rink, which gave Nan an open shot at attracting his interest. Not a bad plan.

"I won't keep you from your lesson," I told George. "I just wanted to see if there was anything I could do to help with tonight's service."

Nan went flying by, flailing her arms. George winced and zipped after her. Over his shoulder he yelled, "Flowers. Mary said she forgot to order flowers." He caught Nan's arm. She swung around, and smack, she ran into his chest. The two went down in a heap. Glad to be standing, I headed back to the office to check e-mail. When rink business was squared away, I tooled back out to the parking lot.

Erica fell into step beside me. "Are we going to the motel to stake out your dad?"

"Nope." I climbed into my Civic and revved the engine. "We're headed to the florist to pick out flowers for tonight's service." Since I already had to meet Danielle at the florist, this wasn't a big deal. Could I multitask or what?

As for Stan, after last night I'd been rethinking his involvement in my near-death experiences. My dad didn't own a minivan. I was positive he had the skills necessary to steal one, but if Stan was going to steal a car, he wouldn't pick something that evoked big families and soccer games. He'd go for a vehicle with muscle.

Also, Stan was a known marksman. When I was a kid, he annoyed everyone by hogging the gun at the summer fair's shooting gallery. He never lost. The man could shoot. While some things about Stan might have changed over the years, I was pretty sure his ability with a gun wasn't one of them. If Stan had been the one looking through the gun's sight last night, I'd be dead. Not exactly a happy thought, but it was reassuring in its own way.

I parallel parked my Civic in front of Sherwood Florist. We walked through the doors, and a wave of perfume wafted over me. The sensation reminded me of a time at one of Pop's senior center gigs. The women rushed the stage, and I got caught in the middle of a dozen heaving, perfumed bosoms.

"Thank God you're here." Danielle raced over, looking like she hadn't slept in days. Her hair was flat, her eyeliner was crooked, and her eyes had a hunted look to them. "Come on." Danielle grabbed my hand and yanked. Hard. Unless I wanted my arm to come out of its socket, I had to go with her.

We dodged knickknacks and potted plants as Danielle yammered, "I heard about the shooting. Thank God you're safe. I know this is selfish, but I was scared you might not want to go outside today. Not that I would blame you. If someone shot at me

I'd stay inside with the shades drawn and the doors locked, but you're a lot braver than I am. Which is why I need you. There are so many flowers, and Marion keeps telling me I'm picking the wrong ones. I don't know what to do."

The woman in question was waiting at a small table in the back of the store. Marion Poste was tall, blond, and very well endowed. Rumor said that the mayor was so captivated by her bust that he never noticed a brain beneath the blond exterior until after they were married. I wasn't surprised Danielle was intimidated.

Marion saw me coming and stood. "Rebecca, my husband told me about the shooting last night. You were lucky to have one of our officers there to protect you. I hate to think what might have happened."

The excited light in her eyes said otherwise. Being the mayor's wife had several perks. Marion's favorite was gossip. The nastier the better.

"I'm here to help Danielle pick out flowers."

Marion gave me an annoyed frown for changing the subject but then got down to business. "Yes. Danielle and I were just ruling out daisies. They aren't an appropriate wedding flower."

Danielle's pout told me a wedding without daisies would be a huge disappointment.

"Why not?" I asked.

Marion sighed. "There is nothing special about a daisy. They grow by the side of the road around here. I refuse to use so unimportant a flower for a wedding."

The I-can't-believe-I-have-to-explain-this tone irked me. Yesterday, I couldn't have cared less if Danielle carried poison ivy down the aisle, but Marion had just turned me into Danielle's floral champion.

I gave Danielle my best sympathetic look. "I think she might be right. This isn't a city florist. I guess you'll have to settle for roses or some other less challenging flower."

Marion chewed on her bottom lip. Finally, she asked, "What does not being in the city have to do with Danielle's flower choice?"

"Chicago florists love taking simple flowers and turning them into artistic creations. Orchids and roses are easy to make look special, but a daisy? I guess they appreciate the challenge." I'm not sure I could tell an orchid from a petunia. That wasn't the point. I gave Danielle another sad look. "I'm sure Marion can make a bouquet of roses look perfectly nice. Right, Marion?"

Danielle opened her mouth to protest, and I casually stepped on her foot. I probably stepped harder than I'd intended since her eyes welled up with tears.

Danielle's distressed expression worked in our favor. Marion put her arm around the unhappy Danielle and gave me a nasty but determined look. "Don't listen to Rebecca, my dear. I can do anything those city florists can do. You'll have the most sensational daisy bouquet anyone, city or otherwise, has ever seen."

Fifteen minutes later, the flowers were ordered. Danielle left smiling, and Marion looked smug. I just wanted to finish my business and follow Danielle out of there. The smell of flowers was starting to make my head ache.

"I know it's last minute, but I need to get some flowers for Sherlene-n-Mean's memorial service. It's tonight," I explained.

"We'd like cheerful arrangements," Erica said as she appeared at my side. She'd been hanging out near the front door during the wedding discussion. "Nothing too formal, and no lilies. Lilies remind people of death."

"Death can't be ignored at a memorial service." Marion pursed her lips. "The press can't seem to ignore death, either."

"Press?" My head snapped up. "What press?"

Marion sniffed and leaned forward in her chair. "Someone at last night's press conference told a reporter about your friend's unfortunate accident. She reported it on her news broadcast. Poor Harry has already fielded a dozen phone calls from other reporters about the story. I have no idea how it got to be a story in the first place."

"Murder tends to get attention," I said.

"I know that," she huffed. "I was referring to the artifacts that brought those obnoxious reporters here. Harry doesn't understand it, either. Fifty years ago, a school stood on that piece of ground. When the new school was built two decades ago, the land was turned into a community park. If Indian artifacts existed, they should have surfaced then. If I didn't know better, I'd think someone planted those items to make the mayor look bad." She looked at me and Erica, sizing us up as potential saboteurs. We must have come up lacking, since she said, "How many arrangements do you need?"

Erica and Marion fought over colors and arrangements for the next half hour. When Marion promised the flowers would be at the rink by five o'clock, I bolted out the door. The air was crisp, cool, and perfume-free. Just what I needed. I also needed food. Last night's pizza had finally worn off, and my stomach was noisily empty.

Hopping into the driver's side, I waited for Erica to strap in. A car zoomed past, and I eased mine out into the street.

"Hey," Erica said, squinting into the distance. "That was Kandie Sutra's car. I haven't seen her since Sunday."

No one had. Not since just before the disco ball in the rink fell and almost killed me. Kandie Sutra and I needed to have a talk.

Maybe it was a reaction to the week I was having, but I didn't pause. I didn't think. I just slammed my foot on the gas and gave chase.

Nineteen

"What the hell?" Erica grabbed onto the oh-shit bar and hung on for dear life. Meanwhile, I pressed down on the gas and leaned over my steering wheel, doing a good impression of a NASCAR driver. Kandie Sutra was back in town after her strange Houdini act, and I wasn't about to let her get away.

Kandie turned into the rink parking lot. I hung a hard left behind her and followed as she zipped around the lot and back out onto the street. She zoomed past the senior center. I followed in hot pursuit. I glanced down at the speedometer. Fifty miles an hour felt a lot faster than it sounded.

A light ahead of us turned red. Kandie slowed, as if ready to stop, but then gunned it. I watched her disappear as my foot inched toward the gas pedal.

"Don't do it." Erica gave her red mane a shake. "If that was Kandie, we'll find her again. She's not good at being inconspicuous."

The car disappeared out of sight, and I sighed.

Erica smiled. "Stopping was the right thing to do. Do you really want Deputy Holmes to slap you with a ticket? He might be hot, but a close encounter with him isn't worth the hundred-buck fine."

"You think Sean Holmes is hot?" The light turned green.

"Sure do." Her smile widened. "He's got rock-hard abs, a chiseled jaw, and that boyishly mussed hair. Not to mention the brooding cop personality. He'd make the perfect hero for my next book."

I almost choked. "Haven't you noticed the powdered sugar and cookie crumbs on his clothes?" Personally, I was amazed his waistline hadn't suffered from his baked-goods addiction. "Cookie crumbs aren't heroic."

Erica wasn't convinced. "Romantic heroes need flaws to make them approachable."

I rolled my eyes. "Sean has plenty of those." His constant desire to arrest me topped the list.

"I thought Sean was the reason you and Lionel aren't an official item." Erica raised an eyebrow. "Did I get that wrong?"

"Totally wrong."

Erica flinched. Okay, I might have said that a little more forcefully than intended, but the car chase had given me a lot of excess adrenaline.

From the corner of my eye, I could see Erica give me a sly smile. "I think the lady protests too much."

My right eye started to twitch. "I have nothing to protest. Sean has been a pain in the neck since the day I moved back to town. He wants to arrest me, not date me. As for Lionel . . ." I blew a lock of hair out of my eyes and sighed. "Let's just say that my desire to sell the rink and get on with my life doesn't do much for our relationship."

"Really?" Her mocking tone said she didn't believe me. "Then the sparks that fly when Sean and you talk are just my imagination?"

Sparks? What sparks? Erica's romance-writing imagination was definitely working overtime.

I tooled by the rink and scanned the parking lot for Kandie's car. Nothing. A twenty-minute drive to her house, filled with innuendo-laced comments from Erica, was also a bust. Kandie had gone back underground. Drat.

Now what?

"Hey. Pull over for a second. I want to see what they're doing."

I glanced over to where Erica was pointing. The park. The two professors from last night were talking to a group of eager-looking college kids. They were armed with plastic yellow, green, and white pails and assorted shovels. I wasn't sure what a professional archaeological dig was supposed to look like, but I pictured something a little more . . . professional. Or maybe something with matching buckets.

We got out of the car and walked over to the dig. The temperature was warmer than last night. No one was wearing jackets as they moved dirt from the big hole to an area fifteen feet away. A couple of kids sat sifting through the bucket-brigade dirt for bits of rock or bone. Big excitement.

"Everyone be very careful," the big, dark-haired professor from last night yelled. "This is the most important Native American discovery in years. We are going to prove to the world that the Chippewa lived in this part of the country even if it takes us months or years of digging."

Erica leaned over and whispered, "This is kind of exciting. Do you think the big guy will let me interview him for research? He's kind of cute."

I guess. If you liked grizzly bears. Still, while the professor wasn't my type, I did find something about him interesting.

I grabbed Erica's arm and walked over to him. "Hi. My friend and I were wondering how long you plan on being in town. Will it really take months or years?"

Grizzly Adams turned and grinned. Then he spotted Erica. She gave him a sultry smile, and his eyes went wide. Pulling at his turtleneck, he stammered, "These things can't be rushed."

"Oh, good. Erica was worried you might leave before she had a chance to interview you for her next book." Erica looked startled. I smiled and kept talking. "She thinks you'd make a dashing romantic hero."

"Me?" His face turned red under all that black fuzz. "Really?"

"Absolutely," Erica purred.

"Are you staying somewhere in town?" I asked. "Erica can give you a call and set up a time to do the interview."

"It might take more than one session," Erica added.

The professor looked ready to faint. "We're all at the Presidential Motel, but I can give you my cell number if you want."

He and Erica exchanged information. It turned out his name was Xavier. While they made small talk, I mentally connected the dots. The picture they created told me Stan was definitely not a murderer. That was good. On the other hand, Stan was up to his perfectly plucked eyebrows in his old swindling tricks. That was bad. Now I just needed to catch him at the right moment to see if my mental calculations were correct.

My stomach growled. Finding my father could wait until after lunch. A meat loaf sandwich might not help me solve Sherlene's murder or figure out my father's complete scheme, but it would make me happy. At this point, happy won.

Dragging Erica away from her new friend, I stuffed her in the car and steered over to the diner. A wave of sound hit us as we opened the front door. It appeared every teenager in Indian Falls had skipped class in favor of greasy burgers and fries. Perhaps my stomach would be just as happy with takeout.

"Ms. Robbins."

I looked around the place, wondering if I'd imagined someone calling my name. Mabel was busy pouring sodas at the counter, and Sammy was putting plates of hot food in the window. Almost every table was filled to capacity with kids wrapped up in their own dramas. I must be losing my mind.

"Ms. Robbins."

Erica nudged me and pointed toward the back of the diner.

Tommy Corwin was standing up in the last booth, waving his hands. He was alone. I grabbed Erica and headed over. I couldn't help it. After my father left, I spent a lot of time in these back booths alone, and I hadn't necessarily wanted it that way. Tommy came across as unconcerned about his place in the teenaged social pecking order, but sitting alone surrounded by laughter always felt lonely and awkward.

"Are you here for lunch, Ms. Robbins?" Tommy's fingers clutched his napkin. "You can sit with me, if you want."

The wistfulness in Tommy's voice made me slide into the booth. "I told you to call me Rebecca."

Erica slid in beside me. Tommy's eyes grew wider. "You're Erica the Red. I love watching you skate. EstroGenocide is really going to kick butt tomorrow night."

"I hope you'll be there to cheer us on." Erica smiled and grabbed a menu.

"Everyone is going to be there. Although I've been thinking that I should probably stay home. Just in case." He looked down at the scarred Formica table with a dejected shrug.

Erica put her menu to the side. "Just in case what?"

"In case of . . ." Tommy's face turned almost the same shade as his hair. He swallowed and whispered, "The curse."

"Curse?" Erica asked, just at the moment that everyone else in the place paused to breathe. A few kids turned and pointed in our direction. Tommy looked ready to crawl under the table.

"A fortune-teller at the festival told Tommy he was cursed," I explained in a quiet voice. "He thinks the curse had something to do with Sherlene-n-Mean's death."

"I didn't mean for the curse to rub off on her. She bumped into me. Honest." Tommy's sentences ran together, but we got the gist.

Thank goodness Mabel arrived to take our order. Erica and I both ordered the meat loaf sandwich. Tommy said he wasn't hungry, but I made him order a banana split. Tommy needed to focus on something besides death curses. It was hard to be depressed when eating a dessert as big as your head.

Erica talked derby with Tommy until the food arrived. A solemn-faced Mabel set my sandwich in front of me. It was at least twice as big as Erica's. Sammy and Mabel must have heard about the shooting. Suddenly, my anticipated sandwich felt like a prisoner's last meal. The thought zapped the hungry right out of me.

I poked at the sandwich with my fork and ate a couple of fries, trying to renew my appetite. Nope. The food sat like rocks in my stomach. Sighing, I pushed my food away and studied Tommy. He was staring at his sundae with a decided lack of interest.

"So, why aren't you all in school?" I asked, ignoring Erica, who had finished her food and moved onto mine.

"Half day." Tommy plucked a cherry off the ice cream and rolled the stem between his fingers. "The teachers have some kind of meetings this afternoon." Tommy studied the cherry for a few moments, then dropped it back on top of the melting dessert. "I know you've been really busy, Ms. Robbins, but did you get a chance to talk to Madame LeManski about removing my . . . you know."

Erica looked up from my food and raised an eyebrow. "Who is Madame LeManski?"

Tommy's shoulders drooped. "She's the psychic who told me about my curse."

"Tommy." I leaned forward. "Did it ever occur to you that she might not be a real psychic?"

"But she is. Everyone says so. She knows things."

I would have laughed at Tommy's reverent tone if he hadn't looked so pathetic. The poor kid looked ready to cry.

"Look," I said. "I promise that I'll go see this Madame LeManski today."

Tommy's face brightened.

"Do you know where I can find her?"

His face dropped again. "No one knows. I figured since you're a detective you could find her."

"Of course she can." Erica pushed the plate away and smiled. "Rebecca is a professional, and professionals don't work for free."

I blinked. Professional? Me? I opened my mouth to protest, but Tommy was already saying, "Oh, I know. I don't have much money, but I'm happy to work extra hours at the rink to cover Ms. Robbins's expenses. Is that okay?"

"Okay." Erica reached across the table and shook Tommy's hand. He blushed at her touch but looked happier than I'd seen him in days. Maybe ever. Erica slid out of the booth, threw some money on the table to cover the bill, and said, "Don't worry, Tommy. Rebecca will have that curse broken in no time."

The minute we hit the parking lot, I demanded, "What was that? I'm not a professional detective. Why did you tell Tommy I was?"

She folded herself into my car and grinned. "Because it made him feel better. Tomorrow, you can just tell him that you found this Madame Whoever and that she chanted while doing cart-wheels and removed the curse. The kid will feel better, and every-one will be happy. What's the harm?"

I understood her point. Only I couldn't do it. I might think the curse was bogus, but the kid didn't. Lying about something that important to Tommy felt wrong, and I certainly wasn't going to charge him for work I didn't do. Just the idea of it made me feel icky. Of course, not helping also made me feel bad. That meant there was only one thing I could do.

"If I'm going to charge Tommy for finding Madame LeMan-ski, then I'm going to do it right." I hit the gas pedal. "Let's go see Pop."

I let Erica and myself into Pop's house and listened for signs of life. Pop's car was in the garage, which meant he was home. That was good, but I knew from past experience that Pop liked to have company over for lunch. Walking in on him and Tilly frolicking in the living room wasn't part of my plans.

I walked into the kitchen and yelled, "Hello?"

"Be right down," Pop's voice called from upstairs. Erica and I grabbed sodas and sat down at the kitchen table. A few minutes later, Pop appeared in a pair of black velvet pants and a black turtleneck sweater. He looked almost normal.

Pop made a beeline over to me. "I heard about the shooting last night. Eleanor was listening to Doc Truman's police radio. Sheriff Jackson gave it to Doc when he took the job as coroner. Eleanor borrows it when Doc is out of town. She invited me over the other day to play police officer, but I was busy."

Erica snorted. I gave her a look that begged her not to encourage him. Not that he needed encouragement.

"I should have called you, Pop. Sorry." I really was. Although part of me wasn't sure Pop would have answered his phone while on a date. "The shooter got away, but Zach got the make and model of the car. That should help Sean find him."

"Sean means well, but I'm not sure he has the instinct to track down a killer." Pop scratched his butt and adjusted his pants. "I heard he plans on being at the memorial service to keep an eye on things just in case the killer decides to show up. A bunch of us from the center will be there, too. Sean is going to need backup if things get out of hand."

Pop and his posse of dentally challenged deputies were probably not the kind of help Sean would need in a crisis. I thought about warning Sean and decided against it. Why ruin Pop's fun?

"Pop, have you ever heard of Madame LeManski?"

My grandfather gave me an excited smile. "Are you looking for a psychic to help on the case? There was a show the other day about a woman who got vibrations from gardening tools."

"How did she—"

I cut off Erica before Pop got sidetracked. "One of my employees was told by Madame LeManski he was under a dark cloud. I promised I'd track her down and have her remove the curse."

"No one is supposed to know who Madame LeManski is. People used to try to guess, but after a while they just gave up." Pop shrugged. "El mystery-o is part of the fun."

"So you don't know."

Pop grinned. "I didn't say that, did I?" He paused to heighten the drama. "Madame LeManski is none other than Louise Lagotti."

I blinked. "Are you sure?" Louise was famous around town for making strange arts-and-crafts projects. She was also one of Pop's former girlfriends. While she and Pop were dating, the woman foisted a deranged looking four-foot-tall Santa scarecrow on Pop and made him display it in the middle of his lawn. In May. I don't know how many birds the thing frightened off, but I know it scared the crap out of me.

"It's Louise," Pop said. "Trust me. She talks in her sleep."

Yep. I had to ask.

Twenty

Louise Lagotti lived in a rambling red farmhouse fifteen minutes outside of town. Had Pop not given us the address, I still
would have known it was her house. Louise's yard looked like a
craft fair threw up in it. The slightly overgrown front lawn was
populated with scarecrows. Some had floppy pink bunny ears and
cotton tails. Others had green shamrocks and glittery hearts protruding from their heads. And, of course, there were Santas. Lots
and lots of Santas.

We dodged a couple of Baby New Year scarecrows on our way
up the front steps and rang the bell. First we heard a high-pitched
yipping. Then the sound of footsteps. Finally, the door opened
and Louise said, "Rebecca, how nice of you to drop by. How's
your grandfather?"

I blinked. Louise's ample body was coated in pine needles, bits
of corn stalks, and hay. Her bouffant champagne-colored hair had
a branch sticking out of either side, giving her a strange deerlike

quality. Thank God hunting season hadn't started. The hunters around here weren't known for their attention to detail.

"Pop is fine."

She gave me a relieved smile. "I'm happy to hear it. We've talked a few times on the phone, but it really isn't the same as seeing someone in person. Between our two businesses, we just haven't had time to dedicate to our relationship. But we will."

I smiled at Louise. Meanwhile, my hands itched to strangle my womanizing grandfather. He told me months ago that he'd broken up with Louise. Apparently, he forgot to give her the memo. Now it was up to me to do it. Just great.

"Pop is really focused on his singing career," I said, trying not to sound as stupid as I felt.

Louise gave me a sage Yoda nod. "Your grandfather and I are so much alike. It's why we're so compatible. We also know when we have to give each other space to be creative. That's what we've been doing."

In *Star Wars*, Yoda was wise and all-knowing. Louise was just deliberately obtuse and a touch deranged. Since shattering her fantasy wasn't going to get me anywhere, and might not even be possible, I said, "We're actually here to ask you a question. Do you moonlight as a psychic named Madame LeManski?"

Louise's gasp told me Pop's nocturnal gossip gathering had been accurate.

She shook her head back and forth, sending bits of twigs and hay flying. "Why would you think I'm Madame LeManski?"

Erica giggled.

I cringed. No way I was going to tell her what Pop said. Kissing and telling was just tacky.

To bad Erica didn't have the same sensibilities. "You talk in your sleep."

A red flush crept up Louise's neck, and her breathing got faster. A whole lot faster. She looked ready to hyperventilate.

Thank goodness Erica was quick to react. She pushed me aside, took Louise's arm, and led her into the house. I followed behind into a dumping ground of hay, glitter, and felt. Erica threw baskets of Louise's crafting stuff off a large armchair and pushed Louise into it. A small brown dog that looked suspiciously like a long-haired rat hopped up onto Louise's lap and started growling.

I took a step back and got ready to run. My week was bad enough without adding rabies to the fun.

Louise took several deep breaths, gave the dog a reassuring pat, and admitted, "I've been dressing up as Madame LeManski for ten years. No one ever suspected it was me until now. Now everyone will know, all because I couldn't keep my sexual urges for your grandfather in check."

Eew. The fluffy rodent growled. He thought it was icky, too.

"No one has to know," I told her. In fact, I would prefer that no one knew. The thought of hearing about her and my grandfather's sexual urges for months to come made me faint. "Erica and I won't tell anyone."

"I won't tell a soul," Erica said, although the gleam in her eye told me the story might make it into one of her books.

Louise blinked up at us. "Then why are you here?"

The dog settled down on Louise's lap. His eyes followed me as I moved a scarecrow head and sat down on the couch. "You gave one of my employees a reading at the festival last weekend."

"Did I tell him to look for love in unexpected places?"

"You said he was under a dark cloud."

"One of my favorite lines. I got it from the Psychic Friends Network. It sounds mystical, don't you think?"

Erica looked intrigued. "So you're not a real psychic?"

Louise threw back her head and laughed, sending the rat-dog into a flurry of yips. "Gosh, no. One year people were complaining that we didn't have a fortune-teller at our festival. Rock Falls had one, and she was a big draw. So the next year I signed up for a booth as Madame LeManski. Got a wig and a bunch of cool makeup, and I even researched some mystical phrases to make me sound legit. Guess it worked, since people show up year after year."

"So you just make stuff up?" I asked, a little annoyed. That sounded a lot like what my dad did for a living.

"Oh, sure." Louise didn't seem overly concerned by the morality of it. "Or at least, I used to. Now I just use the material I've collected over the years. I have three or four lists of fortunes that I use. I go down the list until I get to the bottom. Then I start back at the top. That way if a group of people come to the festival together, they don't get the same reading. That would be embarrassing."

Right. "Don't you think it's wrong to take money from people when you don't have any real powers?"

Louise waved off my indignation. "It's just for fun. No one around here actually believes I can see into the future."

"Tommy Corwin does."

"Who's Tommy Corwin?" Louise sounded confused.

The dog growled.

I sighed. "A tall redheaded kid with glasses who believes he's cursed after coming to see you at the festival."

Louise cocked her head to one side and scrunched up her nose. After a moment, she slapped her thigh, sending her pet flying. The animal scurried behind Louise's feet with an offended bark. "I remember him. He blushed when I read his cards. It was cute." She frowned. "Why does he think he's cursed? I never tell people they're cursed. That would be plain old mean. I don't believe in being mean."

"You told Tommy a dark cloud was hanging over him."

Louise didn't look impressed. "And?"

"And he thinks you're a real psychic." I overenunciated every word to make sure she understood. "Tommy thought your words meant he was cursed. A fact that was reinforced when he bumped into Sherlene-n-Mean just minutes before she was electrocuted in the dunk tank. He thinks his curse killed her." My voice might have gotten a little loud at the end. I couldn't help it.

"Huh." Louise flopped back in her chair, sending bits of scarecrow carcasses flying. "Considering the circumstances, I can understand why he's upset. So, what do we do now? We can't let that poor boy walk around town thinking he's got a psychic plague."

"Wave your hands in the air."

Louise and I looked at Erica as though she'd lost her mind. The way she was grinning, I thought it was highly possible. Either that or the corn husk fumes had gotten to her.

Thank goodness Erica explained. "Say some hocus-pocus and make the curse go away. Then Rebecca can tell Tommy you made everything better and life can return to normal."

Made sense to me.

Louise wasn't so sure. "Why? Tommy isn't here to see it. You can tell him anything you want for all I care."

"I could." Erica nodded. "But Rebecca has this thing about lying."

Louise looked to me for confirmation. I nodded.

"Well, that is a problem. Wait. I've got an idea." Louise

stood up, her eyes dancing with glee. "I'll be right back. Don't go away."

She bolted out of the room with her dog right behind her. I could hear her somewhere in the house, banging drawers and talking to herself. The occasional dog bark added to the noise.

Erica sat down on the couch with me and grinned. "I've had a lot of free time lately because I haven't had any ideas for my next book. After a few days with you, I've got enough material for three or four. Your life is fun."

My life was a disaster.

A few minutes later, Louise returned wearing a triumphant smile. The little dog sat at Louise's feet, looking up at her with adoration.

"Voilà." Louise held out her hand and revealed an arts-and-crafts nightmare.

"What is it?" I dared ask.

Louise's smile dimmed. "It's a voodoo doll."

The only voodoo dolls I'd ever seen were in horror movies, and, trust me, they looked nothing like this. This one was made out of hot-glued Popsicle sticks. A shock of red-marker-coated corn stalks was glued to the top. Pink yarn was wrapped around the torso, giving the sad-looking thing a touch of modesty.

"Of course it is. How clever." Erica pretended to understand Louise's creation. Or at least I hoped she was pretending, because I was lost.

Louise's smile returned to full wattage. "Tell Tommy that Madame LeManski made this for him. As long as he carries this, the curse will leave him alone."

Maybe so, but every teenager in the Midwest would mock him. Not exactly what I was going for. Still, now that the shock had worn off, I thought the deranged doll had possibilities. I took the thing from Louise, thanked her, and added, "You might want to remove the dark-cloud fortune from your repertoire, as well as any other potentially sinister sayings."

"You might be right." Louise bit her lip and chewed. "I just hope the blond lady doesn't need a voodoo doll, too."

"Blond lady?"

"I'm sure I'm worrying for nothing. She arrived looking red-eyed, so she probably had already been crying." Louise sat down on the chair with a thump. The dog hopped up and licked her frowning face. "The woman said she had a choice to make. If she picked wrong, someone was going to get hurt."

"What did you say to her?" Erica asked.

Louise sighed. "The Psychic Friends never covered anything like that. At least not when I called. So I had to improvise. I told her that lightning was going to strike no matter which choice she made. She would have to make the best of things and avoid getting struck herself."

"Why lightning?" It wasn't the first psychic phrase that popped into my mind.

"My mother used to tell me that every time I faced a big decision. Of course, I made it feel more supernatural by saying she had an aura sparking with energy. Psychics on TV are always talking about auras." Louise shrugged. "The woman started to cry. I tried to hand her a tissue, but she pushed me away and ran out, saying fate had already made her choice. Do you think she took me seriously?"

Yes, and I had a bad feeling Louise's babbling about lightning and sparks was more than a metaphor to the crying blonde. I was making a deductive leap with zero evidence, but my gut told me this was the same woman Mabel had seen crying near the dunk tank. Mabel assumed she was the mother of one of the losing pageant girls. She was wrong. The woman was near the dunk tank because she was making a choice between life and death. Lightning striking. In her psychic wisdom, Louise had used the wrong words, and Sherlene-n-Mean died because of them.

"Do you remember what the woman looked like?" I tried to sound casual. The sharp look Erica gave me said I failed.

Louise didn't notice. "I keep my booth dark so people can't tell who I am, so I didn't get a good look. She was short and blond, and she was wearing a dark sweatshirt. I can't tell you what color."

Damn. The dark shirt was a good detail, but the rest of the description fit half the women I graduated from high school with. I got up, thanked Louise for her help, and headed for the door.

"Wait." Louise's voice stopped me inside the doorway. "When I tried to hand her a tissue, I noticed a necklace she was wearing. It looked like a big pink bug with silver wings. I thought that was kind of strange and gaudy, but young women are so different now than they were in my day. Right, King?" She gave the rat-dog a pat. He licked her face and barked his agreement.

I barely blinked at the overly optimistic name for the mangy little animal. My mind was too busy processing news of the necklace. There was one person who fit both Mabel's and Louise's descriptions. I had no idea why she might want me dead, but I was almost certain I'd seen the necklace around her neck.

Shoving Tommy's new voodoo doll into my purse, I grabbed Erica's arm and hightailed it out to the car. The minute Erica climbed in and shut the door I asked, "Does anyone on Estro-Genocide have a big pink necklace with wings?"

"Oh my God." Erica's eyes snapped wide. "It wasn't a bug Louise saw. It's a roller skate with wings."

I swallowed hard and hit the gas as Erica said the killer's name. "Kandie Sutra."

Twenty-one

"You think Kandie Sutra had something to do with Sherlene-n-Mean's murder?" Erica sounded confused.

So was I. Kandie and I exchanged hellos and good-byes. We'd never had an in-depth conversation about anything. What reason would she have to electrocute me? Still, motive aside, when you added the conversation with Louise's alter ego to the rapid disappearance after Sherlene's murder, Kandie looked guilty.

"It's suspicious that Kandie was at the park before Sherlene's death and at the rink later that night just before the disco ball fell. It doesn't feel like coincidence."

I waited for Erica to laugh at my television-cop impersonation. Instead, she asked the question I'd been mulling over. "Now what do we do?"

I wasn't sure. The first case I'd solved was kind of an accident, and I'd figured out the second one moments before the killer blew up my rink. Figuring out who done it before a major crisis was occurring was new territory for me. So I did what any sane citizen would do: I grabbed my cell and punched in Sean's number.

Voice mail.

Crap. Leaving a message wasn't a good option. I was going to sound stupid enough explaining my reasons for fingering Kandie. I had a story about lightning, a necklace, and no physical evidence. If I was going to sound foolish, I wanted a live audience.

Unfortunately, neither Sean nor the sheriff was at the sheriff's department, but Roxy was. Her thickly lined eyes widened as she spotted me. "Deputy Holmes told me all about the shooting last night. He and the sheriff have everyone looking for the shooter's van. Sean even asked me to fax the van's description to the state police."

Roxy's excitement about Sean's fax request made it sound like he'd asked her out on a date. The woman needed help.

"Do you know where I can find the sheriff or Deputy Holmes?" I asked.

Her eyes narrowed. "Why?"

I considered telling her about Kandie. Visions of mascara-laden eye rolling and lots of snide comments made me reconsider. If I thought Roxy would bother to pass along the information, I might subject myself to the humiliation, but I knew better. Roxy would have her fun and never say a word.

"I was just wondering if they had anything new on the shooter," I improvised. "Then again, if they did, I'm sure you'd be the first to know."

Roxy flashed a toothpaste-commercial smile. "And you'll be the second."

Great.

Back outside, I contemplated my options. It was almost five

o'clock. Sherlene-n-Mean's memorial service was scheduled to start at seven. The team had the details under control, but I should really be helping. I called Sean again and left a message asking him to drop by the rink. I made sure to mention the refreshments table. Sean couldn't resist the siren call of a chocolate chip cookie.

The rink was hopping with activity when we arrived, and from what I could see almost everything had already been done. In the center of the rink was a beautiful white pedestal with pink and silver fabric hanging off the sides. On either side of the pedestal were bouquets of flowers. I wasn't sure if I liked Mrs. Poste as a person, but I couldn't complain about her flower arrangements. They were stunning. A few feet to the right of the flowers was a large easel displaying a glossy version of Sherlene-n-Mean's team photo.

In front of the memorial display, George, Typhoon Mary, and Danielle Martinez were setting up folding chairs. Danielle saw me and walked over to say hello.

"It's really nice of you to help out with the service," I said. Danielle had come to a couple of derby bouts, but as far as I knew, she and Sherlene had never met.

Danielle shrugged. "Typhoon Mary called the rectory today and asked if she could borrow some folding chairs. Rich said yes, and he volunteered to help with the service. He's back at the church, composing his sermon."

The religious implications loomed large. Sherlene was a former Catholic nun. Pastor Rich was a Lutheran minister. I wasn't sure if the two denominations had rules about segregation, but our town sure did. Growing up Catholic, I'd been encouraged by my religious educators to stay away from the Lutheran side. At eight years old, you tend to listen when someone says it's for the good of your soul. Still, I was pretty sure in this instance that God would understand.

Danielle, Erica, and I set out trays of DiBelka Bakery cookies and breads on two of the snack-area tables. I then snitched two oatmeal raisin cookies for my dinner. While chewing, I spotted Tommy Corwin coming through the front door. I grabbed my purse and made a beeline for the kid.

"I found Madame LeManski."

The kid blinked twice, and his face went pasty white. He swallowed hard and whispered, "What did she say? Am I cursed forever?"

"Nope. She gave me a message for you." I pulled the craft project from hell out of my bag and handed it to Tommy. "This voodoo doll is going to help you remove the curse."

The word "voodoo" made Tommy look like he wanted to hurl. I took a step back just in case.

"What do I do with it?" he asked, holding the thing as far from his body as possible.

I'd considered this question. Louise's suggestion sucked, but my previous encounter with her creations had given me an idea. "Burn it."

"Really?" The color returned to Tommy's face.

"Yep." I nodded. "Take the thing outside, set it on the ground, and light it on fire. The curse will disappear once the doll is burned to a crisp."

Tommy didn't look impressed. "Is that all? I thought getting rid of a curse would take a lot more effort."

Damn. I should have made the kid carry the doll around. Getting his ass kicked daily would have given him a warped sense of righteousness. Oh well. Too late now. "It's not as easy at it sounds. You have to watch the doll burn and make sure that every part of it is touched by the flames. If even a tiny bit is left unscathed, the curse will live on."

Okay, the last part might have been a bit much, but I couldn't help myself. I could see how Louise got into the psychic thing. Making up hocus-pocus was fun. More like a game. Less like a lie. Maybe I'd found a new career path. If I managed to stay alive and sell the rink, I might consider it.

Tommy bummed a lighter off one of the derby girls and raced outside with his Popsicle-stick pal. I glanced at my watch and yelped. The service started in forty-five minutes, and I wasn't exactly dressed for the occasion.

Flagging down Erica, I said, "I have to run upstairs and change. Do you want to come with?"

"Yes." She looked annoyed I asked. Erica took the bodyguard gig seriously.

Upstairs, I said, "Do you want to change, too? I'm sure I have something appropriate that'll fit you."

"No thanks." She smiled. "The team is going to change in the locker room right before the service. We want to make sure we show off the colors that made Sherlene so proud."

Pink and silver weren't usual mourning hues, but this service wasn't for a typical woman. With that in mind, I shimmied into a bright green sweater dress long enough to hide my scraped-up knee, a silver metal belt, and strappy silver high heels. I even put on a pair of dangly silver earrings and a matching bracelet in Sherlene's honor.

Once we'd gotten back downstairs, Erica disappeared into the dressing room to change into team colors. Meanwhile, I wove through the growing crowed and got two more cookies from the buffet. Fortified, I tried to call Sean. Still no answer. So I broke down and called the sheriff. He might not remember what I told him ten minutes from now, but at least he'd listen to me.

Voice mail. Drat.

"Are you Rebecca Robbins?"

I turned around and almost fainted. Sherlene-n-Mean was standing in front of me with a concerned expression. Or it could have been Sherlene in another twenty years. Now I knew where Sherlene got her height. While Sherlene's mother lacked the flash of her daughter's thick makeup, leather, and metal accessories, she had the same commanding presence. Mrs. Cline wore her hair in a perfectly styled blond bob and sported a conservative black dress that made her look incredibly tall and lean. She also looked incredibly sad.

"I'm glad you could make it, Mrs. Cline." I meant it. The wake and funeral for my mother sucked, but not being there would have been worse. "Sherlene—I mean Shirley—would be happy you're here."

Mrs. Cline's eyes welled up with tears. "Please, call me Joanne. And thank you for being so kind. I wasn't at my best when we first spoke."

"Don't worry about it." I could afford to be magnanimous considering I'd shattered all of the woman's illusions about her daughter in one fell swoop.

Joanne shook her head. "My behavior was uncalled for. You were just trying to do the right thing. You couldn't have known my daughter hadn't told me about her new life." Her voice caught, and her chin trembled.

I did the only thing I could think of to make her feel better. I picked up a bakery tray and asked, "Would you like a cookie?"

Joanne's lips turned upward. "No, thank you. You've gone to a lot of trouble to make this a special night for my daughter."

"The team did most of it. They wanted this to be something Shirley would have appreciated."

"I knew she liked skating, but I thought she'd given it up years ago." Joanne's voice was faint and confused. I grabbed a bottle of water from the snack counter and handed it to her. "Shirley surprised us all when she decided to become a nun. Although I guess I should call her Sherlene, since that's the name she chose."

The bitterness in Joanne's voice struck a chord. It sucked to have someone you loved not tell you the truth. Especially when the someone was family. "She was probably worried you'd be disappointed by her leaving the church. I hated disappointing my mother."

"She made the decision to be a nun after her father died. Her father and I raised her Catholic, so how could I object?" Joanne took a sip of water. "I wanted to, though. Do you know when she left the church, Rebecca?"

Math wasn't my strong suit, but I added up what I knew about Sherlene and said, "She joined the team about three months ago. I'm guessing she left sometime before that."

Someone turned on the sound system, and an orchestral version of "Amazing Grace" rang through the rink.

Joanne sniffled and said, "I went back into the letters she sent me and tried to figure out if I'd missed something. Shirley talked about feeling out of place. She missed skating. I told her to find some friends to skate with. After that she sent me a Bible quote that she said changed her life. I brought it with me, just in case someone wanted to read it."

Joanne took a piece of paper out of her purse and handed it to me. I recognized the numbers at the top. Those were the numbers I'd found in Sherlene-n-Mean's locker. The letter *P* was for Psalm. The verse talked about God training her arms and legs for battle. At the end it mentioned broadening her path and keeping her ankles from turning. The whole ankle-turning thing is a big deal in roller skating. Strong control of your ankles equaled good control of what direction you skated in. Sherlene must have taken the quote as a sign she needed to change her life.

I spotted Pastor Rich walking through the door. Taking Joanne by the arm, I led her to him. "I hope you don't mind, but Pastor Rich is going to be leading the service today. The team didn't know she was Catholic. He'll want to meet you and talk about Sherlene before the memorial starts."

Pastor Rich was surprised, but happy to talk to Joanne. It wasn't every day you realized you were officiating at the memorial service for a derby nun. I left Joanne in his care and headed to the front for a peek at the parking lot. No Sean. Rats.

Suddenly, I heard my grandfather's voice yell, "Fire in the hole." A second later, a loud *kaboom* had me dropping to the ground. Holy shit. I hoped last night's shooter hadn't brought bigger firepower. The sound of Pop's laughter made me look up. Pop probably wouldn't be laughing if I was going to get shot.

"What was that?" George's eyes were wide and worried.

"Pop" was my only explanation.

George nodded and went back inside. I could hear him yell, "It's okay," before the door shut, effectively muting the rest. I couldn't decide if it was funny or sad that people expected my grandfather to cause explosions. I settled on funny, since sad was too depressing, and went in search of the source.

I rounded the corner of the rink and coughed. A wave of black smoke wafted over me. It was streaming out of the nearest rink Dumpster. The sounds of snap, crackle, and pop echoed inside the metal container. Next to the Dumpster, Pop and Tommy Corwin danced around exchanging high fives and laughing hysterically.

"What are you two doing?" I yelled.

They turned. Pop kept grinning. Tommy looked ready to dive into the smoking Dumpster.

"I didn't mean to set fire to the Dumpster," Tommy stammered. "It was your grandfather's idea."

Tommy better hope he got a good job after college. He'd never make it as a criminal.

Pop gave Tommy a wounded look. "You asked me to help you set that doll on fire."

Oh no. "This is about the doll?"

"I tried to burn it, like the psychic said." Tommy's shoulders slumped. "The yarn burned great, but the rest of it wouldn't stay lit. I didn't know what to do. That's when your grandfather showed up and offered to help."

Pop shrugged. "The kid was crying over that doll. He kept saying he was going to be cursed forever. I had to do something, so I helped put together something that would kick that curse in the ass."

I couldn't help myself. I had to ask, "What did you make?"

"Some kind of cocktail thing." Tommy's voice was filled with awe. "It was cool."

"You made a Molotov cocktail?"

Pop smiled. "It's not hard to make. Jimmy and I googled it one day at the center when Marjorie and her friends were hogging the TV. An empty bottle, some gasoline, and a strip of fabric. The Popsicle-stick doll didn't stand a chance."

I wasn't sure if the throbbing ache in my throat was from the acrid smoke still hanging in the air or from holding in a primal scream. There was a killer on the loose, and my grandfather was busy performing a hit on a fake voodoo doll.

"Tommy," I said in the calmest voice I could manage, "go inside and get the fire extinguisher."

"But the curse might not be lifted yet and—" Tommy looked at my face, sighed, and dashed off.

The minute he disappeared into the rink, I turned to Pop. "What were you thinking? There's a memorial service about to start inside and you're out here blowing up my garbage cans." That wasn't my only complaint, but it was a good place to start.

Pop cocked his head to the side. "Huh. The kid was so upset, I forgot about the service. We should have waited. The explosion would have been a lot cooler in complete dark." He sighed. "I'll remember that for next time. Hey, look who just drove up."

My eyes followed my grandfather's finger to the far end of the parking lot, where Stan and Alan were climbing out of Alan's car. I put chastising my grandfather on hold and started toward my father. He had a lot of explaining to do, and now was the perfect time to start. Not taking my eyes off my dad, I headed across the parking lot to intercept him when—oof. My heel caught in a crack, and down I went. Thank goodness I'd had lots of practice falling. I landed smack on my padded rear end, saving my knees from another scraping.

Using the car next to me for leverage, I hoisted myself up onto my silver heels and brushed off my butt. Damn. Dad and Alan were already going inside. I'd have to catch Stan after the service to ask my questions. Well, another hour or two really wouldn't make a difference on that front.

I took a step toward the rink. That's when I noticed the car next to me—or should I say minivan. The van was a maroon Freestar with gray undercarriage, and it was a limited edition. Yikes! This had to be the van Zach chased after. Which meant one thing: The killer was inside the rink.

With no Sean and no sheriff, there was only one person left to catch her.

Me.

Twenty-two

"Pop," I yelled and raced across the lot. "Call Sean. Tell him the shooter's car is here at the rink. I'm going inside to see if I can spot her."

"Her?" Pop's eyes widened. "The shooter is a her?"

"I'll explain later." I left Pop punching numbers on his cell and almost plowed down Tommy as I opened the rink's front door. He went out with his fire extinguisher, and I went in.

The lights were dimmed on the sidelines. "Amazing Grace" played softly through the speakers. Mourners filled the seats, and those who hadn't gotten seats were standing quietly behind the folding chairs. The service was about to start. I found a good spot to observe in the back and squinted in the low light, trying to find Kandie Sutra's blond head. A hand grabbed my arm. I choked back a scream and spun around.

"There you are." George looked relieved. "Joanne Cline refused to let the service start until you were seated. She saved you the seat next to hers."

Before I could protest, George dragged me up to the front row of seats. Joanne was seated in the middle of the row. Pastor Rich was on one side of her. An empty chair was on the other. Joanne dabbed a tear away from her eye and waved me over.

Crap. A front-row seat seemed like a good way to get shot in the back. Unfortunately, I had no idea how to get out of it. Announcing a killer was in the building seemed like the obvious answer, but that risked pissing her off and putting everyone here in danger. Not to mention ruining Sherlene-n-Mean's service.

I did a quick survey of the crowd behind me. Yowzah. Pink, silver, and black spandex was everywhere, along with a significant contingent of fishnet stockings. Erica said the team would dress alike out of respect, but I thought that meant wearing team T-shirts or something. I wasn't sure how respectful fishnets and short shorts were. Still, Sherlene would no doubt have appreciated the gesture. She would have also appreciated the smattering of derby girls who belonged to other teams. I appreciated their attendance, too.

Out of the corner of my eye, I spotted Erica. Anna and Halle were seated with her on the end of the last row. Erica waved. I mouthed the word "Kandie" and glanced around, hoping Erica knew what I was asking. Erica's eyebrows raised, and she shook her head. If Erica hadn't spotted Kandie, chances were she wasn't in the building, and Erica would now be on the lookout. I'd feel better once Sean Holmes showed up, but until then, I swallowed down my urge to run and took my seat.

Pastor Rich touched Joanne's hand and then stood up. He looked serene and handsome in his ensemble of charcoal suit with crisp white shirt. He smiled at the enormous publicity picture of Sherlene-n-Mean and then started talking.

I heard Pastor Rich welcome everyone and thank them for coming, but after that everything was a blur. I was too busy wondering what was going on behind me, which was probably good. Since my mother's death, funerals made me cry—a lot. A redhead crying is a pitiful thing, so I tried not to do it too often.

I heard the sound of the rink's front door closing and glanced back. Eureka! Sean Holmes had made it. He was standing near the entrance, hand on gun, casing the audience. My grandfather stood next to him, doing his best to look intimidating. Funny how life could change. Five months ago, I would have chosen a run-in with a killer over being saved by Sean. Today, I was happy to let him do his job.

George poked me, and I turned my attention back to Pastor Rich. He was pacing back and forth, saying, "Whether you knew her as Shirley Cline or Sherlene Patsy, she was a woman of strength, conviction, and service to others. As a nun, she taught young children and helped her community."

George let out a shocked gasp. So did most of the crowd. One dark-haired woman sitting two rows back on my right shrieked, "Oh my God," at the revelation. I had no idea who the woman was, but she looked really upset. So did Joanne. She grabbed my hand and squeezed it. Hard.

Pastor Rich asked everyone to bow their heads in prayer, and Joanne let go of my hand. I flexed it, trying to restore blood flow, and then started to bow my head. Then I spotted the only other person in the place without her head already bowed. The woman was standing in the back wearing black pants, a black turtleneck, and a baseball cap. She glanced quickly from side to side and began to move toward the sidelines. My body hummed with tension as I watched her inch her way past the mourners. Her hat slipped, and a strand of long blond hair fell out. Her eyes snapped open as she jammed the hair back under the cap and looked around to see if anyone had noticed. Kandie Sutra's eyes met mine, and she froze like a deer caught in Lionel's monster truck headlights. I needed to act. Now.

Sean was still standing near the rink's entrance. I jumped up and opened my mouth to warn him about Kandie.

"Thank you, Rebecca," Pastor Rich's voice boomed.

I blinked as every head turned in my direction.

"I understand how difficult this is." Pastor Rich took my hand and turned me to face the crowd. "We would all love to hear one of your memories of Shirley."

My eyes followed Kandie as she walked over to the girls' bathroom and ducked inside. She was trapped. Now all I had to do was tell Sean and have him catch her. Of course, I was in a trap of my own.

"I was going to check on the music," I said. Yes, it was a lame excuse, especially since the music had stopped playing when Pastor Rich took the stage, but it was the best I could do. I started to flee, but a hand grabbed mine in a familiar vice grip.

"Please." Joanne looked up at me with tears in her eyes. "Hearing you talk about my daughter would mean the world to me."

My throat constricted. One look at her sad eyes and my own started to burn even as my heart was doing a tap dance in my chest. Crap. I was going to cry. Wait. That gave me an idea.

Keeping the bathroom door in my peripheral line of sight, I nodded to Joanne and said, "Everyone here knew Shirley Cline as Sherlene-n-Mean, but she was anything but mean." The bathroom door remained closed. Sean and my grandfather looked at me as though I had lost my mind, but everyone else in the rink was giving me encouraging smiles. Well, except the dark-haired woman two rows back. She hadn't recovered from the revelation that Sherlene was a nun.

I sniffled. "A few weeks ago, Sherlene was here during an open skate to practice. She was speeding along the rink when another skater lost his balance and plowed into her. The skater was terrified Sherlene would get angry, but she helped the boy up and spent the next hour giving him pointers on balance and speed skating." The kid was Tommy. He had been amazed someone so aggressive during a derby match could be so nice to a kid like him. A tear rolled down my face, and my chest tightened. "I didn't know Sherlene well, but I'll always be grateful to her. She . . ." I closed my eyes and took a deep breath. "She took my place on Sunday, and she died because of it."

That did it. The dam holding back my tears broke. George held out a tissue. I buried my face in it and made a less than dignified escape.

My heels clicked against the wood rink floor as I hurried to the carpeted sidelines, crying all the way. Once I hit the back of the crowd, I wiped my cheeks and took several deep breaths to make the tears stop. Nope. Still flowing. Using my overactive tear ducts to get away from the service had a definite downside.

"Your grandfather said the shooter was here." Sean materialized at my side. "I saw the van in the parking lot. Do you know who it is?"

"Yeah. Who do we take down?" Pop held up a fist.

On the rink floor, a couple of EstroGenocide team members got up to talk about Sherlene-n-Mean. George gave them each a tissue and took one for himself.

I explained, "Kandie Sutra was spotted near the dunk tank during the time it was rigged. She skipped town immediately after." A couple of mourners shot me dirty looks, and I lowered my voice to a whisper. "She's back and hiding in the girls' bathroom. Go get her."

The last part was directed at Sean, but Pop was the first to move. He hitched up his pants and stomped over to the bathroom door. He was just about to storm in when Sean pulled him back.

"I'm going in," Sean said.

Pop looked ready to argue, but Sean pulled out his gun. Pop was ornery, but he wasn't stupid. He swallowed hard, took a step back, and said, "Right. You go. I'll stay here and guard Rebecca."

Sean pushed the door inward, stepped inside, and let the door swing shut behind him. Pop and I put our ears to the door. Nothing. The only thing I could hear was Pastor Rich saying thank you and encouraging everyone to share more stories while they mingled and had refreshments.

Still nothing from inside the bathroom.

"Excuse me, but I need to use the facilities," Doreen's voice tittered from behind us.

Pop jumped and spun around. "You can't go in there," he said, throwing his body in front of the door.

Doreen peered at Pop over her glasses. "Why not?" Then she looked at me. "There isn't another dead body in the bathroom, is there?" Her voice was a combination of revulsion and glee. "I just got a serious offer on this place this afternoon. I was going to talk to you about it tomorrow, but another dead body will most likely kill the deal."

A serious offer for the rink. The thought knocked the wind

out of me. Thank goodness Pop still had his wits about him. "You don't have to worry about the deal. There aren't any dead bodies in the bathroom."

"Then why can't I go in?"

"Because." The door swung open, and Sean stood alone in the doorway. He smiled at Doreen. "I was running a safety check. You can go in now."

Doreen hurried into the bathroom, and the door closed behind her.

"Where's Kandie?" I demanded.

"The window in the handicapped stall was open. She must have stood on the toilet and hoisted herself through it."

Wow. The window was near the top of the wall so perverts couldn't see in, and it was tiny. Kandie must have wanted to escape really bad to use that route.

Sean told Pop and me to stay inside and headed outside to search for Kandie. Pop spotted some of his friends and went off to spread the gossip. I went to get another cookie, all the while keeping an eye on the front door in hopes a triumphant Sean would come in. I wanted to hear that Sherlene-n-Mean's killer was in cuffs. Feeling safe would be nice.

"Rebecca." George waved at me. He was with Sherlene's mother, seated at one of the snack tables. I resisted the urge to take another cookie and joined them. George smiled. "I was just telling Joanne that Sherlene had a locker with her belongings here at the rink."

"George said I could have any mementos she kept." Joanne wasn't crying, but her trembling bottom lip told me the waterworks could start again at any moment.

Feeling tears starting to form in my own eyes, I said, "Why

don't I clear out Sherlene's locker right now? It'll just take a minute."

Before George or Joanne could protest, I hurried through the crowd to my office for the combination and across the rink floor to the locker room. I hit the lights and walked down to Sherlene-n-Mean's locker. A couple of spins of the dial and I was in. The locker was just as messy as it had been earlier in the week. Joanne Cline wasn't going to want all of this stuff. I'd have to go through it all and make some decisions.

Something clanked in the shower behind me. My heart wedged in my throat, and my muscles froze. The rustling of fabric sent my pulse into high gear. Either a couple of teenagers had decided to get frisky in the shower or I was in big trouble. Swallowing hard, I turned.

"Hello, Rebecca." Kandie Sutra gave me a sad smile and raised her gun.

Twenty-three

This was the second time in my life I'd had a gun pointed at me, and it still sucked. The first time I was so surprised it took a few minutes for the fear to sink in. This time my arms broke out in goose bumps and the back of my neck broke into a cold sweat. I was terrified. "I didn't see you leave the bathroom. Sean Holmes thought you went out the bathroom window."

"I snuck out when George handed you a Kleenex. Once the service was done, I came in here to wait." Kandie's voice sounded tired and resigned.

"There are a lot of people in the rink. You're going to get caught."

"Maybe." She shrugged. "Maybe not. Does it matter?"

Yikes. An indifferent Kandie was bad and very scary. Hostages had value, but if she wasn't planning on getting out of this alive, I was screwed. With nothing to lose, I opened my mouth to scream. The rink sound system turned on, and Kool & the Gang blasted out "Celebration." The team had wanted to skate with Sherlene one last time. A nice sentiment. I just wished they had waited five more minutes.

Now what?

Trying not to look panicked, I asked the one question I needed answered before I died. "Why have you been trying to kill me? What did I ever do to you?"

"You didn't do anything." Kandie sighed. "And I wasn't trying to kill you. No one was supposed to die in the dunk tank."

Great. I was going to die for no reason. That pissed me off. "Then why the hell are you holding a gun to my head?"

"Because I told her to."

I spun around. The dark-haired woman from the memorial service walked toward me. She was the one who was so upset about Sherlene's former career choice. Other than that, I hadn't a clue who she was. This was getting stranger by the minute.

"Do you want me to shoot her, Linda?" Kandie's eyes were glazed and her shoulders slumped. Unfortunately, her gun hand wasn't getting as tired as the rest of her. That held steady, strong, and right at me.

A surge of hope raced through me as Linda shook her head and took the gun from Kandie.

"Not yet." Oh God! A fresh streak of fear raced up my spine. "Killing her here might make the team stay out of loyalty. I need this to look like Rebecca ditched them and went back to her life in Chicago. That should shake them loose."

Now I was scared and confused. What did the derby team have to do with anything?

"I don't think so." Kandie sounded annoyed. "I've told you

the team likes it here, and no one will believe Rebecca just up and left to go back to the city. Besides, her grandfather lives here. He'll tell everyone that she's missing."

Linda snorted. "Her grandfather thinks he's a combination of Elvis and Ricky Ricardo. He's nuts. No one will ever believe him."

Kandie looked at me and gave a small shake of her head. She didn't agree with Linda, and she was letting me know it. Why? I thought the two were working together. Suddenly, something clicked. Linda must be Linda Salkin—owner of EstroGenocide's former home rink and the wife of the man Kandie'd had an affair with in the not so distant past.

Linda didn't notice Kandie's disbelief. She just kept talking. "Once this shindig is over, we'll take Rebecca upstairs to pack some things. Then we'll get her out of town."

"We can't wait in here until everyone is gone." Kandie's voice no longer sounded indifferent—which I thought was a vast improvement. "The team is going to come back here to shower and change."

Linda frowned. "I hadn't thought about that." She looked up at the ceiling as though waiting for inspiration. I looked at Kandie. She was watching Linda. Since neither woman was paying attention to me, I reached into Sherlene-n-Mean's locker and felt around for something, anything, to defend myself with.

"Okay, change of plans. I'll walk out of here with the gun and Rebecca." Linda smiled at me. "If you call out for help, I'll shoot you. Then I'll shoot your wacko grandfather. Is that clear?"

I think I nodded. The high anxiety level was making me a little light-headed, so it was hard to be sure.

"Good." Linda turned to Kandie. "Wait ten minutes and then follow us."

I stopped paying attention to Linda's other instructions because her gun hand dropped to her side. It was now or never. I sent up a small prayer to the Roller Skating Gods, got a good grip on Sherlene-n-Mean's steel-reinforced boot, and swung.

"Ow!"

Linda grabbed her arm in pain. Her yelp gave me a huge burst of satisfaction as I raced out of the locker room and smack into a very large Roller Derby girl. The two of us went down in a heap.

Skaters zoomed around me as I scrambled to my feet. I dodged two teenagers rolling by holding hands and looked back at the locker room entrance. Kandie peered out of the door, spotted me, and ducked back into the locker room. I didn't have much time. I had turned toward the sidelines to find Sean when a viselike hand clamped around my arm.

"Where the hell do you think you're going?"

Oh crap. I smiled up at the very angry, incredibly tall derby girl holding me in a death grip. "I'm sorry. I didn't see you." Which was true, albeit hard to believe considering the woman's girth. The name on her jersey was Eartha Quake, and I didn't doubt she could cause a quake all on her own. I had no idea what team she belonged to, and I didn't have time to find out. Linda had just poked her head out of the locker room, and she was looking around for me.

"I really am sorry."

Eartha Quake either didn't believe me or didn't care. She gave me a shove and sent me flying toward the center of the rink, away from my pursuers but right into a group of skaters. A pair of strong arms grabbed me before I hit the deck again, and Anna Phylaxis yelled, "You can't push Rebecca like that." She glared across the floor at Eartha Quake.

A snarling Eartha Quake took one look at Anna and skated in our direction. "What are you going to do about it, Twiggy?"

Anna didn't say anything. She just sped forward, stuck out her foot, and sent the enormous derby girl to meet her namesake. Anna high-fived Typhoon Mary just as three unfamiliar female skaters plowed into them both. Several EstroGenocide team members saw their comrades go down and headed for the center of the rink to help. Pandemonium erupted. Skaters were pushed, hair was pulled, and people on the sidelines cheered as though they were watching a real derby meet instead of a rink-floor brawl.

I ducked as a fist flew toward me and looked around for Linda and Kandie. There. The two were skulking around the edge of the rink, heading for the sidelines. They must have decided shooting me in the middle of all these witnesses was a bad idea. Now they were making their escape.

With Sherlene-n-Mean's boot held ready for battle, I dodged two derby girls rolling on the floor and spotted Erica the Red near the sidelines. She was herding nonderby skaters off the floor, away from the melee. Linda and Kandie were crossing the floor near the snack area, approaching Erica's position.

"Erica," I yelled, racing toward her. "Kandie and Linda killed Sherlene." I pointed to where the two were slinking along the rail. "They're trying to get away."

Erica's eyes narrowed. She pushed off from the rail and zoomed toward the duo.

"Don't," I yelled, trying to pitch my voice over the pulsing disco music. "Linda has a gun."

Kandie and Linda spotted Erica a second before she reached them. Kandie's eyes grew wide as Linda reached into her pocket. The gun flashed in the light just as Erica rammed them. The gun flew up in the air and skittered across the rink floor. Erica grabbed Kandie around the waist and pulled her to the ground. Linda jumped over the two of them and went racing across the floor for her gun. I ran into the fray, hoping to find the gun before she did. No one else was going to die. Not if I could help it.

Linda dove for the flash of silver, but an incoming skate got to it first. The gun sped under her grasping hands and slid across the boards, coming to a stop ten feet in front of me. Linda scrambled to her feet and charged. I willed my high-heeled feet to get there first. We dove at the same time, only the gun wasn't there when we arrived. Another foot had sent it flying toward the back wall.

Linda pushed to her feet while I grabbed her black sweater and pulled. Hard. Linda almost lost her balance, looked down, and kicked. Her pointy-toed boot made contact with my hip bone. Yow! Pain exploded in my side, and I bit my lip to keep from screaming. I wasn't about to give Linda the satisfaction.

She turned and started toward the gun. Ignoring the serious ache in my hip, I launched myself at Linda and wrapped my arms around her waist. She lost her footing and screamed as she went down—right on top of me. I shoved her to the floor and gasped for air. Linda rolled to her knees, pulled back her hand, and sent it flying.

I turned my head to the right, but not fast enough. A zing of pain slashed across my cheekbone. Yeouch. Now I was pissed. I grabbed a fistful of dark hair and started pulling. Linda screeched, and I pulled harder. She slapped and clawed at me, but I didn't let go. This was the woman behind Sherlene-n-Mean's death. She'd ruined my mother's disco ball and taken shots at me. She deserved whatever she got.

Linda landed a punch to my jaw. For a second, my vision

blurred and I lost my grip on her hair. She pulled away and got to her feet. She was halfway to the gun when I remembered Sherlene-n-Mean's boot. I grabbed it off the floor, cocked my arm back, and let it fly.

Ha! Direct hit.

The boot made contact with the back of Linda's head, and she crumpled to the floor. Pushing my aching body upright, I walked past a groaning Linda, leaned down, and picked up the gun. My fingers tightened on the handle as I pointed it at Linda. "I'm sure Deputy Holmes will confirm this, but you're under arrest for the murder of Sherlene Patsy."

Twenty-four

Sean did confirm it. He showed up moments later, cuffs in hand. Someone had shut off the music, leaving an underscore of shocked murmurs and the occasional cry of "I can't believe it."

Sean asked Linda to turn around and added, "Linda Salkin, you're under arrest for the murder of Sherlene Patsy, the attempted murder of Rebecca Robbins, illegal use of a firearm, and criminal destruction of private property."

Oops. I'd missed a few of the charges.

Linda glared at me as Sean put the cuffs on her. "I want my lawyer. He'll tell you Rebecca is wrong. I didn't murder anyone. Kandie did that all on her own."

Sean didn't look impressed. "You can call a lawyer from your jail cell."

"Where is Kandie?" I asked.

Sean pointed toward the snack stand. "I cleared out the people and cuffed her to a chair. Erica's standing guard. I was going to take her to my car, but I thought you could use some help."

I could have used help earlier, too, but I was alive. That was all that mattered. Sean escorted a protesting Linda to the exit, and I headed for the snack stand. Erica smiled as she saw me, but then her eyes dropped to my hand and her smile faded.

Oops. Sean had forgotten to take the gun. I put the pistol behind my back and studied Kandie. She was slumped on a red snack-table chair with her hands cuffed behind her back. She looked up at me, and I gasped. Now that I wasn't filled with fear, I understood what I was seeing. The unfocused, red-rimmed eyes reminded me of a jock I'd dated in college. Kandie wasn't just unhappy. She was stoned. The empty pain pill bottles in her house suddenly made sense. So did the physician's name on those bottles: J. M. Salkin, Linda's husband. The pieces were starting to fit together.

I sat down on a nearby chair. "Kandie, are you addicted to pain medication?"

Next to me, Erica gasped.

Kandie looked ready to deny it, but then she gave a dejected nod. "I started taking the pills when I broke my leg. Between the surgeries and the physical therapy, I was always in pain, so I took more than I was supposed to. Then I couldn't stop."

"And Linda's husband wrote prescriptions for you."

"I slept with him, and he gave me pills." Kandie sighed. "I tried going off them a couple of times, but the pain was really bad."

A responsible doctor would have seen the problem and gotten her help. Instead, Jay had gotten laid. Nice guy.

A tear slipped down Kandie's cheek. "I didn't want to help Linda, but she threatened to report Jay to the medical board and have my medication cut off. I didn't know what to do. Jay begged me to help him, so I told Linda yes. It didn't seem so bad at first. Linda just wanted the team to come back. No one was supposed to die."

"You slept with her husband, and she kicked us out of the rink." Erica sounded angry and a touch confused. "Why would she want the team back?"

Kandie looked down at her shoes, so I answered for her. "Money."

The Toe Stop's profit margin had risen since EstroGenocide took up residence, even though my rink was under construction for much of that time. Now that the Toe Stop no longer had a hole in one side of the building, I was pretty sure those numbers were going to climb. Linda's marriage had to have been on the decline pre-Kandie. From what I had seen, she wasn't the type to let her business go down the drain, too.

Now that Kandie had started talking, she didn't want to stop. Not even when Sean arrived to take her and Linda's gun to the station. She admitted to rigging the dunk tank. Zapping me was the first part of a disastrous plan to make the derby girls abandon ship. Step one: Shoot electricity through my body. Step two: Have Kandie freak out and tell the team she didn't feel safe at the rink. One or two more "accidents" and she'd convince them they needed to leave for their own safety. Instead, she'd killed one of her friends and the rest of the plan fell to pieces. Linda was the one with crappy aim at Lionel's place. Since scaring me hadn't worked, she'd decided to remove me—permanently.

"Did you drop the disco ball or did Linda?" I asked. I'm not sure why it mattered to me, but I needed to know who was responsible for destroying something my mother loved.

"I don't know who did that." Kandie looked genuinely confused. "I thought Linda must have snuck into the rink, but she said she didn't. Maybe she lied."

Calling Linda a liar would be easy, but somehow I didn't think Linda lied about this. Why would she? Which meant someone else had dropped the ball. Now that all the pieces were in place, I had a feeling I knew who that someone was.

Once Sean and Kandie disappeared out the front door, Erica turned to me. "I think I may have to use you as the inspiration for one of my characters. Like it or not, you're a hero."

The word "hero" made my insides squirm. A real hero would have prevented the brawl in the first place. "You helped," I said.

"Nope. Kandie gave up without a fight," Erica said. "Linda didn't. I knew she was crazy, but I had no idea how crazy. Good thing you know how to fight dirty or things might not have turned out so well."

"I don't know how well things turned out." I looked around the rink and surveyed the damage. Snack-table chairs were overturned, and cookie crumbs and napkins littered the floor. Pieces of ripped clothing were scattered across the rink floor. Several derby girls sat nursing their war wounds on the sidelines amid a haphazard stack of St. Mark's folding chairs. Not exactly the scene you'd expect to see after a memorial service. "Linda and Kandie ruined Sherlene's memorial service. That sucks."

"Are you kidding?" Erica gave me a beatific smile. "Sherlene-n-Mean would have loved this."

I picked up a broken chair off the ground, and for the first time in a long time, I laughed. Erica was right. Sherlene-n-Mean's service would go down in Indian Falls history. What was better than that?

. . .

Friday's funeral for Sherlene-n-Mean was simple and brawl-free. Lionel and I stood in the back. Pop made sure to get a spot up front just in case anything interesting happened. He was feeling a little put out that I hadn't invited him to be a part of Linda's capture. As if I had a choice. To his disappointment, the only real drama came when Father Mike appeared at the gravesite and insisted on officiating. Now that Sherlene's former status as a nun was public, the Catholic church was claiming dibs. Pastor Rich was gracious in stepping aside, but I did notice one hand clench tightly at his side.

After the funeral, Joanne invited everyone to Papa Dom's Italian restaurant for lunch. I asked Lionel to save me a seat and made a quick detour to Ten Little Pins.

Guy looked nervous the minute I walked through the door. "Rebecca." He walked around the counter and headed toward me. "I thought you'd be at the funeral. I wanted to go, but someone had to take care of things here."

"What about your mother?" I asked, looking for telltale signs of smoke. She was the real reason I was here.

"Mother?" Guy pulled at his dress-shirt collar.

"Yes, Guy. Your mother. The one who snuck into my rink and tried to drop a disco ball on my head." It wasn't a souvenir-seeking fan Laurel Loveless saw by the Dumpsters on Sunday night. Fern Caruso had taken the opportunity to sneak in the back door in an attempt to put me and my business out of commission. Given the way Guy was sweating, I knew I had guessed correctly. "I think it's time to call Sean Holmes."

Five minutes later, Sean arrived to take Guy's statement. His

283

mother had bragged about the disco ball drop the minute she got home. She wanted to show Guy how a serious businessperson behaved. Which is why Guy acted so nice on Monday. He was scared he'd be blamed.

"So why did you come see me Sunday night?" I asked.

Guy looked down at his scuffed loafers. "I was going to file a lawsuit against you on Monday if you didn't remove your arcade equipment. It was my last attempt to prove to my mother I should be in charge."

Since I wasn't going to press charges, and Sean was going to pick up Fern and take her to jail, Guy was going to get his wish. Too bad he was too unhappy to celebrate.

The smell of garlic and tomato sauce greeted me as I walked into Papa Dom's. Having smelled the same aromas after the rink cleaning, I was ready to eat my weight in pasta. Lionel waved at me from a booth situated away from the mourners, and I headed over. He had arrived on my doorstep about an hour after last night's excitement died down. He'd been attending a sick cow; otherwise, he'd have gotten there sooner. Twelve well-meaning citizens had left him voice mail messages describing my capture of Linda Salkin. He gave me a stern reprimand for not calling him, applied cold compresses to my bruises, kissed me senseless, and tucked me in for the night. Then he took up residence in the guest room. Not ideal, but having him nearby was better than nothing.

Pop slid into our booth with a big grin. "Rebecca, how do you feel about running for sheriff?"

I blinked. "What are you talking about?"

Pop bounced up and down in the booth. "Lots of people have

asked if you'd be interested in running in the next election." He pulled out his phone and held it up. "See, I've been getting texts all morning."

I didn't want to look. Being an elected official was the last thing I needed. "I don't think so, Pop. If anyone is going to replace Sheriff Jackson, it should be Sean Holmes." I don't think Sean would fare any better than I would at politics, but at least he knew the job and how to fire a gun. The last part I might remedy, but the rest—no way.

"That's what I told them." Pop wedged the phone back into his leather pants and shrugged. "But don't be surprised when folks keep asking. People around here trust you. Unlike some I could mention."

As if on cue, my father walked through the door. Leave it to Stan to skip the funeral but show up for the free food. He scoped out the room, spotted Joanne, and made a beeline for her table. She was seated with George and Typhoon Mary, looking dazed and unhappy. The minute Stan appeared at her side, she sat up straight and smiled. Suddenly, Mrs. Cline looked very alert.

Oh no. I jumped out of the booth and walked over to join them.

"I can't imagine what it would be like to lose my little girl," Stan said. He was holding Joanne's hand and giving her a warm, understanding smile. "I want you to call me if ever you need anything."

He handed her his card just before I wedged myself in between them.

"I hope you don't mind if I talk to my father for a minute, Joanne. He and I haven't spent much time together lately." Not waiting for Joanne's response, I grabbed Stan by the arm and marched him to a table on the opposite side of the restaurant.

"Mrs. Cline has had a hard time. She doesn't need you making things worse."

"I was offering my condolences."

"And your phone number," I shot back. "Joanne doesn't need your kind of help."

My father stiffened. "What kind of help is that?" He had the nerve to sound offended.

"The kind that buries Indian artifacts in the park to make a buck."

Stan went still, then looked around the room to see if anyone was listening. Leaning forward, he quietly asked, "How do you know about that?"

"A bunch of people saw you in the park Sunday morning. Your clothes were covered in mud. There were only two places you could have picked up that much mud—either by the dunk tank or in the hole for the commemorative fountain. I'm guessing Alan's motel will be booked for months due to the historic find." I let the word "historic" drip with sarcasm. I couldn't help it. My father had always excelled at rewriting history to suit himself. This recent adventure had elevated that skill to an art form. "What's your cut? Is it worth going to jail?"

Stan actually went pale. "I'm not getting a cut." I sat back in my chair and waited. Beads of sweat appeared on his forehead. "Okay," he admitted. "I was supposed to get thirty percent of the profits for a year."

"Did Alan pull out of the deal?" The kid didn't strike me as a welcher.

Stan sighed. "No. The Indian stuff came from a friend of mine. His uncle gave the pieces to him years ago and said they were from a local Indian tribe. My friend was grateful to get rid of the junk until he saw the press conference. He figured I was behind the archaeological find and threatened to go to the police if I didn't give him my cut. I had no choice. If he went to the police, Alan would get thrown in jail. Prison would break that kid's spirit."

Translation: If you tell the cops, you ruin Alan's life forever.

Great. I blew a strand of hair out of my face and considered my options. History demanded I blow the whistle, but how did I know the Chippewa tribe didn't live here at some point? Who could say for certain? As jealous as I'd been over Alan's relationship with my father, I didn't want Alan to go to jail. The kid was sweet in a dorky kind of way. Besides, while I hated to admit it, part of me was relieved to discover that Stan's fatherly interest in Alan was driven by financial need.

"Okay," I said, trying to sound stern. "I won't go to the cops. For now. But the next time you pull a stunt like this, I'm turning you in."

Stan gave me one of his commercial-worthy smiles and laughed. When he realized I wasn't joking, his smile disappeared. "No more angles or slick business deals for me. I'm going straight. From now on, I'm going to be the most upstanding citizen this town has ever seen."

I laughed and looked around at the town's citizens assembled here. Pastor Rich and Danielle were in a corner booth with Father Mike. None of them looked particularly happy about the situation, but no one would admit it.

In the center of the restaurant, my grandfather was kneeling in front of Joanne, singing "Love Me Tender" at the top of his lungs. A bunch of senior center women shot daggers at Sherlene's mother for securing Pop's undivided attention. Meanwhile, Joanne looked as though she didn't know whether to laugh or cry. Something told me she might do both before Pop was done.

Not too far away from them was George, waving his arms in the air like a conductor. He was describing his newest strategy for tonight's derby bout. Typhoon Mary just nodded while Erica and Anna cracked jokes with the team. Then there was Lionel. He was tightening the wrap on Halle Bury's sprained ankle. Lionel noticed me watching him and smiled.

I couldn't help but smile back. The guy had a killer smile, and he was a good person. They all were. If Stan wanted to be Indian Falls's number-one citizen, he had his work cut out for him.

"I know I've said I was going straight before," Stan continued, "and I slipped. This time I'm on the up-and-up. I'm going to be a model citizen. You can hold me to that."

I looked back around the restaurant at my friends and then back at my father.

Hold him to it? "You bet your ass I will."

Twenty-five

Turns out Pop wasn't exaggerating about the sheriff thing. The rink's answering machine was filled with pleas, campaign suggestions, and preemptive requests to clear parking tickets off records. Sheesh. While I liked asking questions and being generally nosy, I wasn't ready for a shiny badge or a public office.

The phone rang. I barely got the receiver to my ear before a voice yelled, "Rebecca, you can't possibly run for sheriff. You'd ruin this town."

The voice of reason. Too bad it came in the form of the sheriff department's receptionist, Roxy Moore. She made me want to lash out irrationally. Lucky for her, I wasn't in the mood. Besides, she was the perfect person to get the word out about my political disinterest.

"I'm not running for sheriff, Roxy. Not now. Not ever."

I could hear Roxy regrouping on the other end. "Well, good," she said. "Some people in this town think that being a busybody who sticks her nose into everyone's business is qualification enough. But, it isn't. I'm glad you're thinking straight for once."

I *was* thinking straight, which is why I hung up the phone and went out to get the rink ready for tonight's grand reopening. George and the team had stayed late last night to make sure all traces of yesterday's memorial service and brawl were gone. The flat track for the derby bout was already in place. There wasn't much left for me to do but straighten the sound booth, organize the rental skates, and make sure we had enough popcorn and pizza for all. Once that was done, I laced up my skates and hit the floor.

Air whooshed by me as I pumped my legs and sped along the flat track floor. The navy dress I'd worn to the funeral flapped against my legs, and I zipped around the far side of the rink and back to the middle. My hip and face still ached from my battle with Linda Salkin, but I didn't care. I just pumped my legs harder and enjoyed the solitude and the feeling of being alive.

Feeling daring, I spun around and, skating backward, catapulted myself into the air. After one turn, I hit the floor with both feet. My arms flailed as I tried to keep my balance . . . and I did. The jump sucked in the technical department, but I'd stayed on my feet. It was a sign. Not that I really needed one. For the first time in a long time I knew what I needed to do.

I zoomed back into the office and picked up the phone. After three rings Doreen answered. Sitting at the desk, looking at the picture of me and my mom, I said, "The Toe Stop isn't for sale."